BLADEMAGE ADEPT

The Blademage Saga

Volume 3

Chris Hollaway

Thanks:

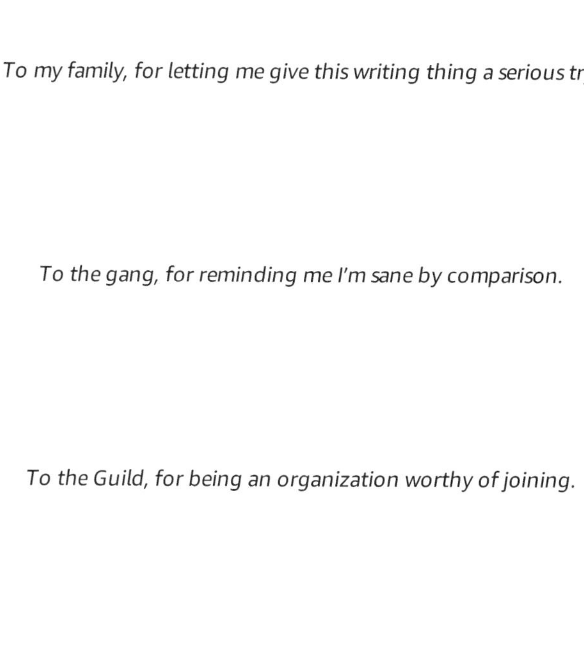

To my family, for letting me give this writing thing a serious try.

To the gang, for reminding me I'm sane by comparison.

To the Guild, for being an organization worthy of joining.

To Ken and Paul, without either, I would not know any measure of success.

CHAPTER 1

"Are you awake up there?" Kevon called, leaning back and shielding his eyes from the late afternoon sun.

The crow's nest rocked lazily, the wind and the water in an uneasy truce.

It won't last long, Kevon thought. *I should let her get some rest, at least.* He had only been sleeping well the last few days. He'd had a week of pushing back the constant press of the sea, climbing to the top of the mast to distance himself from it long enough to court a few moments of oblivion. Only the touch of iron or steel brought any lasting relief from the weight of the magic that threatened to take his sanity, or his life. Mirsa had no such relief.

"She hasn't stirred in hours," Alanna remarked, emerging from belowdecks. "I've already been up to check on her once."

"How do other Magi stand crossing the seas?"

"It's more comforting a thought than some might imagine," the assassin smirked, twirling a dagger absently. "We should be nearing the coast soon enough. She can rest easy then." She clicked her teeth together at a young deckhand that passed by closer than others had dared, and he yelped and stumbled away. "They should have guessed who we were when we signed on for this voyage," she laughed. "We have yet to eat any of them, and still they cower."

"Let them be," Kevon scolded. "They're risking their lives even associating with us, with *me*. After our first night on board, I'm not sure I blame them."

"The others were uncomfortable with the sorcery you

and the witch wrought, bending the seas to make our escape. They chose to take their chances elsewhere." Alanna shrugged.

"In the middle of the night. Without a boat?" Kevon asked.

"Assassins are resourceful," she purred, her jade-green eye boring deep into his soul as her fingers twined with his.

Kevon's pulse quickened, and the mostly healed wound at his back ached in time with his hammering heart. The look in her remaining eye had begun to remind him more of Marelle in the previous weeks. She was still a much different person than she'd been the season they had met over two years ago.

I don't imagine she's having the easiest time adjusting to who I am now, he thought, recalling their shared hatred of the Mage that had taken loved ones from both of them. *Our roads both led to the same destination, to Holten's destruction. That should make things easier. Why isn't it?*

The boat rocked on a swell, and Kevon swayed into the mast. Alanna turned away at his sharp intake of breath from the light impact against his back. Her fingers slipped away through his like the last grains of sand in an hourglass.

"*I'm trying*," she said, slipping back into the passageway that led to the lower cabins.

The Warsmith thought about following her. There was a time he would have abandoned everything to be with the woman she had been. There were still times he considered it, but there was always *something* that stopped him. His fear of the unknown, his duty to the Realm, the journey they had undertaken to decipher the ancient text. He took a few steps after her before succumbing to hesitation, and turned to walk to the railing and overlook the sea.

"Ha! Ye're a pig!" the Dwarven ambassador chortled from further down the railing. The ship pitched again, and Kylgren-Wode wrapped another loop of the rope that secured him to the ship's side around his arm. "No, that's not right. A turkey?"

Kevon braced himself against the rail, and tried to make sense of the dwarf's mumbling. "A chicken?"

"Aye, I suppose. Why ye think a chicken is more afraid than a pig is a mystery. Never kept pigs fer their eggs."

I've given up trying to understand them, but I see what Bertus meant. Kevon smiled and shook his head. The two dwarves were the only ones on board that no one hesitated to talk with. Their easy manner and odd perspectives were an amusing combination no matter who you were.

"Yer likely right te be afraid of that one, and she of you. There's something te be said fer that though," Kylgren-Wode advised.

"Bertus said something about training?" the Warsmith asked, eager to talk about something other than Alanna.

"How do ye think the boy is?"

"Well, I hope. My family's lives may depend on him." Memories of the Sending Pholos had helped perform to transport the young Warrior to the North Valley flashed through his mind.

There were disturbances that someone new to the Plane of Fire might have left, Pholos had told him. No evidence of Holten's death, but surely his passage.

Tensions had mounted after the battle near the waterfront. Kevon and his friends had barely gained entrance back into the city before accusations of heresy from inside the Warrior's Guild were leveled. None of the guardsmen that were there that night stood against him, but few spoke out on his behalf, fearing retribution from both of the Guilds. By the time Pholos returned with his concerns about Holten, there was time to work a Sending on Bertus to see to Kevon's family, and evacuate to this ship the others who supported the Warsmith. They'd set sail for Alcron under cover of darkness, Kevon helping Mirsa work Water magic to hasten their departure.

"I ken show ye the basics, but I'm no Stoneguard," Kylgren-Wode offered. "Once we're back on solid ground."

"I look forward to it." Kevon began walking toward the aft of the ship, to the higher decks, removing his steel-laced wristbands as he went. Halfway up the stairs, as the first cuff slid free, the press of the ocean's power engulfed his mind.

Unprepared, the Mage stumbled, and thrust his arm back into the wristband, wiping away the forces that had nearly overwhelmed him. He finished the climb to the highest deck, and sat in the center on the polished wooden planks to think.

First the ring, and now these? More prepared, Kevon removed the wrist braces and felt the swell of power beneath him, held more easily at bay by the extra yards of distance and focused concentration. He reached out and took some of the magic, pressing outward along the surface of the waters for miles, until he tasted the dank sand and felt the sea slapping against the insolent shore that rose from it to the east.

"Almost there," he whispered, pushing away the magic before he was tempted to drink more deeply from the offered power. He slipped one cuff back on, and was still fighting the press of the sea from below. He poked at each of the strips inside the remaining cuff. Four had no effect, the remaining two shielding him completely from the magic like he'd come to expect them all to do.

If this pattern holds, they will not protect me as I require for much longer. The exhausted Mage stood and gazed toward the eastern horizon, hoping the land he'd sensed was not too far beyond it. *Tomorrow, the day after at the latest.*

CHAPTER 2

The protection afforded by the bracers ended in the middle of the night. Kevon woke screaming belowdecks, drowning in power that tossed the ship like a toy upon the sudden waves.

The Warsmith struggled out of his twisted bedroll, looking for something to latch onto to quell the madness. His sword skittered across the floor as the craft rolled, and after it slid past his flailing grasp three times, he snatched the hilt. Absorbing the shock of the now familiar jolt, he wrapped himself around the scabbarded blade until the ship, and his mind stilled.

He prowled the hall, blade in hand, checking on the rest of the passengers and crew. Aside from bruises and scrapes, no one below had any injuries. Kevon climbed the stairs to the deck, and opened the door.

"Haul on that like it was yer life, not his!" Kylgren-Wode called, grinding his iron-shod boots against the deck at the end of the stout rope that looped over the railing.

Kevon rushed over, steadying his mind in preparation for releasing the sword to help with the rope. He let go, pushed back against the sea, grabbed onto the rope, and pulled with the others.

The shaken sailor latched onto the railing as he reached it, taking the weight off the rope. The nearest crewmen leapt forward to complete the rescue, Kylgren-Wode among them.

"Clear skies, calm seas, and then this?" The ship's captain muttered from behind Kevon. "I've half a mind to dump all of the Kærtesian scum overboard."

"One more day," Kevon snapped, turning to glare at the

captain, motioning for Alanna to stand down. “Another day and we won’t need you, or your ship.” He recovered the sword, shouldered his way past the irritated sailor, and headed back belowdecks.

Mirsa sat in silence, letting her mind wander only far enough to skim the surface of the ocean’s power. The spell Kevon worked churned ocean water heavily against the vessel, shoving them along with furious speed. He drew power from the depths of the sea, and from around her, leaving a small bubble of calm where she could keep watch for hostile magic that could interfere with his concentration. The steel laced armbands he wore kept the magic he worked hidden from her senses, but the pressure against the hull was more than enough evidence. Vast amounts of power were being used to speed them toward their destination.

“An hour more, at this pace,” she announced. “Still no signs of other Magi, but we should be within sight of other ships very soon.”

“Sails?” The captain asked.

Kevon shook his head. “Ready them; wait until you spot another ship.”

Twenty minutes passed before a shout from the crow’s nest signaled contact with another vessel.

Opening eyes that would have only distracted him moments before, Kevon shifted his focus to easing the ship’s speed without capsizing it. He funneled away more of the energy surrounding Mirsa, and pointed to the top of the mast.

“I’m all right,” the Master Mage argued. “The deepest part of the ocean is well behind us. As long as I do not seek it out…”

The Warsmith had wondered as much, if the lessening of the sea’s insistence had been a product of his increased skill, or the shallowing of the ocean floor. “As you will. Be ready.”

Kevon finished easing the surrounding seas into normal

currents, and signaled the captain. Shouts rang out, and sails unfurled to catch the breeze that angled them on toward their destination. He ended the spell, and grasped the hilt of his sword to disconnect himself from the magic completely.

Mirsa felt the power of the sea press up against her, but stop at a manageable level. Her breath quickened, then fell back into its normal steady rhythm. The nausea returned, but she focused on her breathing until it passed. When she felt more composed, she stood and made her way to look over the upper deck's railing, ahead to the shore that lined the horizon.

CHAPTER 3

Bertus poked at the fire, stirring the coals before adding a few more broken branches. The skewered rabbits on the crude spit above it were nearly ready, but the hunt and their preparation had cost him the greater part of the day.

Savage, he mocked himself, looking at the bloodied stone shards he'd had to use to clean and skin his meal. He crowded closer to the flame, feeling the chill of the evening beginning to settle in again. *At least they let me bring my bedroll.*

The Seeker rotated the sizzling carcasses a quarter-turn, and looked around. He strode over to the base of a large tree at the edge of the clearing, and grabbed on to a low-hanging branch. He pulled himself up, and spotted another branch that would hold his weight. The effort required was negligible. He had not climbed a tree in years, but his Warrior training had hardened most of the correct muscles.

Twenty yards from the ground, a glimpse through the foliage brought both him and his youthful daydreaming to a halt. A farmhouse with smoke rising from the chimney lay to the north, something he had not seen before he'd left the track to search for food earlier in the day.

I couldn't possibly make it there tonight, he decided. The smell of roasting rabbit wafted up and mingled with the pine. His gurgling stomach reminded him that he had other obligations to fulfill. He noted the direction of the dwelling, and climbed back down to his dinner.

Bertus's stomach growled in protest as he pressed on past midday, emerging from the forest onto the track within sight of the farmhouse. He hoped that the owners had supplies and equipment to spare, and would deal in coin. He unstrung his bow and tucked it under the strap that held the quiver of arrows at his back.

The Warrior waited while the farmer leaned on a shovel and looked him over. Deciding that Bertus was all right, the man called the baying mastiff to heel, and motioned the Seeker to follow him to the house.

"Weapons outside," the man cautioned as he leaned his shovel against the wall and opened the door. "Ma never held with them, I reckon we won't, neither."

Bertus nodded, lifting the quiver-strap over his head and lowering his gear to the sanded wooden deck. There was only one person in the valley he had cause to distrust, Holten. He left behind everything but his coin pouch.

"Comp'ny!" the man shouted ahead as they walked through a formal room and down the hallway past several closed doors. "Set 'nother place!"

The table, a monstrosity at least six feet wide and well over twenty feet long, was larger than any Bertus had seen outside the palace in Navlia. Half of the available space was taken up, and one of the women who were bustling about was just placing an extra plate on the end when he and his escort entered the room.

"Welcome," she said over the murmurs of the others at his appearance in the room. She cast an appraising glance, and smiled. "You're new."

Familiarity tickled the back of the Seeker's mind, the speech and features too similar to ignore. "You're Alma."

Too famished to explain, Bertus refused to answer questions until after the meal was over and he'd helped clear the table and clean up the kitchen. Most of the family returned to their outside duties, and the Seeker was left with Alma, one of the other women of the house, and another fellow that refused to wander far from Kevon's sister's side.

"Who are you, and how do you know Alma?" the other man demanded, as soon as they had taken seats in the living area after the meal.

"Martin, calm down," Alma advised, smoothing her skirt and lifting her gaze to Bertus. "He's going to tell us."

"First of all," the Seeker began, "I must know. When was the last time any of you saw Holten Magus?"

"Almost three years a..." Martin started. "Kevon! You know Kevon! Wait..." Martin bit his lip, thinking. "A Warrior. The last Warrior that came to this valley was before..."

"Yes," Bertus admitted. "I'm a Seeker. Kevon sent me here, to find you, Alma. And your mother."

Alma's eyes dropped. Martin frowned. "Last winter..." he began.

"I'm sorry. I understand. As awful as it sounds, it makes things easier. We need to leave here, at once."

"Now see here..." Martin stood and took a step toward Bertus. "You know nothing of what..."

"You may not know me, but I know you. You're a better fisherman than I am, though not as good a cook." Bertus turned to look at Alma. "She is the finest seamstress in the valley, perhaps even before her mother's passing. Kevon rode out of here more than two years ago on his father's mare. He needs you to trust him, to trust me. You must leave this place, to journey across the Realm, across the seas, to him. To safety." Bertus stood and squared his shoulders toward Martin. "He is my best friend, and I will see this done as he asked."

"I believe him," Alma said, standing beside Martin and sliding her arm around his to clasp his hand. "We need to go."

"Yes," Martin agreed. "*We* do."

"I have enough coin to buy just about anything we need, but we need horses more than anything right now." *And a sword,*

Bertus thought, longing for the weight of the ancient blade he'd grown so used to carrying at his side.

"Coin is not as precious here as it may be in the rest of the Realm," Martin cautioned. "We have something better."

"The whole farm?" the boy asked, eyes scrunched up in disbelief.

"Yes," Martin sighed. "And all of the sheep. We only need three saddle horses, three saddles, a sack of oats, and all the food and water your father can spare. Quickly."

"I'll tell him," the boy said, wheeling the borrowed horse around toward the road. "I'll probably get a whipping though, for lying."

Bertus flipped the boy a gold coin from his pouch.

The boy caught it, looked it over, and tossed it back. "That'd get me a whipping for stealing. No thanks, mister."

The Seeker laughed as the youth galloped down the road to try and convince his family that they were trading into a new farm.

Martin had Bertus help saddle their plow-horse and load it up with supplies they already had on hand. Alma brought out changes of clothing and blankets, along with an assortment of knives from the kitchen. She handed Bertus a long, sheathed skinning knife, which he immediately affixed to his belt, giving a different kind of comfort than the simple iron band that he wore on his right hand.

They had gone through the house and packed away everything that was small enough to take, and useful or valuable enough to barter away later, when the boy returned with his father.

"What's all this nonsense?" the man demanded, jumping down from his horse to glare at Martin and Bertus.

"The offer is good, but I don't see what we asked for," Bertus snapped.

"The boy was..."

"Telling the truth? Yes."

"I'll have to..."

"This delay was not part of the bargain," Bertus scratched his arm, drawing the man's attention to his sword-brand. "I have the authority to seize anything I may require, in the name of Prince Alacrit. I had hoped to avoid doing that."

The boy, who had already dismounted and was helping Alma finish packing, turned his head to conceal a smile.

"I'm sorry, many pardons," the man stammered. "I accept, I'll prepare..."

Bertus's icy gaze followed the man as he fumbled with the reins and climbed unsteadily back into the saddle. "Hurry," the Seeker hissed.

Hours later, Bertus directed Martin and Alma off the track near the beginning of the high mountain pass that led out of the North Valley. "That's far enough for today," he announced. "It's best to start out easy, get used to the road."

"We'd not make the top of the pass before nightfall, at any rate," Alma agreed. "Besides, the 'Dancing Sheep' is less than a day's ride from here."

"Kevon made it sound like no one..."

"Things have changed since Kevon was here last," Martin said, swinging down from his horse and stepping over to help Alma dismount. "I went halfway to Eastport already this year to get a new ram for our flock."

Alma cupped Martin's face in her hands. "We made it through last winter. We'll make it through this." She laughed. "Whatever this is."

Suddenly self-conscious, Bertus led the horses a short distance away and began caring for them as the others lit a campfire and started preparing supper.

"You never really mentioned what this is all about," Martin commented, brushing stray breadcrumbs from his tunic as he finished his meal. "We've taken this all on faith. I think it's time we knew what was happening."

"Normally, I would wait for Kevon to tell you himself," Bertus began. "I can't keep this from you that long, though. Kevon is no longer in Kærtis, or even on Purlon."

"Where?" Alma squeezed Martin's hand tighter, and leaned in closer to the fire, squinting across the flames to Bertus.

"Across the sea, fleeing from Holten Magus and the authorities in Eastport." After waiting for the initial shock to fade from his companions' faces, he continued. "Kevon has defied the Warrior's Guild, and has no doubt angered whatever Councils the Magi have to maintain order among their ranks. In addi..."

"Wait." Martin interrupted. "How can Kevon even be accused of defying the Warrior's Guild?"

"He currently holds the rank of Adept, and is skilled enough to advance to Blademaster, if they would only let him attempt it." Bertus chuckled. "He helped train me, even after he revealed himself as a Mage."

"Is that why Holten Magus was pursuing Kevon? Why neither of them have returned?" Martin stood and began pacing about.

"With any luck, Holten Magus perished in the realm of flames he fled to when he could not defeat us."

Martin's hand moved to the knife at his belt. "How dare you speak of..."

"You did not know of his plans, just as Kevon did not, at first," the Seeker explained, motioning for Martin to calm himself. "Here, you likely heard nothing of the orcs and demons that we faced over the last two years, or the true monsters behind them. Your Holten Magus was foremost among them."

"I heard rumors about creatures that attacked under cover of darkness, but saw and heard nothing on my journey," Martin admitted. "I assumed they were just children's stories."

"It was no story that bit my friend in half. The nightmares we hid from at night were as real as the two of you. It still unnerves me to greet the dark without torches or castle walls."

"I'm sorry I doubted," Martin crouched by the fire again beside Alma. "But none of this explains how Kevon has gotten so far in the Warrior's Guild without being able to use a sword."

"That's the thing everyone is so upset about," Bertus laughed. "He has been using swords. And magic. Not at the same time, really. It's complicated. And there's this," he flashed the ring on his right hand before waving it off. "It's a long story, and we'll have time to talk about it more on the way back to Navlia."

CHAPTER 4

Flakes of ash drifted down onto Kevon's shoulders, and he brushed at them, managing only to streak his tunic with more of the greasy grey soot. He reined his horse in, and turned back to wait for the others.

By the time Alanna pulled alongside him on her mare, he was nearly through rinsing out the cloth he'd been using to cover his mouth and nose. The covering was snugly back in place when Mirsa and the dwarves rolled up in the wagon.

"We can't continue in this," Kevon cautioned. "We need to find shelter, and hope for the wind to shift again in our favor."

For the first time since the plume began nearly three days ago, the falling ash now obscured the erupting peak to the east.

"It should discourage unwanted followers, at least," Alanna remarked, brushing soot from her mouth covering.

"The folk of Malcaea are not likely to be deterred by this," Mirsa countered. "Our horses are barely slowed by the ash, as we sit and suffer."

Kylgren-Wode snuffled through his thick mustache. "Reminds me of the smithing district in the Hold."

"We'll push ahead," Kevon decided. "Stay close to the wagon."

Alanna rode to the other side of the wagon, and Kevon began his spell.

A dome of Wind and Movement coalesced over the group, moving along with them, stopping the falling ash, but obscuring their view.

"Gah!" Kevon exclaimed, shifting his concentration to churn the settling ash away from the front of the dome. After a minute of adjustments, the dome was shortened and flattened, dropping down to just above his eye level, allowing the ash to swirl from the edges of the barrier down to the ground, but sparing the horses and his companions from breathing it in.

"Better," he decided. "Let's move while this holds, and hope we find something else before much longer."

The abandoned forge was not sealed completely against the falling ash, but did not require the constant attention of the Magi to maintain, as the spell had. Kevon sat near the open end of the structure until well after dark, rising occasionally to patrol around the building. Only when the falling ash slowed and the crescent moon poked through the clouds did he wake Kylgren-Wode to take over the watch.

The Warsmith settled into the corner between where Alanna had spread her bedroll, and where Rhysabeth-Dane sprawled across Mirsa's sleeping form, snoring faintly. He gazed out at the countryside, blanketed in dull gray ash, lit by the slowly brightening moon. The still night air hung hot and dry against his skin, and Kevon smeared streaks of ash across his forehead wiping at the thin film of perspiration. He drained the last few tepid mouthfuls from one of his water skins, and drifted off to sleep.

The ground beneath Kevon's bedding shifted as he slumbered, loosely packed earth near his shoulder dipping while the compact earth under his head remained firmly in place. He awoke with a sore neck from the unusual sleeping position, his shoulder and arm dug down below him, his neck resting flat on the bedroll on the lip of the depression.

"What in the world..." Kevon threw back the blanket and rubbed at his neck. "Stupid..."

His punch at the dirt in the bottom of the dip resounded

with hollowed tones. "Eh?"

Disappointment turned to curiosity, and he pushed dirt to the edges of the hole, uncovering a wooden surface.

"What's that?" Mirsa asked, stirring from her blankets.

"I'm looking..." Kevon peeled his bedroll from its place, and began scooping handfuls of dirt from the depression, and piling them in the empty corner. "A box?" He reached the edges, and scraped enough from below the top that he could grasp the short sides with his fingertips and wriggle it a bit. "I've almost... There!"

The box slid free, the considerable weight inside it shifting with a dull clunk. Kevon strained, sliding his fingers from the sides of the box to the bottom, finding a better grip. He hefted the container up to the side of the hole he'd dug, and pushed it away from the edge.

"Someone's coming back fer this," Kylgren-Wode said, peeking over Kevon's shoulder as he opened the box, revealing hammers, tongs, half a dozen iron bars, and various iron and steel scraps.

"Yes," Kevon frowned, looking to the still, cold forge across the open room. "I don't imagine anyone would just leave this here..." He closed the box, and stood, moving to the open end of the building.

"We're low on horseshoes and nails, there won't be a better chance to resupply than now." Kevon glared through the ash-filled sky to the east, where the outline of the volcano, and its thick plume still blocked most of the morning sun.

"There's coal in the bin outside," he told Alanna. "A pair of upturned barrels out back," he pointed to Kylgren-Wode. "Could we manage to fill them with water somehow?" he asked Mirsa.

"Do ye think we should let the Mage come in fer lunch?" Kylgren-Wode asked, pausing the bellows before speaking.

“Ten spare shoes and a pouch full of nails,” Kevon fished the glowing arc from the coals and used a punch to tap out the final two nail holes on the shoe. “I’m ready for lunch.” He dipped the finished shoe in the nearby water barrel, swirled it around until it stopped sizzling, and set it and the tongs atop the anvil.

“I’ll get them,” Alanna slipped out of the building and around the corner toward where the wagon was set up against the side wall, top and sides draped with canvas to lessen the damage from falling ash.

Alanna, Mirsa, and Rhysabeth-Dane returned to the forge as Kylgren-Wode opened the provision sacks to dole out bread and dried fish.

“More fresh water,” Mirsa handed Kevon one of the full water skins she carried. “I worked up a fountain out back while you were clanging around in here. We can fill up everything before we leave.”

The ground rumbled. Kevon stepped outside and peered through the haze. “I think the ash will be worse before it gets better,” he sighed, spotting the thickening column rising from the now glowing peak to the east. “Perhaps we should make a few more improvements.”

“Ready?” Mirsa asked, chuckling at Kevon’s bleary-eyed gaze.

“Mmhm…” Kevon mumbled, placing a hand on the upraised ridge of slate he’d spent the bulk of the last two mornings moving from the deposit Mirsa had detected earlier.

“Raising the far supports,” the Master Mage advised, and Kevon could feel the magic moving through the earth, granite pillars on the other side of the forge corkscrewing upward to nearly twice the height of the building.

Without speaking, Kevon pulled up on the slate slab, drawing it upward with his Art as he pushed his focus downward to gather more power to work the spell. He used none of his own energy for the magic, what little effort he did expend was to gather the latent forces from below. The slab groaned upward under his direction, his fingertips trailing along the upward-moving stone, retaining contact with the energy deep beneath them.

The link shattered as the slate worked free of the dirt it had been resting in. Kevon's focus shifted to the Movement rune he had already prepared, and he stepped aside, no longer comfortable in the stone's path without the extra magic at his disposal. The slate remained balanced in the calm air, balanced by gravity and the slightest touch of Kevon's magic. A puff of air tipped the slab toward the forge and waiting supports, and Kevon let it.

Hand still on the edge of the falling stone, Kevon felt the weight shifting, and latched onto that energy. Twisting the stone's own momentum into fuel for his spell, he focused on multiple points across the flat surface, and *pushed* upward, adding his own reserves to the rune, slowing the slab's fall before it *clack-clacked* against the raised supports on the far side of the forge.

The supports on the near side spiraled further from the earth to meet the face of the slab. "It should hold," Mirsa called.

Kevon released his spell, shaking from the intense exertion. The Movement rune dimmed in his mind, and he heard the other Mage talking.

"I know we've done more complex work with stone, but the terrain here is ill-suited," Mirsa said, laying hands on the resting slab.

"We have no way of knowing about other Magi in the area, and I'm afraid of working any larger scale Earth magic so close to the volcano," Kevon agreed.

Mirsa lowered the supports so that the midpoint of the slate was barely above the corner of the existing building, then paused. "The end supports are too far apart. Can you lower those on the end, while I bring up the new ones?"

"Sure," Kevon wheezed, stumbling a few steps toward the

other end of the slab before he found his footing. He reached the stone pillar at the back corner, and placed a hand on it. The connection with the power below formed, and he split his attention between maintaining the link, and monitoring the pressure and stress on the slab above. The supports on Mirsa's end lifted, and the slate groaned. Kevon forced the twisted pillars on his end back into the ground, slowly, matching Mirsa's speed. In the space of a few minutes, the new roof was level across the front end of the smithy. Both Magi shifted their focus to the supports at the back, Kevon lowering his, and Mirsa handling the one on her end, as well as the pillar in the middle by the other end of the building.

"All right," Mirsa called. "Enough!"

Kevon stepped back, and could barely see daylight between the old roof and the new covering. "It's good!" he called, but Mirsa was already fusing the slate and granite with short, powerful bursts of Earth magic, stabilizing the structure further.

"Can we go back in?" Rhysabeth-Dane struggled with the horse she was holding away from the action, and coughed as she inhaled ash when she spoke.

CHAPTER 5

Sparks flew from the impact. Kevon moved the glowing steel half an inch, and struck again. Another movement across the anvil, another shower of sparks. A last tap near where the glow of the metal dimmed, and Kevon tossed the blade back into the furnace.

"When did you learn to do this?" Kevon asked Kylgren-Wode. He turned over the guard the dwarf had crafted while he'd been resting earlier, and nodded. The twisted layers of re-forged scrap gave the piece a distinct look, and would be eye-catching once the final polish was done. The way the crosspiece curved down around the front fingers and rejoined the handle at the base was strange, but functional. The three rivets that sat near the anvil looked at least as good as Kevon could have done himself.

"Things no one else wanted te bother with used te be my specialty," the ambassador chuckled. "I'll have yer grip carved as soon as we find some decent wood."

"I'll have to draw some metal up from the tang to match this, but I've always tended to be heavier there than most," Kevon commented, poking at the glowing blade a few times with his tongs before fishing it out of the coals.

"When will this ash end?" Alanna grouched, peering toward where the mountain should be.

"There has been no new eruption in two days," Mirsa commented, moving to a safe distance from the sparks, beside the assassin. "With luck, the skies should clear by tomorrow."

“Not that seeing the boys all sweaty with their shirts off has been *bad*,” Alanna quipped, throwing Mirsa a sidelong glance. “I just wish they’d be a little quieter about it.”

“Outside in the ash, or inside in the heat, stuck in the corner wrapped in a blanket to shield myself from iron bits... still in the ash.” Mirsa fixed her gaze on Alanna’s good eye. “I, for one, will not miss any of this.”

“Trust me,” Kylgren-Wode laughed, applying the last of the thick clay to the precariously balanced blade. “I’ve done this more than once.” The dwarf wiped a bit of clay from one of the edges of the blade, and turned it over to inspect the other side. “It’s ready. Now I’ll work the bellows...”

“We’re hardening it, I get that,” Kevon snapped, not bothering to hide his annoyance.

“Something about the different temperatures...” Kylgren-Wode shrugged. “The way I’ve always seen it done. If you didn’t like Dwarven craftsmanship...”

“No, it makes sense...” Kevon placed the blade in the glowing coals, and set the tongs aside while the metal heated.

“There?” Kylgren-Wode peered over the bellows-handle at the glowing iron.

“Not quite...” Kevon watched as the light golden glow on the sword edges began to take on a rosier hue. “Now.” He picked the blade up with the tongs, and dipped it point-first, into the water barrel near the open end of the smithy. He swished it around until the water stopped hissing, then eased the end with the tang in slower, taking care not to agitate it as much as with the blade end.

“What are you smiling at?” Kevon asked, shaking his head at the dwarf.

“Just happy yer blade didn’t shatter,” he chuckled. “It’s going te be a good one.”

“Temper with this stuff still on it?” Kevon asked, deferring to the dwarf's judgment.

"Te light straw," Kylgren-Wode nodded, leaning into the bellows, pumping the handle at a smoother, measured pace.

Kevon placed the blade back into the coals, and scowled at the ash-muted light that still streamed into the room. "This part would be easier in a cave."

The bellows continued their even motion, even as the dwarf's moustache twitched with irritation.

"It'll need a stout grip," Kevon commented, scraping the last of the fired clay from the blade's fuller. "The tip is still heavier than I expected."

"Alder," Kylgren-Wode grumbled, fussing over the placement of the tools and the newly-made fuller-jig back in the box. "Been passing them fer days before we stopped. Best thing for it, until we find some Ironwood."

"The patterns are..." Kevon traced a finger along the wavy borderline of dark and light metal that rippled along the length of the weapon between the outer edges and the depression of the fuller.

"The same as ye'll see if ye look close at yer axe," the dwarf lectured, packing away the rivets, leather, and a length of bright red ribbon he'd produced from somewhere. "Different metal, doesn't mark as easy. Same methods."

"And you're sure that I won't want to sharpen it here?" The thickened edges that ran nearly to the top of the depression in the blade would take a good deal of filing to bring to a working edge.

"Yer learning the war-axe," Kylgren-Wode shook his head. "Two hands from the tip, all the sharpening yer going te need."

Kevon nodded, feeling the thickening at the end of the weapon, the slight flaring that lent extra weight, but thinned the metal for easier sharpening. The variations in coloring appeared as tongues of cold flame, different on each side of the sword-tip, but similar enough. The weight distribution would be more like an axe or hammer, the cutting reserved for the end, the length of the blade more for blocking and breaking. A flicker of familiarity lurked for a moment at the edge of his awareness, but fled as he noticed it.

"I like it."

CHAPTER 6

The better part of the morning consisted of sorting out breakfast and clearing the layers of ash that had settled over everything in the wagon during the night. Rhysabeth-Dane doled out the last of the ship's biscuits and hunks of cheese they'd traded for before they left the port almost three weeks prior. Kylgren-Wode unlatched the back gate of the wagon, stowed the partially finished blade, and let the horses eat hay from the end of one of the uncovered bales.

Kevon patted down the fresh earth over the re-buried box of tools. The remaining stock and scrap that was left in the box was supplemented with a pouch of coin that was nearly twice the value of the supplies they had used for repairs and new weapons. Had the owner been present, the improvements they'd made over the week they'd spent there might have paid for the iron they'd taken. Without such an agreement, Kevon felt guilty even leaving as much silver as they had.

Mirsa sat outside, looking over the Dwarven librarian's shoulder as she studied the ancient book and her notes.

"Eat," Rhysabeth scolded the Master Mage before hunching back over the text.

"It's not agreeing with me..."

"It is not just for you..."

"Hush," Mirsa cautioned, looking around to where the others made preparations for departure. "No one knows..."

"They are blind," Rhysabeth-Dane agreed, glaring over her shoulder for a moment. "But they do need to know."

"When the time is right."

"If you're talking about leaving, the time is right now." Alanna knocked the caked ash from the soles of her boots before picking up her saddle and disappearing back outside as fast as she had appeared.

Mirsa gnawed off a bite of cheese, and washed it down with a swig of water.

The Dwarven librarian nodded as she began arranging her notes and books, packing them away for travel.

Kylgren-Wode helped Mirsa and Rhysabeth-Dane stow their belongings and lifted them into the back of the wagon before securing the gate. He snugged the harnesses of both of the stout draft horses before he climbed up to the seat and took the reins.

"What are ye waiting fer?" he roared at Kevon and Alanna, already in their saddles and standing by. "The mountain te belch again?" He jerked his thumb sideways for emphasis, pointing to the thinner column of steam and ash that billowed in slow motion from the peak far to the east.

The Warsmith smiled and clucked with his tongue, turning his mount onto the pallid track, Alanna moving alongside as the ashes swirled up and about in his wake.

"Never thought I'd be looking forward te getting back on the sea," the ambassador grumbled, waiting a moment for the grey cloud to settle before following his friends southward.

"What about now?" Mirsa prodded Rhysabeth-Dane as the wagon rattled along the mountain road that wound down to the port city below. "Can you feel this mountain?"

The latent Earth power had been pressing against Mirsa's mind for the greater part of an hour, but the tiny librarian just shook her head. "I'm glad to be near it, but it's not my mountain."

Mirsa pressed her senses outward, searching for any trace of the oddly structured power that had surrounded the Dwarven Hold, but found nothing, and severed the link before the magic could overrun her. “Interesting,” she mused, squeezing Rhysabeth closer to her side.

CHAPTER 7

"And good fortune to ye," Kylgren-Wode shook the stablemaster's hand and scooped up the pile of silver coins from the table. He walked back outside to where Mirsa and Rhysabeth-Dane waited by the emptied wagon.

"It'll be enough te get us there," he grumbled, "but not much else."

"The elves are the next piece of our puzzle," Mirsa declared. "We'll have to go from there."

"We'll not be going anywhere if they don't find a ship willing te carry us there," the Dwarven ambassador grumbled, jerking a thumb toward the waterfront district. He stooped and scooped up the remaining saddlebags containing their scant belongings, and tossed them over his left shoulder, wiggling back and forth until they settled into place. Shifting his axe harness to the right until he felt balanced, he rested his hand on the haft of the weapon and glanced over at his companions. "They may already be sailing fer that island in the time it takes fer us te get te the water." He grunted and took a few halting steps to punctuate the joke before dropping into an easy stride down toward the sea.

Rhysabeth-Dane covered her mouth and peeked at Mirsa with glimmering eyes before grabbing hold of the Master Mage's hand and lurching after their companion.

"They say you're the man we need to talk to," Kevon said,

stepping up to the bar and sitting down.

"Who says?" the man beside him asked, lowering his mug.

"Every ship captain who's heard the words 'passage' and 'Mage' in the same conversation, for starters," Alanna answered, taking a stool on the other side of the man. "Seems you have a pet Mage of your own, if the stories are true."

"He wouldn't like being called that," the man laughed, "But there's a lot of things Reko doesn't like." The man stood and extended a hand to Kevon. "Yusa's the name, Captain Yusa. But you already knew that."

"We did," Kevon admitted, "But what we need to know is if we can buy passage on your ship."

"Where are you headed?"

"We'd rather discuss it in..."

"Excellent!" Yusa clapped Kevon on the shoulder, and tossed two coppers onto the bar before gulping down the last of his ale. "Secrets is extra..." he whispered over the background noise of the small tavern, and turned to leave.

Alanna glared at Kevon, who could only shrug and follow the ship captain out onto the street.

"I don't know about 'extra'," Kevon commented as he caught up to Yusa and matched his stride. "There could be trade opportunity where we're headed though, Alanna here could help with that, make it more than worth your while."

"The elves are particularly fond of Heartmelons, which will not grow on their home, but are abundant here. They..."

Kevon smiled at the brief slice of personality that showed through the assassin's toughened guise.

"I'll help," she hissed. "But you'll make it worth *my* while. Both of you."

Captain Yusa stopped and glanced around before speaking. "Travel to the Glimmering Isle is something that is simply not done. I..." He looked over Kevon and Alanna for a minute, then laughed. "I'll see what Reko has to say about it. Then I'll probably do it anyway."

◆ ◆ ◆

"Yer certain of this Yusa? And this 'Reko' ye've never met?" Kylgren-Wode scowled as the longboat approached the pier. He blew the fresh shavings off of the alder grip he'd been whittling at, and tucked it in a pocket with its twin.

"Who can be certain of anyone?" Kevon asked. "It may have been different for you in the Hold, but we have all felt the sting of betrayal. We'll feel it again. The important thing is to be prepared for it."

"The games ye play are with yer lives, we gamble instead with honor." The ambassador agreed. "Deception in the Hold would only feel like a knife in yer back, it wouldn't really be one."

Alanna's glare hardened, her face flushing half a shade in an uncharacteristic show of outward emotion.

Kevon and Kylgren caught tossed lines from crewmen and helped secure the boat on the pier.

Captain Yusa waved the two aside and climbed up from the boat himself. "No offense," he offered, brushing himself off and standing tall before the group. "I studied the Arts for a season, to no real effect. I still like to stay clear of metal. Sometimes I feel a connection to the sea. I'd hate to lose that."

"No arguments here," Kevon smiled. "Have you made your decision?"

"Master Reko is not completely convinced, but I am captain of my own destiny." Yusa laughed. "I've spent too long fishing and following the coastlines. The men are ready for adventure, as am I. We'll reprovision, and sail with the morning tide in two days."

CHAPTER 8

Bertus knocked on the door well after the farmerfolk had left for the morning, a break in the routine of the previous few days. After riding from before dawn until after dark nearly every day the last week, the horses and the tempers of their riders were sorely in need of a break.

"Ready!" Alma smiled, opening the door and shouldering her share of the provisions. Martin grunted and hefted his saddlebags before following her out into the hallway.

"Breakfast is already on the table," Bertus announced, taking Alma's satchel and one of Martin's saddlebags.

"I hope it's strips of smoked venison and lukewarm water!" Alma's eyes glinted mischievously as she slid past Bertus down the hallway toward the little inn's common room. Martin chuckled and followed her out to the table near the fireplace.

"No," Bertus whispered as they disappeared around the corner. "That's lunch."

"Now that there seems to be no hurry," Alma began as Bertus set down the bags and took his seat at the table, "Perhaps you can tell us more about why we have been hurrying."

Bertus waited until the innkeeper left the pitcher of milk and dish of butter and returned to the kitchen before beginning to speak.

"What would you like to hear about first? Our battle with the Orclord? The ambush by fanatic Magi in the palace in Navlia? Or the showdown with Holten that burned down part of Eastport?"

"Begin with our connection," Martin suggested. "Tell us

about Master Holten."

"Holten sent Kevon across the realm with a message that would have ended in his death. With a trinket that suggests your 'Master' had been involved in other serious crimes against the Myrnar. After years of hiding behind a curtain of iron and steel, Kevon finally faced his past not more than three days before I arrived in your valley." Bertus cut a piece of ham and speared it with a fork already laden with scrambled egg.

"But Holten lives?" Martin asked as Bertus chewed.

"Mmm." Bertus swallowed as he shrugged a shoulder. "The battle was… unusual. Kevon and another Mage slung fire at Holten, and he at them. Then… he seemed to turn to living flame, and escaped to another place, one opened by magic. Kevon and the other Mage seemed to think that he may have died there, but sent me to fetch you, should it not be the case."

"It is good that we are far from there," Martin agreed, reaching to hold Alma's hand. "Though Holten was never one for sentiment, he was practical, and would likely use it against his enemies." His eyes narrowed. "Now, what's this about an Orclord?"

The torch lights and skyline of Smara showed against the southwestern horizon as Bertus sat watching the sun sinking behind it. The horses had been stabled hours ago, supper eaten and cleared away. The relaxed pace of the day had helped ease the tension that had been growing in his mind since they'd fled Laston, and given him time to think about how to proceed the next few days. Outsiders in Kron were treated differently than residents; catered to, but charged dearly for it. Smara was the center of that practice, and the most extravagant by far.

"Beautiful, isn't it?" Martin asked, walking up behind him.

"No." Bertus shook his head. "I've seen the sights in Eastport, feasted in the palace in Navlia, roamed the halls of the

Dwarven Hold." He sighed. "Your home was beautiful. I'm sorry you had to leave it, sorry that I was the one to tear you from it."

"I'd much rather lose my land than my life," Martin assured Bertus. "You may have saved us, or given us a fighting chance. That is no cause for sorrow."

"He should have sent someone else. Someone older, stronger..."

Martin laughed. "The Kevon I knew, those years ago, would have looked up to you. From what little you've told us of your travels, I can only assume there is much more we've not heard." His face grew somber. "I'll do whatever you ask, follow wherever you lead, if you will keep my Alma safe."

Bertus shrugged. "South, then. Until we have to choose to turn east for Navlia, or continue on to the frontier. The palace will have improved defenses after the last attack, but we'd stand out more there than we would blending into one of the units Carlo is commanding on the edge of the wastelands."

"Until we must decide," Martin agreed. "We should turn in for the evening."

CHAPTER 9

"Faster," Alanna whispered, a thin sheen of sweat on her brow visible in flickers from a distant torch.

Kevon grunted, weary already from the evening's exertion, but thrust yet again.

The assassin shifted to the side, dodging the blunted wooden practice knife by the width of two fingers at most. She ducked as her student shifted his weight and slashed to the side, passing through the space where her head had just been. She rolled her neck as she straightened, smiling at the slight *pop* as the tension eased. A raised knee impacted Kevon's arm on his reverse slash, stalling his attack. The precise application of force at his wrist and elbow caused him to cast aside the wooden knife, and after a few twists of the captive arm, the Warsmith found himself face-down on the dirt floor, unable to act except for twitching at the pain of the leveraged arm.

"You want to *protect* her," Alanna mocked, pressing herself close upon Kevon's prone form to whisper in his ear. "You can't even protect yourself from me." She squirmed a moment longer, as if to emphasize her complete control of the situation, before releasing Kevon's arm.

Alanna rose and let Kevon struggle to a seated position and rub at the pain in his arm. "I was there when Carlo taught you not to fear getting hurt. That's a start." She sat on a nearby crate and leaned against the wall. "The less you fear, the easier decisions are to make, in combat, in life." She ran her fingers through her hair, pushing it back from her face, and wiped a smudge of dust from underneath her good eye. "But I don't know how to teach someone not to fear death."

This is the only way I can see to get through to her, Kevon thought, glaring at the parody of his love that sat sneering at him from less than two sword lengths away. *The only way that Alanna has mentioned Marelle's return as even possible.* He closed his eyes and thought back to the evening they met, years ago just outside the North Valley. The children they had been then would be terrified at what they had become. The evening walks, the stolen glances between Elburg and Eastport whorled through his mind, a blur of green eyes and satin ribbons, punctuated by clacking wooden swords and sprinkles of her laughter. Their last evening together in Eastport, the folded note he still kept in a pouch, in a pocket close to his heart.

So close to getting her back, Kevon's teeth clenched at the realization. *If fear is all that is standing in our way... I would rather die than lose her this time.* He rolled his right shoulder in a few slow circles, recovered the stick-knife, and climbed to his feet.

"Again."

Alanna woke, stifling the scream that nearly escaped her lips. Fragments of the nightmarish memory forced themselves into her, white-hot shards of reality that had severed Marelle almost completely from the world. If the assassin thought hard enough, she could remember things from Marelle's life, but aside from the occasional twinge of guilt, the shopkeeper's daughter had effectively died the same day as her father.

Kevon snored softly beside her. The two had fallen asleep, exhausted from the brutal combat practice.

She felt his fingertips resting against the small of her back, and cursed the part of herself that wished his arm was draped around her waist. Wriggling away, she sat up, stretched, and pulled her boots on before venturing outside.

"Yer awake!"

Alanna faked a smile and instantly regretted not staying in the room and trying to take advantage of Kevon. “Good morning, Ambassador.” *At least the other one is quiet,* she thought, glancing over to where Rhysabeth-Dane studied in a corner by Mirsa. *If she weren’t so fond of the Mage...*

“The last crates of Heartmelon are waiting to be loaded on the ship,” Captain Yusa announced, looking up from the map spread out on the common-room table. “If we can get them and ourselves aboard in the next two hours, we’ll be on our way.”

Alanna folded two strips of bacon from a platter beside Mirsa into one of the thin, chewy griddle-cakes they’d become familiar with since leaving Eastport, and took a bite. “Give me a few minutes, and the ambassador and I will help you with the loading.” Still chewing, she returned to the room, where Kevon was starting to stir.

“Shh,” she cautioned, strapping on the last of her usual weaponry, a small brace of throwing knifes across her lower back, hidden easily under her light jacket. “Rest a bit longer. We’re starting on the last loads to the ship now.”

His grunts of protest were cut short by two fingers pressing between his shoulder and collarbone. The area was already sore from the previous evening’s practice, but radiated pain in twinges all the way down his arm as Alanna pressed him back down against the bunk.

“I’ll be back,” she laughed, as the Warsmith sulked, defeated.

Kylgren-Wode led the way out into the pre-dawn gloom, where the beginnings of light to the east showed scattered banks of fog below at the waterfront, out into the bay.

“Hold,” Captain Yusa barked, as they reached a curve in the road that overlooked the docks below. He waved his cloak in front of the torch he carried in a cryptic fashion, and peered out at the sea.

One of the ships nearer to the shore than most blinked a

light several times, and the same pattern of light flashed from below them on one of the docks. Yusa nodded and continued down the road. "They're ready."

Alanna peered down at the waterfront, pretending not to notice the movement behind them in a shadowed alley. She followed behind the others, flicking her arm so that a knife slid free of its wrist sheath into her waiting hand. "You trust your crew?" she asked the Captain as she closed within a few steps.

"Good men, all." Yusa affirmed. "I'm a fair Captain. Sometimes business is slow, but I've never had problems. Reko might have something to do with it."

Anger at the Mage's name flared, Alanna's grip on the throwing knife tightened. "Well," she whispered, "Someone's been talking."

She whirled, throwing her knife as the two swordsmen rushed from the alleyway. The leading assailant grunted at the weapon's impact against his chest, but did not fall. The second blade blossomed from his throat, a third glancing off the second man's shoulder.

A pair of long, curved knives whispered free of their sheaths, and Kylgren-Wode stepped alongside Alanna, axe at the ready. The remaining attacker ducked back into the shadows, and his warning cries were answered by at least two other nearby voices.

Stalking over to the alleyway, Alanna surveyed the emptied street, and recovered her knives. "Guildsman," she spat, tearing the sword-amulet from the fallen Warrior. "I'd have used archers, but luckily, we're not up against me."

"Kevon?" Kylgren asked, poking his axe at the corpse.

"We've not outrun our fame, it seems," Alanna agreed. "I'm going back for the others. Can you two make it to the docks without me?"

"They'll be fine," the black-cloaked figure standing beside Yusa laughed, whirling aside as a thrown dagger passed through where he'd just been.

"Master Reko!" Captain Yusa motioned for Alanna to stop,

and turned to address his associate.

"Captain." The hooded Mage held up his gnarled ebony staff, and a piercing brightness began shining from its tip. "I saw the commotion from the ship. I suggest we all return there."

"I'll gather the others, and meet you shortly." Alanna glared at the newcomer for a moment before dashing back toward the inn.

Her skin crawled, even knowing the veil she could not see or feel was in place around them. Alanna led the way out of the inn, peering about to check for signs of danger. Kevon jostled her from behind, turning her toward the waterfront, making room for Mirsa to come through the doorway, deep in concentration. A calm-looking Rhysabeth-Dane followed, only the slightest wrinkle of concern touching her face, offering a guiding hand to Mirsa as they strolled down the darkened streets.

"Alacrit's favor does us no good here," Kevon whispered to Alanna, the words hollowed and fading almost as soon as they left his lips.

"The prince's good will barely extends past the Inner Cities," she sighed, "In a rival nation, it's worse than nothing. We'll have to make do with our steel and *sorcery*."

A block down the road, they saw a patrol of militiamen burst into the inn they had just left. As soon as the last one entered the building, Kevon took Mirsa by the arm. "Let's go," he whispered, jostling the Mage from her spell. The companions stayed close to the buildings lining the street, scurrying across crossroads when directed by Alanna.

A hundred yards short of the docks, alarm horns started sounding. Confused townsfolk peered out into the streets, or rushed inside, slamming doors and barring them shut.

"Run."

Kevon pushed back his tunic sleeves, turning to face up the road from town, ignoring for the moment the completed sword hanging at his side, and the hammer looped at his back. Half a dozen mercenaries emerged from an alleyway the party had passed less than fifty yards back. Within seconds, a blazing sphere two feet in diameter was suspended between Kevon's outstretched hands. With a dramatic flinging gesture, the fireball rocketed toward the cluster of men, detonating with a thunderclap and a shower of sparks just over where their pursuers had flung themselves to the ground.

"Illusion," Kevon whispered to Alanna, who stood beside him, throwing knives at the ready. "I said, *run!*"

Alanna and Kevon caught up with Mirsa and Rhysabeth-Dane halfway to the boat. The dwarf squealed a bit as Kevon scooped her up and shouted for the Mage to hurry. Two flashes of steel, and two crossbowmen fell back from their positions on nearby rooftops, injured or dead. The assassin palmed her last throwing knife in her left hand, and grabbed Mirsa's arm with her right, dragging the Mage along behind her.

Crates of Heartmelon sat unloaded near the longboat, which held Captain Yusa and one of his crew. Kylgren-Wode and the dark-robed Reko stood at the end of the dock, waiting for the others.

"Dare we grant them passage?" Reko asked Yusa. "They seem to be trouble."

"You think everyone is trouble, Wizard." The Captain retorted. "We'll see what is what once we get aboard."

"Avert your eyes," Reko commented as the last four passengers ran past him to begin jumping aboard the boat. The lightning-bright flash that pulsed from the end of his staff lit up the morning in all directions, causing the remaining pursuers to slow, unable to see clearly.

As soon as everyone but Reko was aboard, the craft lurched seaward, already free of its moorings. Yusa and his crewman unshipped oars and prepared to start rowing, but an unseen force still propelled them out toward the ship. As Reko's form dwindled in the distance, and their pursuers closed in on him, the Mage vanished, along with the magic that he had been pushing them with.

"A reasonable advantage, that," Yusa mused, and began calling out time and rowing on toward their destination.

"Wait," Kevon cautioned the Captain, and reached within himself and down into the water to craft a spell much like the one Reko must have been using. The runes flared to life in his mind, and the boat leapt forward in the water, carving a path toward the ship.

"Still enough to be profitable, without those last crates," Yusa mused as he sat at the desk in his cabin, revising numbers in the ledgers Alanna had helped him organize. "A few of my crewmen with family there should be able to return to their homes after this, I'm not so sure I'll be welcome in that port."

"My apologies for that," Kevon offered. "There are some decent folk that have misread my intentions, and some less than decent ones that know them for what they are. Both would like to see me dead."

"Wouldn't have anything to do with you practicing the Arts and wearing a sword, would it?" Yusa chuckled. "Reko may be somewhat judgmental about that when I tell him."

"Then why..."

"He has a way of finding things out. We've been together for years now, this crew has no secrets from him. With his temper, it's better that way." Hefting a gnarled walking stick that lay across the desk, Yusa thwacked the cabin wall twice. "Reko!"

"Am I a servant, to be summoned thusly?" the Mage growled, lurching into view next to the desk.

Kevon startled at the black-robed Mage's appearance, having felt nothing indicating the working of magic on the scale required for Sending, even over such a short distance. *Illusion,* he decided after a moment of frantic thought. *Concealed Illusion, very well done. It's the only explanation.* A lump rose in Kevon's throat. *So he already knows.*

“Does someone want to explain to me why we were attacked openly in the streets?”

“You alre...”

Kevon motioned for Mirsa to be silent, wanting to allow the unfamiliar Mage to keep his secret for at least a little longer. *Wanting to keep secrets, I understand.*

“The attacks were directed at me,” he explained. “When we were still in Eastport, it was discovered by the authorities that I can use magic, as well as a sword.”

Reko’s form tensed, his carved ebony staff lowering toward the group.

The others shifted defensively, Alanna’s last throwing knife flashing into view in her hand. Kevon alone made no move, but smiled at Reko as the pale, hooded Mage ‘reacted’ to information he already knew.

“Easy,” Yusa chided. “I may not know everything about these youngsters, but they’re not our enemies. Why judge the boy for an accident of birth, if that’s what it is? Besides, if he were so dangerous, he would not have needed our help to get away. I may not know magic as well as you do, but I know *people*.”

“Someday, you may be wrong,” Reko sighed, raising his weapon to a less menacing posture.

“Not today,” Captain Yusa said, rising from his seat to lean over the desk. “Though it seems there is more explaining to be heard.”

CHAPTER 10

The sights, sounds, and smells of Smara were more impressive than its evening skyline. Warehouses and silos were fronted by the attached market stalls that lined every street. The main streets were wide enough to allow two wagons each direction, and ample foot traffic.

"The first block would hold the market square in Navlia," Bertus murmured as they entered the city, and every crossroad was a glimpse of something grander than the one before. Wagons being loaded from swinging chutes hanging from silos made the Warrior wonder if the people of Kron had enlisted dwarves to help build some of their structures.

Bertus leapt from the saddle and handed his reins to Martin, motioning for the others to stay while he edged to the corner of a booth and peered around the corner.

Half a block down a side street, grain flowed from a burlap nozzle that hung from a silo chute into a waiting wagon below. One of the green-clad farmerfolk stood conversing with the driver of the wagon, working a lever that seemed to control the flow, as the wagon inched forward.

Bertus backed away from the corner before the wagon finished filling.

"What is it?" Alma asked as he retook his reins.

"Britger-Stoun," he answered, shaking his head. The common-speaking nephew of Bargthar-Stoun had been in the Hold until Bertus had left with Mirsa and the others. The Warrior had only seen the dwarf a handful of times, but the scar across his face was evident from even this distance. Bertus did the calculations in his head. Riding hard without a wagon, the dwarf should still be over two weeks away from here.

"Get us rooms. There," Bertus said, pointing to an inn on the next block. He shoved a coin pouch at Martin, and climbed back into his saddle. "I'll be along shortly."

Bertus wheeled his mount around to watch the others ride down the street toward the inn, casting a sideways glance as Britger's wagon crossed the intersection behind him, headed east. After a minute, the Seeker turned to follow the dwarf and his wagon.

Bertus hung back as the wagon exited the city, following only when he could barely discern its outline in the distance. He set out at a rapid pace, not wanting to look suspicious. He decided that he would confront the dwarf if he overtook the wagon.

Two miles down the road, the wagon turned north. When Bertus reached the turnoff, he could see the wagon turning back to the east, disappearing behind the high rows of corn. He spurred his mount to a lope, eager to know how the dwarf had managed to make it across the Realm in so short a time.

The track to the east went a short distance to a small farmhouse and a medium sized barn with a cut stone foundation. Fresh tracks led to the barn, and Kevon dismounted and checked the doors. They were barred from the inside. He hitched his steed to the railing in front of the house, and knocked on the door.

After waiting a minute for an answer, he returned to the barn and circled around, finding a smaller unlocked door in the back.

The floor in the barn was also the same cut stone as the exposed foundation. Shafts of evening sun pierced the shadows, revealing thick layers of dust, and a ramp that led down into darkness.

Bertus unbarred the door to let more light in, and peered down the ramp, into the gloom that extended to the end of his vision.

A pile of torches lay on a small table. Aside from a handful of tools hanging from pegs on the wall, the table was the only furnishing in the building.

Bertus returned to the horse, and retrieved flint and steel from his saddlebags. Once back in the barn, he lit a torch, and started down the ramp.

Cautious at first, the uniformity of the downward track eased part of the Seeker's concern, while intensifying his interest. The stonework was reminiscent of the Dwarven Hold, but Bertus guessed that it was much older.

The ramp turned to the northeast, and leveled out. The smooth stone became uneven, like walking on tree limbs laid side by side. Bertus looked down, and saw the smooth stone cylinders he stood upon. He kicked at one, and nearly fell as it turned forward, and the ones he stood on slipped in reverse, sliding him back.

Steadying himself against the wall, he felt, more than heard, a drumbeat fading into the distance. A faint glow down the tunnel was almost lost in the torchlight. Bertus crushed the lit end of the torch against the wall, putting it out. Through the smoke of the extinguished torch, he could still see the receding light. The tempo of the drumbeats was more noticeable now that the flames of the torch were not hissing in his ear.

After two minutes of staring after the departed wagon, the tunnel was dark and silent. The only glimpse of light came from the bend in the tunnel behind him.

Treading carefully until he reached the smooth stone of the ramp, Bertus retreated into the barn, barring the large door and exiting out the back. Coming around the corner of the barn, he noted the sun beginning to sink behind the corn, and wondered if he would be able to make it back to town before full dark, rejoin his charges before too much time passed.

"At least we found out how he got here so fast," Bertus

chuckled, patting down the bag after replacing the tools he'd taken from it. He scratched the horse's mane, and moved to unhitch it from the rail.

"Ah really wish ye hadn't."

Bertus looked over to the doorway of the house, into the sights of a loaded Dwarven crossbow. "Britger-Stoun? I thought it was you."

"Hero." The dwarf harrumphed, lowering his weapon slightly. "Ye've seen more than ye should have. More than any man."

"I've stood before the Seat of the Earth, and mocked your king."

The crossbow drooped further.

"I've helped a heretic Mage advance through the ranks of the Warrior's Guild. Peeking into your barn is the least of my sins." Seeing no further reaction, he continued. "Kylgren-Wode and Rhysabeth-Dane sail to the east with my companions. I was sent to collect my friend's family."

"I was sent to buy grain," the dwarf grumbled, scratching the puckered ridge that tracked across his right jawline. "Several loads of it."

Bertus's mind swam. "If this is even your second load, the trip takes what? One day each direction?"

Britger nodded, swinging the weapon down, removing Bertus from danger. "The world cannot know of this. If they knew the places..."

"Your people bear us no ill will," Bertus shook his head. "Your uncle has sent advisors to assist us. Wondrous as this secret is, it is yours to keep. It's a pity that tunnel does not lead to the south, though."

Britger-Stoun held fast for a few moments before the corners of his mouth turned up in a smile.

"I still don't like it," Martin said as the blindfold tightened about his face. His and Alma's hands were already bound behind them, and another dwarf worked at covering her eyes.

"Ye'll be freed once we're on our way, in the tunnels. Nothing to see there." Britger laughed.

Martin sat back against the bale of hay and appeared to relax, leaning into Alma, who was now kerchiefed securely.

The wagon lurched ahead and rumbled down the roadways the last few miles to the secluded barn.

Armed dwarves burst from the farmhouse, making sure that the passengers were secured before opening the barn door and lashing an odd-looking contraption into the back of the wagon.

Bertus stared at the two large stretched hide drums that hung suspended by leather harness, filling almost half of the back of the wagon. Hooded brass lanterns were lit and hung from hooks in the front and rear of the wagon.

Britger-Stoun fussed with the harnesses of the muscular ponies that led the wagon, and made sure that the reins of the three horses following the wagon were tied at the corners and midpoint of the rear of the conveyance. He drove the team down the ramp and continued on to the rough stone bumps that Bertus had walked upon when he'd followed the last wagon down into the tunnel.

"All right," Britger announced. "Untie them."

Bertus loosed the knots that had been tied rather forgivingly around Alma's wrists, and allowed her to release Martin.

"Where…?" Martin rubbed his eyes and peered back at the ramp that coiled up and around the corner, then ahead to a darkening infinity.

"Are ye going te gawk, or drum?" Britger growled, handing Martin a pair of age-worn sticks tipped with milky-white spheres. "Slowly, at first, until yer horses get used te it."

Martin scowled, rubbing his wrists before accepting the sticks. Testing the drums, he tapped one with a globed end, resulting in a hollow *toom*.

One of the ponies snorted, and the wagon lurched ahead

and to the side.

"Steady!" Britger snarled. Martin waited for the horses to calm down.

"Not them, you!" the driver flicked the tip of a rein that cracked like a whip inches from Martin's ear. "They don't understand Common!" A string of curses in his native language spilled forth, and the ponies stamped uneasily. "Drum!"

Anger at their treatment over the last few hours flared, and Martin swung the drumstick with all his might, and the sound boomed around and through him. He struck the other drum, and the slight variance in pitch rose and twined around the other tone that was just starting to fade.

"Better!" Britger-Stoun called through the thrumming din. "Now, *steady!*"

Half a dozen beats on each drum, and Martin's arms were already starting to burn. Before he knew it, the base of the ramp was lost in the darkness behind them, the wind picking up at his back, blowing stray strands of straw past where he pounded on the giant instrument. He leaned against the hay bale behind him, watching the horses galloping along behind in time with the beating drum between them. The tone of the drumbeats evened out as he found the correct rhythm, and a new sound rose below the deep thrum that seemed to shake itself through his entire body. Too scattered to be a whistle, too low to be a squeak, he shook off the image of hundreds of tiny millstones grinding away at nothing.

The sound ebbed, and the whistling wind tore at the hanging lanterns. The swinging light sources threw odd shadows at the seamless walls and ceilings, but Britger and the stout ponies kept the wagon barreling down the center of the path. The ringing of shod hooves against stone settled into a soothing rhythm that accented the drumbeats. Britger pulled the brake, and the wheels slowed and locked, but the speed they traveled at increased.

Hours passed, and the burning in Martin's arms had long since faded to numbness. Each drumbeat struck as true and as firm as the last, as the first. He wondered if he would be able to stop when asked, if he truly controlled his arms at all. The speed they traveled, judging by the wind at his back, was unnatural at best. He dared not slow down, nor waste a breath on trying to shout a question into the wind behind him.

Bertus sat alongside Britger, peering ahead into the unchanging distance. His eyes watered from the strain, and dried in the wind. The musty air was punctuated only with occasional horse flatulence. Traces of fine dust swirled and caked on the front of their clothing, collecting in wrinkles of fabric and escaping as the riders shifted position.

Glints of silver spiked the sides of the tunnel, and Britger-Stoun's hand moved again to the brake lever.

"Hold fast!" he shouted, releasing the brake. The wheels turned back slowly at first, the horses groaning at the increased drag, then charging harder to compensate for it.

The wagon lurched as it passed between the shining markers. Wheels that had begun spinning backwards surged forward, threatening to drive them over the team that led the way. Britger pulled the brake lever again, and the ride resumed its maniacal familiarity.

"That's the only break in this line," the dwarf yelled over the whistle of the wind. "We've only lost two teams te it this generation!"

Bertus's knuckles whitened as he gripped the rail and the seat-board tighter, ready for the journey to be over.

"Are you all right?" Alma asked Martin, the wind nearly tearing the words from her lips as she spoke them.

The focused drumming kept him from answering, but even in the flickering lantern light, she could see that all the color had drained from Martin's face.

"Let me help."

Climbing under Martin's swinging arm, Alma slid in front of her husband, nestled her back against him, and scooted back onto the bale of hay he sat on. She twined her arms around his, feeling the beat, sensing the rhythm that drove them onward toward their destination. After a minute, her fingers overlapped his hands and wrapped around the drumsticks, grasping them firmly enough that Martin could let go.

His connection to the strange phenomenon severed, Martin sagged, slid further back on the baled hay, and slipped into unconsciousness.

Three awkward beats, and Alma found the rhythm. The team coursed ahead, steadier than before. Smooth stone walls masked the miles that their journey devoured. The headwind they fought was the best indication of their progress, and even that seemed unreliable, at best. Her hair whipped around her face, streaming behind like a frayed pennant, but her eyes were closed. She felt, rather than saw the drums, focusing only on her breathing and the music. The whine of whirling stone cylinders mirrored her breaths, ebbing and flowing with eerie similarity.

Martin woke hours later when Britger-Stoun called out from the front bench.

"Steady!" the dwarf called, turning to make sure he'd been heard. "We're almost there."

The first opposing drumbeat took Alma by surprise. Her concentration and hands were both shaken by the unfamiliar beat. No sooner had she recovered from the surprise, than another beat pounded into her. She could feel the wagon slowing, the decreasing wind from behind her let her lean back into Martin, who was only starting to sit up.

"Keep drumming!" Britger screamed, moving his hand to the wagon's brake.

Alma sat forward, tightening her grip on the drumsticks, and smoothed out the tempo, a task made far more difficult now that the trance she'd been in for the last few hours had been broken.

The drumbeats from ahead sped up, building until there was one for every two that Alma struck. The wind calmed, and the air freshened.

Britger released the brake lever, and the wheels rolled lazily forward, lurching the wagon only slightly as they burst into a large lighted chamber. "Ho!" he called, and the drumming from the chamber stopped a few beats before Alma managed to control herself.

"*Bertus-Oscare!*" Britger-Stoun shouted as scowling dwarves swarmed the wagon, snatching the drums and sticks away from Alma. The king's nephew shouted a few choice words in his native language before pointing to the blindfold hanging around the Warrior's neck. "My apologies," he growled.

"About time," Bertus said, slipping the blindfold up and over his head. It was an hour later, and several spiral ramps, ear-popping pressure changes, and creaking stone doors lay behind them. The familiar sights and smells of the Dwarven Hold's stable surrounded him, and he leapt down to greet the hostlers and help with the care of their horses.

"A-Ah..." Britger-Stoun stammered. "I'm sure Uncle will want te see ye straightaway."

Bertus laughed. "When this is finished. We'll not keep him waiting as long as last time."

Martin and Alma followed behind Bertus as they were led through the winding tunnels and passages that led to the chambers of the Dwarven King. The Warrior called out greetings to those he knew in the rudimentary Dwarven he had learned on his last visit. Work stopped as the procession passed, cheers of welcome mingled with murmurs of confusion at Mirsa's absence, and the addition of the two newcomers.

"Behr-toos!" Bargthar-Stoun cried out, leaping from the Seat of Earth before the group was halfway across the chamber. The overexcited ruler backhanded a guard that stumbled into him near the base of the stairs that led up to the throne, and motioned for the rest of them to stay where they were.

"Heee-Ro." The king stopped a few steps before Bertus, and extended his arm in a formal greeting. "Muhr-sah?" he asked, peering over Bertus's shoulder to his companions.

"Mirsa still journeys with Kylgren-Wode and Rhysabeth-Dane, Highness."

Bargthar-Stoun nodded as Britger translated. "*Anch seite?*", he asked, pointing to the knife at the Warrior's hip.

"Your old sword?" the King's nephew asked.

"The first leg of my journey was magical, I was forced to leave it behind."

Bargthar-Stoun nodded at the translation and pointed to one of his guards, yelling something that Bertus could not understand. The guard bowed, then fled from the chamber.

"*Hoo*?" Questioning eyes squinted at Martin and Alma.

"Alma, sister to Kevon, and her husband, Martin."

The dwarves argued back and forth for a time, as Martin and Alma fidgeted.

"What is it?" Bertus prodded Britger-Stoun in a lull in the squabble.

"Yer people don't abide the use of iron and sorcery, do they?"

"No, they do not," Bertus sighed. "If you are unable to help us, I understand."

The dwarf's eyes widened. "Our people have been waiting fer him since before the wars. We have te help ye."

CHAPTER 11

"I still don't like it," Reko declared as the cabin door closed behind Kevon and the others. "We should not have to risk so much for them, when it would be so easy to turn them over to..."

"Not your decision, I'm afraid." Captain Yusa chuckled at his friend. "I value your counsel, but you are not always right."

"I'd like that to stay between us," the Mage growled, vanishing with a gesture and a soft *whoosh*.

Yusa strode to the cabin door and opened it. "Tea, now," he told the sailor standing closest to him. He returned to his desk to wait for the herbal brew, rubbing at his neck.

'Captain?" Kevon asked, poking his head through the still-open door.

"What now?"

"If we're causing trouble between you and your..."

"Nonsense. Arguing with Reko is one of my favorite things. Despite the headache it usually brings." He kneaded at his neck a moment longer, stopping just shy of the scar at the base of his skull. "Was there something else you needed?"

"I was hoping to speak more with Reko," Kevon confessed. "I'm not having as much trouble so far this voyage, but was wondering how he copes with the sea so well."

Yusa laughed. "We don't sail to the north! I tried once, nearly drove him mad. Never seen him so upset. No, we stay to the shallows. If the weather is calm, you can always see the bottom below us. That's one headache I don't need."

"I'm grateful for that, then," Kevon admitted. "Our last voyage was not an easy one. It came close to claiming my sanity, and our lives."

"We'll be out of the shipping lanes soon, and beyond my experience. What lies between here and the Glimmering Isle is a mystery to us all."

"I only hope the Isle has more in the way of answers than mysteries for us," the Warrior sighed.

"How's that?" Yusa asked, waving Kevon to silence as he answered a knock on the cabin door, and took the tray from one of his crewmen. "Please continue," he said, pouring two cups of the steaming brew from the silver pot.

"It's nothing, really," Kevon shrugged. "A riddle, a cipher, in a book we've been given."

"Nothing?" Yusa sputtered, wiping flecks of tea from the corners of his mouth before focusing his stare at Kevon again. "Your idea of 'nothing' involves assassins, and lighthearted journeys to the Glimmering Isle?"

"It's complicated,"

"You mean magic, I assume. Nothing like a book worth killing over to make a fellow's thoughts turn to sorcery."

Kevon nodded, and sipped the hot tea, the bitter undertones almost hidden by the minty taste. "We think it is a book of spells, but we're unable to read it. We have only a fraction of it translated, our only guess is that the next part lies with the elves."

"My guess is you'll have to lock the book away in an ironbound chest to keep Reko from trying to help. His love of games and puzzles is disturbing at times."

"We're not ungrateful for what you've done to help us," Kevon said carefully. "Or Master Reko, either, for that matter. It's just that..."

"Trust is a funny thing, lad. I understand."

The wind died on the third night out, and Kevon woke as he felt the magic begin to work in the water all around the ship.

He shrugged into his tunic and boots, and stumbled up the stairway to the deck.

Crew members tended their duties with only the slightest hint of unease. The last stars of the morning were still visible through the lessened obstruction of now-furled sails.

Reko and Yusa stood near the helm, studying the darkened horizon. Spotting him, the captain waved him over.

“Three more days, if we can find the wind again,” Yusa declared. “You’re close to finding your answers, boy.”

“Help would not be refused,” Reko whispered from the darkened folds of his cowl.

Obliging, Kevon formed the runes to support and steady Reko’s spell, and tapped into the magic he felt already at work.

The initial contact with the other Mage’s mind was unlike anything Kevon had experienced before. A glimpse of order, focus, and clarity led into the well-controlled working of magic, more precisely done than he’d ever seen Mirsa work. He steadied his own mind, and felt the power he offered pressed into service, a carefully measured acceleration that was undetectable by his other senses.

More than able to sustain the minimal drain, Kevon opened his reserves wider, drawing upon them to insulate his being from the crush of Water power pressing in from his connection to the sea. Prepared, he siphoned energy from the water, holding it at a mental arm’s length, while Reko channeled it away to maintain and increase the potency of his spell.

The sun was nearing its apex when Reko eased out of the spell, the ship listing forward as the magic propelling it dissipated. The wind increased as the ship slowed, and Yusa barked orders to his disconcerted crew.

Kevon slumped, the hours of focused magic revealing their strain in a manner he was unaccustomed to. He leaned on the nearby railing, and looked to Reko.

“I’ll be in my quarters,” the Master Mage whispered, as he turned and strode to his cabin.

I know I’m not the strongest Mage on Ærth, Kevon thought,

watching the other Mage walk, untroubled by the effort of the previous hours. *But using magic usually tires me less than anyone I've ever been around. What is-*

A glimpse of a Movement rune poked at the edge of Kevon's awareness before vanishing. He peered at Reko, who was just disappearing into the cabin.

"Get some rest, lad," Captain Yusa said, stifling a yawn. "You've had a rough morning. The crew will handle the rest. He shook his head as if to wake himself further, and shouted at a slow moving crewman.

Kevon took a few deep breaths and managed to make it from the railing to the stairway belowdecks, and stumbled down to his quarters with the renewed rocking of the vessel. He managed to remove his boots, and thought he heard Alanna say something from the bunk above his, but the words made no sense to his reeling mind. He grumbled halfheartedly, and sleep took him.

"Eat this," a familiar voice said, and he felt the press of wooden spoon and the slosh of scalding liquid against his lips.

"Mmmf..." he sputtered, tasting the rich broth, and startling to semi-wakefulness.

"I could just poke a hole in you and pour it in," Alanna suggested. "It would be much faster."

Kevon forced a small smile, and accepted a spoonful of the broth before the darkness reclaimed him.

Quite a lot of strain.

More than his share of watches.

Protecting us all.

Fragments of conversation intruded on the void, swirling

into visions of the speakers in an elaborate dance around Kevon.

"Keeping up with his combat training," Alanna whispered, gliding across his vision in a dress he'd only seen Marelle wear.

"Haven't even touched yer axe," Kylgren grumped, sitting at the edge of his sight.

"The water's growing deeper," Mirsa paced, Rhysabeth-Dane close at her heels.

"Another day, if the map is right," Yusa grumbled, wandering away from the others, gesturing to crew members who were not evident in Kevon's vision.

"Quite the mystery," Reko murmured, glancing from Kevon to the grimoire that Mirsa and Rhysabeth kept hidden, now clutched in his pale hand. Flat, grey eyes stared at Kevon from the depths of the black cowl. "Who are you?" the Mage hissed, fading and solidifying, growing larger as the other apparitions in Kevon's mind shrank away.

The world spun, tottered back and forth as Reko's form swirled apart, sloshing into nothingness. A flurry of motion, shafts of light and darkness spraying through the gritty void, giving way to coarse warmth, gentle lapping, and at long last, creeping oblivion.

The sounds of the sea coaxed Kevon from his slumber, but the bed he rested upon lay steady. Sunlight and a fresh salt breeze pressed against his face, and he drew the rough blanket closer about him.

The low shelter held three more pallets with spread bedrolls, and through the gaps in the walls, Kevon could see another structure nearby. He shifted, and through the open front of the shelter, he could see the ship stationed off shore.

"I'm telling you, with unicorn blood, you could brew a potion that would heal him completely."

"We didn't even know unicorns existed for sure until

today, and you want to start killing them already?" Mirsa shrieked in frustration. "We don't know what's wrong with Kevon yet, Reko. Let's not risk angering the elves yet."

"They've not shown themselves since we landed, who knows if this is even the right island?"

"He's awake."

Kevon glanced at where the quiet third voice had come from, and Rhysabeth-Dane peeked around the edge of the shelter to look into his eyes. She wriggled her fingers at him in greeting, and smiled.

"I'll return later," Reko announced. "Tend to your companion."

Mirsa rushed in, bringing along a waterskin that she held to Kevon's lips. "Drink now, while you're awake."

"I'm fine, let me hold..." Clumsy fingers grasped at the skin, almost knocking it from Mirsa's grasp. Fatigue at even the small action washed over him in waves.

"You've been asleep for four days. Let me do this." Mirsa tucked Kevon's arm back to his side, and poured mouthfuls of water into him.

After a few swallows, Kevon shook his head. "We've arrived, then?"

"This must be the place," Mirsa nodded. "Alanna is scouting into the trees, but we've been here almost two days, with no sign of an elf."

"How do you know?"

"Can't you feel it?" Mirsa whispered, looking past him, toward the back of the shelter, away from the shore. "The Light... is different. Just like in the Hold. Solid, pure, restrained. I'm guessing we're near the..."

"Awake?" Captain Yusa emerged from the other shelter and made his way over to the group. "Good! Perhaps we can start moving soon, and unload the cargo from my ship!"

"Unlikely," Mirsa commented, lifting Kevon's arm and releasing it to flop back down to his side. "He'll need to regain his strength."

"And here comes some help with that," Yusa stopped short of the shelter's entrance, looking off to the side.

Kevon closed his eyes and breathed while the others remained silent.

"What, is he dead?" Alanna griped.

A smile formed as Kevon opened his eyes and saw the assassin leaning around the corner of the shelter, three fat squirrels strung from her wrist. Colorful tubers poked out from the mouth of a sack in her other hand.

"Here..." Alanna snapped. "Take... care of this." She shoved the sack and brace at Yusa. "Why don't the rest of you go... somewhere?"

Mirsa stood and walked past Alanna, handing her the waterskin as she passed by. "It's all right, Rhysabeth," she chuckled, reaching back to take the scowling dwarf's hand. "I'll get the fire going, and then we can study some more."

Alanna waited until the others were out of earshot before she approached Kevon. She sat by his side. "We need you at your best, and soon," she whispered. "Not everyone here is what they appear to be."

Heavy eyelids drooped, and Kevon's mind fluttered.

"Here," Alanna said, pressing something to his lips, a piece of dried leaf. He chewed a few times, and she gave him another mouthful of water from the skin.

"What..."

"Just wait," she said, pressing her fingers to his lips. "Wait for it."

Minutes passed. Kevon's stomach trembled, and his cheeks grew hot. A prickling sensation began in his feet and hands, and the fog clouding his mind started to part.

"Medicine?" Kevon asked, sitting partway up.

"Not quite," Alanna grimaced. "Mild poison, if taken in larger doses. Interesting at lower ones though."

Kevon blinked, and shook his head, his mind beginning to race. "What were you saying? Not everyone..."

"The Mage, Reko?" Alanna harrumphed. "I thought he was

odd on board the ship. But here?” She lowered her voice even more. “He doesn’t leave any footprints.”

CHAPTER 12

"What do you mean, you have to help me?" Bertus asked, his gaze moving from the king to his nephew, and back.

"Come!" Bargthar-Stoun shouted, dragging Bertus toward the steps that led up to his throne. "Mmm." The ruler of the dwarves nodded his head and pointed to the last tapestry on the right hand side of the chamber.

Bertus walked toward the picture, details becoming clearer as he approached it.

An army of orcs populated the bottom third of the panel, twisted forms of many sizes, cruel weapons brandished as they marched upward. The middle third of the tapestry was blasted landscape, rocky terrain scattered with the bodies of orcs and dwarves. The top third was rank upon rank of Dwarven warriors. An impressive shield-wall snaked across the panel. The shield-bearers wielded warhammers, behind them, three lines of pikemen. Beyond that, crossbows and spears filled the hands of the Dwarven host as deep as the embroidered hanging stretched.

Bertus walked closer, catching a glimpse, a glint of gold, a splash of brightness in the otherwise dark work. When he'd come close enough to make out the details of the figure near the center of the Dwarven line, he gasped.

A man, nearly as broad as a dwarf, though head and shoulders above them all, stood in front of the defenders. A sword, alight with flames, decorated with a red ribbon, was raised above his head, as if ready to strike down at the oncoming horde. From the palm of his other outstretched hand, streaks of white and gold radiated in all directions.

The figure's features were too vague to matter, but Bertus did not need any more details. "Kevon?" he whispered.

"I still think we should notify the prince first," Martin argued.

"This action is perhaps more urgent, and it would allow the message to be delivered by a trusted commander," Bertus asserted. "That'll give me time to seek out Kevon, and get him back here to cement our new relations with the dwarves."

The third day after their arrival at the Dwarven Hold, Bertus and Martin stood over a map of the continent, still arguing over troop deployments.

"This commander, Carlo?" Martin asked, "Won't think we've overstepped our bounds?"

"A company of battle-ready dwarves to help shore up the defenses on the frontier should ease his mind," Bertus shrugged. "He'll have to see things our way."

"I still don't see why you can't come with us."

"I'm going to be on a ship, hours out to sea, by the time you even speak to Carlo." Bertus explained. "Kevon wants you safe, and you'll have Carlo to escort you back to Navlia." He pointed to the lines radiating out from the Hold on the map before them. "There is only one exit closer to Navlia than the frontier, and Carlo's not there. It makes a difference."

Martin nodded, glancing over the map once more. "These breaks in the line to the frontier, are they cause for concern?"

"Not with the troop sledge we're running," Britger-Stoun interjected. "It'll be slower starting, without horses, but safer scraping across the breaks."

"Has the advance team from Eastport returned?" Bertus asked the king's nephew.

"I heard the drumming as I was leaving the chamber. They should be reporting soon."

"Good, I'm anxious to get moving again." He rested his hand on the hilt of the sword he'd been presented that morning, a replica of the blade he'd carried on his first visit to the Hold. Inches shorter and visibly thinner, the heavier gray metal the dwarves used balanced much the same as the other blade had in his grip.

"Two Stoneguard, four regulars, and the two of us?" Bertus asked Britger.

"Aye. The ship's crew is being hired out. We've no knack fer it."

"How many can you spare for the frontier?"

"Bargthar-Stoun has committed ten Stoneguard and fifty regulars te accompany yer friends. He's preparing fer supply runs te follow them every few days, also."

Bertus nodded. "That should be enough for the short term. If the tapestry in your throne room holds true..."

"More are preparing," Britger reassured him.

"The others are back from Eastport," Alma said, poking her head through the doorway. "We've all got two changes of lighter clothing for the frontier, too."

"They'll have to do aboard the ship for me, then." Bertus chuckled.

"Not going with us?"

"We'll see each other again, at the Palace in Navlia. I'll bring Kevon along, too."

"Then I'll see what we can get altered for you before you leave," Alma ducked back out and was gone.

"If we are to need Kevon and as many troops as the tapestry suggests, neither one of our missions can fail." Bertus leaned back over the map, his eyes darting east of the port city, along the path Kevon might have taken. "Where are you?"

CHAPTER 13

Kevon peered across the campfire, watching Reko through the pulsating lens that his perception had become. His skin crawled, another recent side-effect of the poison leaves he'd continued to take to remain awake and alert.

Reko sat in the same spot as he had all evening, on a driftwood log they'd been using as a bench. Mirsa sat on the other end of the log, Rhysabeth-Dane at her side, shuffling pages of parchment and comparing them to other books and notes.

"We'll begin the trek inland tomorrow, then." Yusa affirmed, glancing toward Kevon.

"I'm still weak, but well enough to hike." He responded, his gaze remaining locked on the Mage across from him.

"Sure you wouldn't like any?" Alanna waved a bowl of the stew toward Reko.

"Certain." He sniffed. "I have my own rations back aboard the ship. And my own bed." The Mage stood, and glanced around at the others. "Until the morning." He raised his staff, and vanished.

"Powerful, to do that unaided," Kevon commented, shifting his gaze to Mirsa.

"Concealed, as well," she added. "I've seldom felt him work any of his magic."

"Strange, but he's been a loyal companion for years," Yusa laughed. "Quite a few scrapes he's gotten me out of, that's for sure. Quite a few others I would swear he had a hand in."

"We had a companion much like that," Kevon closed his eyes and lowered his head. "Not a Mage, but..."

“An incredible ally.” Mirsa finished.

“I’m sorry I was never able to meet Waine,” Alanna offered. “It seems he changed everyone he met, for the better.” She stood and stalked around the fire to where Reko had been sitting. “One thing we may need to ask your friend, though,” she said, looking to Captain Yusa, “Is why he doesn’t leave footprints.”

“I suspected Illusion before, on the ship.” Kevon added. “A Sending between rooms when seconds of walking would do... was hardly practical. But what I suspected then makes no sense in this situation. We would see prints where we had not seen him, instead of none where he had been.”

“Or where he appeared to be?” Mirsa asked.

“That may well be,” Kevon nodded.” Projecting himself into our midst, while hiding his true self? Difficult, but not impossible.”

“But it is impossible,” Yusa fumed. “I’ve known him for years, before I got my ship, before I trained at...” he scratched his head. “No, it was after I abandoned my studies, and the Arts. A year or better after that. But still!”

“It seems your friend Reko would be the best to ask about this, the next time we see him,” Mirsa decided. “How long have you been watching him?”

“I always keep my eye on the nearest Mage,” Alanna smirked. “I noticed the footprints yesterday, but have felt uneasy around him since our first encounter.”

“I’ve heard some of the reasons why you have cause to distrust practitioners of the Arts, and understand,” Mirsa fidgeted, and looked up at Alanna. “I hope to be a part of the reason you can trust some of us again.”

“Tolerate? Perhaps.” Alanna answered, returning the Mage’s gaze. “But trust?”

“It’s not just Magi that Alanna mistrusts,” Kevon interjected. “But we have the furthest to go to regain any measure of that trust.”

“I trust we’ll all need a good night’s sleep under our belts to strike camp and head inland in the morning," Yusa barked. He stood, glanced at the untouched sand in front of the log where Reko had sat, and shook his head. "Here's to hoping we can get it."

Kevon led the way, working ever inward and upward toward the shrouded center of the island. Stretches of clear path were punctuated by webs of vines and brush that the Warrior reluctantly hacked aside with his saber.

"We rest here," he called to the others, staggering as he reached the third waterfall of the morning, the first that they could not step over and around. He reached out and filled his cupped hand in the thin cascade, sipping, then splashing the rest over his face to wash away the sweat and sap from the vines.

"Still no sign of Reko," Yusa grumbled. "I don't know if he'll even be able to find us this far away from shore.

"Or if we'd want him to," Alanna muttered as she entered the clearing, watching to make sure nothing was behind them.

Kevon sat by the falls, his back to the stone face that rose a good twenty feet above them. His breathing grew ragged and short.

"Here," Alanna pushed a small flask at him, and he drank.

"What is..."

"It's the only thing keeping him on his feet, Wizard," Alanna snapped. "The faster we can get him to any kind of civilization, the better."

Snatching the empty flask, Mirsa sniffed at it. "This is..."

"Bonesage tea," Alanna said, eye locked on Mirsa. "It's more than anyone else here has done for him."

"*We're* not trying to kill him!" Mirsa shouted, taking a step toward Alanna before seeing the bared dagger in the assassin's hand.

"Enough!" Kevon straightened as the tea took effect, and stood up. "No one is trying to kill me. Did she force it down my throat?"

Mirsa looked at her feet and shuffled uncomfortably. "Did you at least brew it with milkweed sap?"

"I always carry fresh milkweed sap with me," Alanna scoffed. "Not all of us have that luxury."

"We'll find something here!" Mirsa pleaded, scanning the surrounding vegetation. "I'll brew up a potion..."

"I only have three leaves left," Alanna sighed. "We're almost out anyway."

"We have to start right away!" Mirsa opened a bag and began pulling out smaller pouches.

"We need to move now," Kevon said, stepping across the stream and hefting the saber. "We'll figure out what we need to do when we stop for the night."

Rhysabeth-Dane blotted a damp cloth against Kevon's forehead, leaning in to see if she could make sense of the fevered murmurs that escaped his lips. She shrugged her shoulders at Mirsa, who'd looked up from the potion she was tending.

"Nothing yet?" the Mage asked.

The dwarf shook her head, and wrung the cloth out before dipping it in the bowl of cool water that sat beside his bedroll.

"How is he?" Alanna asked, ducking under the makeshift canopy.

"Do you have the things I asked you for?" Mirsa snapped.

"I'm not sure," Alanna answered. "These plants are different than those on either continent we've been on. I'd only just begun to get familiar with the foliage when we left..."

"Give me what you do have, and bring some more water." Mirsa glared a moment longer before returning to her work.

Alanna emptied a small sack onto the crate that they were using for a table, sections of vines, flowers in full bloom, and clusters of unopened buds spilling and sprawling across each other.

Rhysabeth-Dane folded the cloth and pressed it against Kevon's forehead. She rummaged through her things, finding the book she wanted and returning to the crate. She flipped through the text, whispering now and again in her native tongue, sniffing a blossom here, tasting a bit of sap there. She continued flipping through the book, and making notes of her own on loose parchment.

"What are you doing?" Mirsa scolded. "You don't know what any of those are! You could..."

"Bonesage tea is a rare treat for my people," Rhysabeth-Dane giggled. "As are many things that would kill you. Very few things that grow in the earth can harm us. I have already identified half of these, and have ideas about the rest." She lifted a spiky, reddish leaf. "Bloodthistle, for example. Sharpens the mind more than Bonesage, while paralyzing the body."

Mirsa cleaned the tools she had been using, and set them aside. She rinsed out a small stone bowl, and brought it over to the dwarf.

"If you were going to heal Kevon, with the supplies we have here, what would you use?" She held the bowl out to Rhysabeth-Dane.

The dwarf plucked three petals from one of the larger flowers, and half a dozen smaller buds from one of the clusters Alanna had retrieved. "These would ease his symptoms, but we would need much more than Alanna has gathered."

"Perhaps not," Mirsa picked up one of the smaller sections of vine that lay on the crate. "This is not poisonous?"

"Just bland," Rhysabeth wrinkled her nose.

"That's fine," the Mage replied, whisking back over to the rock shelf at the back of the shelter where her laboratory was set up. She picked up a small granite pestle and crushed the flowers into a tacky paste that she scraped into a glass container with a wooden spatula. She upended the vine over the mixture, squeezing the sap from the top of the vine section to the bottom. Thick drops oozed from the cut end, globs of the greenish fluid spattering atop the peach colored paste. She poured fresh water from a skin up to the etched line in the glass, and stirred it until there were only a few clumps left. After placing the glass into a bronze holder, and igniting a small piece of wood beneath it with a wave of her hand, she returned to Kevon's side.

She wrung out and replaced the cloth on his forehead before settling into her own bedroll nearby. "Wake me in an hour?"

Rhysabeth-Dane nodded, and continued reading.

CHAPTER 14

Carlo startled awake, the twitch of his arm sending the shield leaned against his desk thudding to the dirt floor. Cursing softly, he shook the debris free of the symbol that had helped reinvigorate the southern garrisons, and had helped push the lines of the frontier further south than they had been in generations.

"What is it?" he growled, his step back from the desk sending the spindly chair sprawling in a swirl of dust behind him.

The Novice that peered into his office wheezed thinly. "Dhwa..." he croaked, choking on his words in the grimy heat. He shook his head, doubling over, resting one hand on a knee, the other against the doorframe. "Follow."

"What is this?" the commander asked as they reached the doorway, shielding his eyes from the shifting glare of the polished plate some of the Dwarven contingent wore.

"Reinforcements from our friends to the north," Martin called from behind the third rank of dwarves. "Sent on the authority of Bertus the Bold."

The sea of armored dwarves clanked and parted, allowing Martin and Alma to walk through to greet Carlo.

"Alma?" Carlo squinted studying the girl's face.

"Yes, how did..."

"I know Kevon, and knew your father. Come with me."

One of the Common-speaking dwarves shouted a string of commands to the rest of the host, who split into groups and sought the shade of nearby buildings. He followed Carlo and the others to the commander's office.

“Bertus could not come himself, then?” Carlo asked, closing the door once the dwarf and his other guests were far enough inside the cramped room.

“He’s taken a smaller group of dwarves through Eastport, to try and follow Kevon,” Martin explained.

“What trouble has your brother gotten himself into now?” Carlo asked Alma.

“People saw him use magic, and weapons,” she whispered. “They had to flee. He used magic to send Bertus to us.”

“And you collected an army of dwarves along the way?”

“Bertus has dealt with them before, it seems. They helped us get here quickly…”

“On foot? In full armor?” Carlo interrupted Martin. “I don’t see how that…”

“There are things we won’t be able to tell you,” Alma began.

“Your family and their accursed secrets!” Carlo roared. He picked up the fallen chair and sat at his desk. “So. What exactly *can* you tell me?”

“I’ll have to see Prince Alacrit right away,” Carlo shook his head. “Convince him to not turn on the boy.” He looked at the Dwarven translator. “Your forces will have no issue as support here, and reinforcements as needed?”

“Ye’ll have a hard time keeping the Stoneguard from the fighting, but the rest will do whatever there is need fer,” he answered. “Our king has ordered fer the words of Bertus, and those he trusts, te be as they were his.”

“Your Stoneguard can bloody their axes at camp three,” Carlo grunted. “We’ve been taking casualties there almost daily. Who knows, by the time we find Kevon, they may well finish the push across the wastes for us.”

“I will inform the others before we leave.” The dwarf bowed and ducked out of the room.

"We?"

"The dwarves are determined that we shall not fail, since they learned of Kevon," Martin offered. "Some legend they're all riled up about."

"Let's hope that Alacrit feels the same," Carlo sighed. "And hoping is one of my least favorite things to do."

CHAPTER 15

"The tea tasted better."

Kevon coughed and retched, somehow managing to keep the foul-tasting potion from coming back up.

"This will fix part of what the tea did to you," Mirsa scolded. "You should be feeling better by noon."

"Good." Kevon struggled to his feet, fumbling with his swordbelt, wondering at the red ribbon tied near the base of his sword's guard.

"You need to rest!" Mirsa stepped between Kevon and the shelter's exit.

"I'm sure that Holten and his followers are resting today."

"If we can wait until you recover, we'll be able to move faster."

"And if we find an elf that knows more about plants around here, I'll recover faster." He sighed. "I don't like feeling half dead any more than you like looking at it. We're moving."

Rhysabeth-Dane packed away the potion-making equipment, cleaning the instruments more thoroughly than Mirsa herself might have. By the time the dwarf was done, the rest of the camp had been struck, and everyone else was done with breakfast.

"Ahem," Mirsa chuckled. "You wanted to move?"

Kevon opened his eyes and pushed off of the tree he'd been leaning against.

"We just need to keep heading inland. Getting close... I can feel it."

I'm feeling it too, Mirsa thought, reaching down to take

Rhysabeth-Dane's hand. The sensation flickered at the edge of her mind, but would not take solid enough form for her to examine properly. "Like in the Dwarven Hold, but different..." She looked at Rhysabeth-Dane, who only shrugged and shook her head.

Shortly before noon, Kevon led them out of the undergrowth onto a wide path that they could see winding down a valley to a sandy cove.

Yusa muttered under his breath, then chuckled and shook his head in the direction of the shore.

Not five minutes further up the path, they made contact with the elves.

The soft, unfamiliar speech startled everyone but Alanna, who had just spotted the trio, and had a palmed blade ready to throw.

Kevon struggled to focus his eyes on the Elven noble before them, her inhuman perfection distorting in pulses against his heartbeat. He heard Mirsa's tongue stumbling over a few lisping phrases before the Mage admitted, 'I'm sorry, I don't know the entire greeting ritual..." The greenery on the lead elf's tunic seemed to Kevon to rustle as though growing from the garment, rather than simply having been embroidered on it. *I really should be more concerned about those two,* he thought, glancing to the noble's escorts, lean, stern Hunters whose casual half-drawn bows represented possibly the greatest threat to life and limb they'd faced in recent times.

"How strange," Kevon commented, as his gaze shifted back to the lead elf's face, and her piercing light yellowish-brown eyes. "No shadows." He sighed and slumped to the unshaded ground before the trio of elves.

The lead elf placed a hand on the shoulder of one of her escorts, and whispered something in her native tongue.

Without hesitation, the Hunter was in motion, headed up the path, bow slung and arrow re-quivered.

Mirsa's mind worked frantically to grasp at the fragment of speech she'd heard. "*Elder?*" she whispered.

◆ ◆ ◆

Mirsa felt the elves approaching well before they reached the door. The other inhabitants of the city poked at the corners of her awareness, almost like another Mage thinking of an unconcealed spell across a room would, but she could feel the newcomer bending the caged Light around them as he moved. The effect was less powerful than the waves of hammered energy she'd felt in the Dwarven Hold, but more focused, purposeful. Her eyes locked on the door just before the knock announced their arrival.

Relaniel entered first, but her companion swept around her to where Kevon lay unconscious on the bed in the center of the room.

"He hasn't moved since we got here," Mirsa commented as their noble escort reached her side. She watched the newcomer lean over Kevon, throwing no shadow, as several of the locals here did not. "He bends the Light..."

"Aelion Lithtaure," Relaniel commented, watching the Elder herself. "One of his names, means 'bender of light', in rough translation." She took a seat between Mirsa and Alanna. "Our healer, our seer, the Hand of M'lani."

"M'lani..." Alanna muttered, thinking back to the stories another lifetime ago. "She's supposed to be..."

"She *is* the matron of my people, much as L'drom is to the little one there," Relaniel said, looking to Rhysabeth-Dane. "I realize that truths quickly become stories in the world of Men, and that they have no claim to any one of the creators."

"Fascinating!" the Dwarven librarian made shushing motions at herself as everyone but Kevon turned her direction at her outburst. She stopped her scrawling notes for a moment. "Would I be able to speak with you about my personal research later?" she whispered across Mirsa to the elf.

Relaniel nodded once, a faint smile playing across her lips.

"There is much wrong with this man," Aelion announced. "Poison, fatigue, and other severe damage to his body and spirit that I cannot fathom the enduring of. He should be dead. Many times over." He ran his hand over Kevon's forehead. "Yet there is something... keeping him here. Drawing him here. What little energy he has left points..."

Aelion turned to address the others directly. "I'll do what I can to heal him. Even so, it will not be quick, and may not be complete." The elf waited for signs of acceptance from all present before continuing. "Then I will begin. You may, or may not want to observe."

Relaniel fidgeted and stood along with Mirsa. "I've seldom seen this, very few have, and never outsiders!" she whispered to the Mage. "It is the highest honor."

Alanna stood and exited, scowling. Rhysabeth-Dane peered over toward Kevon, but returned to studying one of her texts.

The healer moved between Kevon and the window, stepping in front of the rays of light that barely touched his sleeping form. The rays shone on unobstructed by the elf's intervening body, and Aelion stretched his hand out to rest on Kevon's chest.

Outlines of what should have been shadows around the Elder glowed to double their brightness. The reverse shadows thrown by the two lit torches in the room flared out and away from Kevon, while the intensified rays from the window crept up further on the blankets covering him.

Aelion closed his eyes and spoke in low tones. Undeniably Elven words floated to Mirsa's ears, but flickers of images reminiscent of spoken magic fluttered at the corners of her awareness.

The anti-shadows brightened further. The ambient light in the room did not lessen, but grew flat in comparison to the living brilliance. Wavering torch-fueled images writhed, stretching and curving in exaggerated horseshoe arcs that pulsated toward where the Elder's hand rested on Kevon. The fluttering mismatched rhythms of the lights steadied, and fell into a regular 'one-two... one-two' pattern, and Mirsa felt her own pulse matching the light, and Kevon's heartbeat.

The light flowed slowly into Kevon, and his color improved a shade, as the rhythm slowed and grew more stable. The extra light dimmed away by degrees as Aelion's speech drifted into silence.

"This is all I can do for today," the elf announced. "When he is well enough to consider moving, we will see if performing the ceremony on the grand dais would help speed his recovery."

Aelion nodded to Relaniel, and circled around to the door. "Until tomorrow."

CHAPTER 16

Bertus rushed to the ship's railing, throwing his arms around it to stop himself as a swell pitched him forward. His heart leapt as he spotted the thin ribbon of land ahead. His chest and arms ached from the impact, and the strains of the previous weeks.

"We're almost there," he called over his shoulder to Britger.

"My friends say yer not there yet, and not going te be fer a while," the dwarf chortled, pointing to the two Stoneguard that stood nearby, padded clubs at the ready.

Grunting, Bertus pushed off from the railing, turning and taking three short steps toward the middle of the deck, getting enough space between himself and the edge that he felt comfortable maneuvering. He caught the club that the Dwarf-King's nephew threw him, and twirled it a few times to limber his wrist. The Stone-Oak shaft was heavier than any sword he'd used, but lighter than the hammers the dwarves were accustomed to. Early on in the voyage, he'd used that to his advantage, turning the lack of a complete follow-through into a half-second respite to evade the next attack, or launch one of his own. After the first week of sparring sessions, his Stoneguard mentors had adjusted the speed and responsiveness of their attacks. Mercifully, they'd also begun wrapping the ends of the weapons with thick cloth to spare the inconvenience of broken bones.

Bertus charged the pair of dwarves, veering toward the one on his left as he approached. The Stoneguard on the right took a step back and brought his club up in a defensive position, waiting to see what would happen next.

Swing for the knee... There it is... Bertus thought as the dwarf moved to attack. *These little guys don't like it that I'm taller than them, do they?*

Bertus leapt over the attack, lashing out with his right foot and smashing the unsuspecting defender in the face as he drubbed the other dwarf a glancing blow on the side of the head and shoulder. He pivoted on his left foot as he landed, his right tracing an arc on the deck behind him until he'd turned back to face the two dwarves. Setting his left hand down for an instant to steady himself, he grinned.

"Ye'll only get te do that once," Britger-Stoun called from his perch on the upper deck.

"Once is all I needed," Bertus laughed. "Now they know I can do it, they'll be watching for it."

The two Stoneguard stepped further apart, shaking off their injured pride, moving to not quite opposite sides of Bertus before they started closing in.

Bertus dodged and parried the attacks for a good ten seconds, landing a solid strike on each of his opponents before he let anything slip through his guard. A sudden blow to the ribs, then three more hits in quick succession toppled him to the deck.

"What're they saying?" Bertus asked, sitting up to lean against a crate, and touching his split lip to see the blood on his fingers.

"That on land, ye'd not have lasted half as long," the scarred dwarf said, descending the stairs to stand by Bertus. "I must agree that they are not at their best here at sea." He smirked a moment longer. "They like ye though, they're not holding back."

Bertus shook his head, pain exploding at each change of direction. "I'll have to remember that."

"We should prepare te go ashore," Britger motioned to the east, where silhouettes of sails and circling gulls thickened. "The sooner we find yer friends, the sooner we can get back te the Hold."

Bertus checked his pack, counted the coins in his purse before he got ready to leave his cabin to go ashore. He had enough water for two days, enough to eat for four, and more than enough money to spend to find out where his friends had gone from here, if anyone knew.

He steadied himself on the handle of the cabin door as the ship rolled a few degrees more than it had been, then opened it and emerged into the noonday heat.

Britger-Stoun was helping the crew pull the gangplank back onto the deck, and the others were coiling the mooring lines.

"Shouldn't we be..."

"I didn't make it halfway te the shore," Britger chortled. "A deckhand from another ship seen two dwarves, and some men a while back. Said they were headed te the south. So we sail south."

Bertus nodded, touched his lip, winced, and returned to his cabin.

CHAPTER 17

"Don't these accursed dwarves ever sleep?" Carlo whispered to Martin, as they passed out of earshot, walking on the outskirts of the camp.

"Some of them," Martin reassured the commander. "The regulars, I've seen asleep, for certain. I think the Stoneguard sleep in shifts every few days, when no one else is watching." He shrugged. "I could be mistaken."

"They don't shirk, I'll give them that much," Carlo admitted. "Makes all of this easier on us."

The first few nights had been near chaos as the soldiers, civilians, and dwarves had been unfamiliar with each other's habits, and the workings of such a diverse group. By the end of the first week, the routine was formalized. The five soldiers under Carlo's watch scrambled to care for the horses and establish a perimeter. The three Dwarven regulars set up tents and started fires for cooking. Martin, Alma, and the Dwarven translator prepared the evening meal, and cleaned up, usually with the help of the Dwarven soldiers.

"Tell me more about this book they were so concerned about," Carlo turned to Martin, once they were far enough from camp.

"I only know what Bertus told us, that it's ancient, cryptic, likely powerful." Martin admitted. "They were seeking elves that could read older script."

Carlo nodded. "They'll be sailing for the Glimmering Isle, then. With a sizeable head start."

"They were fleeing Eastport, when they sent Bertus," Martin offered. "Perhaps they did not sail there straightaway."

"Mmm." Carlo grunted. "Perhaps. "We'll see when we find them."

"There's a stream up ahead," Martin pointed toward where the faint gurgling could just be heard, and then patted a pouch on his belt. "I have an extra line, if you're interested."

"Another time," Carlo sighed. "The men get unpredictable about this time of evening, when there is no clear task ahead of them, and soldiers from an unfamiliar faction sharing camp."

"I'd wondered," Martin laughed. "The dwarves have been acting different since we met up on the frontier." He scratched his head. "Except for the Stoneguard. Nothing seems to bother them."

"Good luck," Carlo said, turning back toward camp. "I'll send a detail if you're not back before dark."

Martin walked toward the stream until Carlo was well out of sight, then turned aside and slipped deeper into the forest.

"*Dubrath pak-ta!*" one of the Dwarven soldiers muttered as one of Carlo's men bumped against him and almost stumbled into the fire. The other two Dwarven regulars chortled and jostled one another.

"Accursed runts," another of the soldiers under Carlo's command hissed.

"Stay your tongue!" Alma pointed at the man with a mostly empty ladle, sloshing gobbets of soup on his uniform. "They are here to help us. Far from their homes, out in the open, this cannot be easy for them." She smoothed her apron. "But you..." she pointed at the dwarf who had spoken.

"*Skooze.*" He tilted his head down in acquiescence.

"Just like children..." Alma sighed. She glanced at the Dwarven Stoneguard, who had sat watching the incident without reaction. "And you..."

One corner of the dwarf's mouth turned up in a smile, and Alma couldn't help but laugh.

"Ye handled that well," the Dwarven translator said, sopping up the last of his soup with a crust of bread, and sloshing the wooden bowl through the tub of wash-water as he finished his meal. "Learn the language, ye'd make a fine ambassador."

"And deal with this… wonderfully juvenile behavior… constantly?" she asked.

"Ye've got the words of a diplomat already," he shrugged. "And the ear of our King. A handful of seasons in the Hold, ye'd be a great help te both our peoples." He shuffled his feet before looking back up at her. "Some might expect fer the sister of the Blademage te be more than a farm wife."

"I'll not mention that affront to the other farm wives I know," Alma glared at the dwarf. "And what my brother is or is not has no bearing on what I do with my life." She thought a moment. "Besides dragging me back and forth across the Realm, obviously. Making me consort with dwarves and soldiers, probably getting me mixed up in more magic than I care to think about, eventually. Damnation."

"So ye'll consider it!" the dwarf laughed, and slapped Alma on the back. "We'd be lucky te have ye."

Alma shook her head as the translator worked his way over to his countrymen, slapping heads and chastising the soldiers in their native tongue.

"No luck fishing?" Alma asked as Martin entered camp empty-handed, under the watchful eye of the visible Dwarven Stoneguard.

"Not tonight," he answered, flashing empty palms for all in the camp to see.

"You'll do better next time," she reassured him, scraping the last of the thickening soup into a bowl and handing it over.

"Only another two weeks, at this pace, until we reach Navlia." Carlo said, depositing his empty bowl in the washbasin.

"Only." Martin smirked. "This way is easier on the arms, I suppose."

"Enjoy the journey, boy." Carlo barked. "Destinations are seldom what we expect."

Martin shrugged, and sat on one of the makeshift log benches around the fire to eat his meal.

"He gets like this when things change that he can't control," Alma confided in hushed tones as she began washing the used bowls. "I'm surprised it's taken this long, given the circumstances."

"Your brother was the opposite," Carlo remarked, scooping up a dishcloth and drying the bowls Alma finished with. "Even when he was keeping secrets, he was in the thick of things. The only times he was withdrawn were because of a woman. That's clearly not the case here."

"No," Alma agreed. "It took more than a year for Martin to adjust to life away from his Master. It seemed like he was finally settling in to the way our lives had turned out,"

"Then... this..." Carlo finished. "He hasn't even seen any real action yet. I'll make sure the others know to keep watch on both of you, should anything happen."

Alma shook her head. "Things will happen as they must."

Carlo folded the cloth and placed it by the stack of dry bowls. "And rarely as we prepared for them," he chuckled. "Sleep well."

CHAPTER 18

"Ahh..." Alanna sat back against the trunk of the tree, one leg dangling off the broad branch that held her. Below, the lowest level of the Elven city moved, all bright colors and graceful rhythm. She stretched, yawning, and her fingers brushed against the longknife at her belt. She whipped it from its sheath, whirling into a crouch, blade inches from the neck of the dwarf that peeked around the corner.

"Put yer knife away," Kylgren-Wode admonished her, sitting on the side of the branch that had a living railing woven from smaller branches and vines. "I had te get out of the middle of that," he grumbled, indicating the bustle below. "And I don't fancy going much higher."

Alanna sheathed the weapon, but remained crouched as she turned to survey the scene below. "I found the pattern," she commented.

"The what?" the Dwarven ambassador's face scrunched in annoyance.

"The shadows. Some elves cast them, some don't. I found the pattern."

"Oh. Ahem. That pattern. Yes?"

"Some of the commoners, a few of the children, more of the nobles," Alanna explained, "But *all* of the Hunters."

"Well, that makes..."

"And the younger children," Alanna interrupted, "Flicker. Shadows like sputtering candles, some of them. As if they haven't learned to control it yet."

"It would be useful fer hunting, sure," Kylgren-Wode commented. "Traipsing through the woods, no shadows fer the game te see, or enemies, at that."

"It may be a requirement to be a Hunter," Alanna mused. "It makes sense."

Neither spoke for several minutes.

"Miss your cave?" Alanna asked.

"It's a *Hold*!" Kylgren-Wode huffed. "Not a cave. Fer the love of..."

Alanna winked and allowed a partial smile to writhe across her lips.

"Wait. Yer..."

"Not even I am immune to this place," Alanna sighed. "Certainly not with... Well, maybe they're still there." She stood, and helped the dwarf to his feet before jogging across the branch and stepping up to another. "Hurry."

Sunlight sparkled through the glade, the near-noonday light brightening the entire clearing. Rhysabeth-Dane sat under a tree at the far end, near papers and books spread on a flat rock, trying to eat an apple. She threw the apple, her curses lost on the breeze, and reached into her satchel for another.

Two bites in, the three unicorns who'd chased after the discarded fruit returned, and began nuzzling the Dwarven librarian once more. Another thrown apple, and the only phrase that remained intact from across the meadow was 'unicorn stew'. When the unicorns returned, Rhysabeth-Dane scratched their muzzles a minute before waving them off and sitting down to resume her research. Looking over her shoulder to make sure they were gone, she pulled an apple out of her cloak pocket, and continued eating.

"I think she's adjusting better than the rest of us, they won't even come near me," Alanna admitted.

Kylgren-Wode said nothing, eyes locked on the small figure in the distance.

"When are you going to tell her?" Alanna asked, poking the dwarf in his ribs.

"Ye don't understand," Kylgren-Wode grumbled. "Things

are done differently in the Hold. I'd need permission fer..."

"We're not in the Hold," Alanna interrupted. "We're up in a tree, on top of a mountain, on an island between two realms that each have people looking to kill us. We're kind of living by our own rules."

She looked to the sky. "It's almost noon. I'll... go watch Kevon's treatment, if you go talk to her."

When the dwarf made no movement, Alanna grabbed him by the collar of his shirt and spun him to face her, lifting him to his tiptoes and bending down to look into his eyes. "She is awake, and able to hear you. Not everyone has that luxury. Shall I drop you over the edge, or are you going to climb down yourself?"

"Climb! C-climb!" Kylgren-Wode gasped, grasping at the vines on the railing.

"Good luck," Alanna whispered, kissing the dwarf on his forehead before releasing him. She turned and trotted down the skyway toward the center of town.

"Crazy..." Kylgren-Wode trembled, both hands clasped tightly around the railing for a few moments longer before he spotted a climbing path down a nearby tree.

Alanna moved between the milling elves, making her way toward the ivy-covered dais. Kevon had already been deposited on the smooth wooden table at the center, the litter he'd been transported on lay off to the side. Relaniel and Aelion stood nearby, watching the sky, waiting for the proper time.

She slipped past two shadow-less Hunters, toward the front, where mostly the children gathered. Despite their spritely appearances, Alanna noted that each of them did indeed cast a shadow, making the unlikely scene before her the most comfortable one she'd witnessed in days.

Alanna began to wonder when the sun was going to reach its apex, when the entire assembly of elves fell silent at precisely the same moment.

“We begin,” Relaniel said, glancing past Kevon’s sleeping form to where Alanna stood.

Alanna peered left, where the elf’s gaze had alerted her to Mirsa’s silent arrival. Less concerned with the Mage than usual, she returned her attention to the dais.

Aelion, back turned to Alanna, raised his arms and began speaking in the harsh dialect that he used for the ceremonies. Relaniel spread her hands wide, as if embracing the entire gathering.

“This is new,” Mirsa whispered as two decorated Hunters approached from one side, and two nobles closed in on the dais from the other direction. One of the nobles had a shadow, but it flickered fitfully, and disappeared as they approached and joined arms with Relaniel.

Arms woven together like cords of thick ivy, the crescent of elves shuffled toward Aelion, reaching out to him while he continued the ritual, unaware.

Mirsa jumped as the elves on the ends of the crescent made contact, and completed the circle. The caged Light magic in the area crystallized in her mind, her own personal illusion, as she reached out for it, but could not make contact with its surreal brightness.

Alanna witnessed only the visible portion of the event; the brightening of what should have been shadows beneath those gathered around Kevon, the stretching and fusing of those energies into a pulsating band around the table.

Then the shadows of the Elven children ahead of her began to wink out. Twisting her head from side to side, she noted the elves gathered nearest to the center had all thrown their arms wide, their backs arched, faces tilted back toward the sun. The ground all around her glowed, obliterating both hers, and Mirsa’s shadows. The occasional flicker in a fold of cloth on Mirsa’s robe was the only evidence of shade that reassured Alanna that they had not been completely bewitched by the ritual.

The light from the bystanders pulsated inward, building a bright front that stretched in toward the whirling ring of light already building to an uncomfortable intensity. The inward flow met the outer boundary of the inner circle, and fused with the brighter light.

The pulsating energy swelled. Mirsa gasped, and felt the life in each ripple. Each heartbeat of every contributor surged their energy forward, filling the container constructed by Aelion and his acolytes. Pulses quickened, riffles of light leapfrogging each other in a bizarre race toward the center of the mystical vortex.

In moments, the construct in the center was nearly full, the only visible protrusion of light was between the circle and the group of Elven children ahead of them. Giggles erupted from several of them as the last wisps of brilliance squeezed into the center, and the wobbling circle snapped into a calm, warm-looking disc.

Aelion raised his hand over Kevon, and the disc of light rose from the floor, unimpeded by the legs of the table that held his unconscious body. As it rose through the tabletop, the edges of the formed light softened, curling inward to envelop and surround Kevon, molding to his shape. Currents in the light-casing mirrored the inner workings of his body, blood circulating, organs pulsing, and for a few moments the effect made him appear translucent. The pulsing light settled inward, and was gone.

The five elves joined with Aelion staggered back, releasing each other. Only Relaniel stayed, the other four melting into the dispersing crowd. Aelion's assistant leaned against the table to steady herself.

After a minute, only the two elves remained in sight, leaving Mirsa and Alanna to approach the table to see to Kevon.

"I've never seen it so deserted," Alanna commented. "Even at night."

"Everyone that was here has just given of their lives to attempt this," Relaniel explained. "It is taxing, to say the least."

Mirsa noticed wisps of gray at Relaniel's temples, and recoiled.

"Fear not, our life forces are much sturdier than yours. The children, especially, look forward to these rare occasions."

"There is nothing more I can heal," Aelion announced. "Sleep and food are the only things that can help him now, besides..." He trailed off, and shook his head.

Alanna opened her mouth as if to ask what the elf had meant, when Mirsa cried out.

"Mmmph..." Kevon mumbled, eyelids fluttering, but never fully opening. He tried to whisper, but choked on the words.

"Water?" Alanna asked, looking past him to the well at the edge of the clearing that surrounded the Grand Dais.

Kevon shook his head, lips moving again. Alanna leaned in closer to listen.

"Outhouse."

CHAPTER 19

"We should see yer island ahead, any day now," Britger-Stoun remarked, wiping dribbles of water from his beard.

"I wish I had your faith," Bertus answered, gazing toward the horizon, grip tightening around the railing-post he clung to. "At least we have the wind again." He shuddered, thinking of the two days they'd spent becalmed, drifting on the northeasterly ocean currents.

"It would be nice to spend more than an hour on shore this time," Bertus griped, recalling the brief excursion in the southern port town. Only Britger's quick thinking had saved them from being marked allies of Kevon and the others that were accused of nearly burning down half the town and slaughtering a handful of innocents. The dwarf had denounced the actions of his brethren, and offered coin to all who could detail their crimes. After learning of their cargo and violent escape, they'd returned to the ship and set sail for where they thought the Glimmering Isle might be.

"Wait... there's..." Fear gripped Bertus, causing the words to catch in his throat. Even though the winged figures wheeling through the bright midmorning sun in the distance could not be imps, his nightmares pushed to the forefront of his perception. "Gulls..." he whispered, relaxing, then scrambling to his feet, crying out.

"To the north!" he yelled, waving and pointing to the soaring specks against the horizon.

"Not te the south, like we expected?" Britger-Stoun laughed, the jagged line that divided his face writhing in his merriment. “Let’s hope ye spotted the right place!”

Bertus moved to a corner of the deck where he could avoid the increasing activity of the deckhands, but still keep an eye on their destination. As the ship turned to the north, it lost some of the more westerly wind. The crew continued to turn the ship with the wind, then edge back north, working their way slowly around the leeward side of the now visible island.

Hours later, the wind blocked by the island, sails furled by the crew, the ship drifted slowly toward the harbor to the east.

“Seems ye’ve pointed us in the right direction,” Britger-Stoun commented, peering ahead to where another ship bobbed in the evening light.

“We’ll see if we make it by dark,” Bertus mused, listening to the commotion below as the crew prepared to unship oars and row. “No moon, and the anchor hasn’t caught. It wouldn’t do to drift all night.

“One day away from the mountain is the same as another,” Britger-Stoun grumped, “But the sooner ye find yer friends...”

“Agreed.”

“The big one is bad enough,” Britger-Stoun griped, “But this one rocks like a child’s toy!”

“Sit down, and it will rock less,” Bertus admonished the dwarf. They’d begun to launch the longboat as soon as the morning had brightened enough, later than he liked because of the island blocking the majority of the sunrise.

They’d verified that they were in the right place by shouting across to the other ship before dropping anchor the night before, though the other crew had been wary of them at first.

“Bend yer back into it, lad,” Britger-Stoun teased Bertus as the longboat began moving toward shore.

The Warrior looked past the ship's crewman that manned the other set of oars in the boat to the two Stoneguard seated at the rear of the vessel. "And they are…?" Bertus asked over his shoulder.

"Ill-suited fer most labors," the King's nephew laughed. "As ye will no doubt discover."

One of the Stoneguard locked eyes with Bertus, and mimed an exaggerated rowing motion. He elbowed his companion and burst into rolling laughter, further disturbing the balance of the boat.

A longboat from the other ship awaited them on shore, and what, by all appearances, seemed to be the captain of the vessel greeted them, helping pull their craft up onto the beach.

"Friends of Kevon?" Yusa asked as soon as all of the passengers had disembarked.

"Yes, I'm Bertus, and this is Britger-Stoun," Bertus clasped arms briefly with the newcomer.

"Yusa, captain of the fine vessel moored out yonder. My men will be returning there shortly, but I can help with introductions to our other friends," he said, gesturing to where the three Elven Hunters stood, only half-blending into the trees at the end of the beach.

Without so much as a word, the bearing of the two Stoneguard changed from that of good-natured bullies to professional soldiers. From their limited nonverbal communication, Bertus was able to spot two other Hunters stationed apart from the rest, better hidden than the ones near the obvious path up toward the center of the island.

There was something odd about the elves that Bertus could not quite put his finger on, but he said nothing. He straightened his sword belt, slung his packed saddlebags over his shoulder, and began the sandy trudge to the path further up the beach.

Captain Yusa hurried to walk alongside Bertus, while Britger-Stoun hung back, followed closely by his Stoneguard escorts.

Shadows...

The thought drifted across Bertus's mind as he realized what the Elven oddity was. The trees the elves stood by threw long morning shadows, but the Hunters themselves did not dampen a single glimmer of light. For some reason, the first thought that came to Bertus was a poorly cast illusion by Kevon, and he could not help but smile.

"Aye, beautiful, are they not?" Yusa asked, spotting Bertus's smile.

Having been focused on weighing the combat effectiveness of his own group versus the five elves he knew about, Bertus had not noticed that two of the elves near the path were female. His eyes moved to the one he judged to be the leader, the oldest of the group. Her arms bore vine tattoos that snaked from the backs of her hands, up, around, and disappeared into the short sleeve of her woven fiber vest. Beneath the barest exposure of midriff, a skirt woven of the same material rode from low on her hip to mid-thigh. Tattoos on her legs simulated the shadows on the rough bark of the trees that grew nearby. Her long, honey-blonde hair, plaited on the sides, gave the impression of wind-blown wheat stalks.

"When they choose to be seen, I would have to agree." Bertus altered his stride, making sure his swinging arms were further clear of his weapons than usual, noting the easy grace of the Hunters with their half-drawn bows.

"There were others to be with you," the younger Elven Huntress addressed Bertus. "A woman, an older Warrior, at the least."

"We were separated. Please take us to Kevon."

The elf's expression darkened a moment before she nodded, and turned up the path.

Bertus followed, watching the elves that drifted to their flanks and kept pace. Nearly out of sight, two of the other Hunters trailed behind them.

"Your friend has almost recovered," Yusa reassured Bertus.

"Recovered?" Bertus stopped, and grabbed Yusa by the collar. "Recovered from *what*?"

"The strain…" Yusa gurgled, prying Bertus's grip loose enough that he could speak. "The magic, the responsibility, the poison."

"What poison?" Bertus yelled, and the surrounding elves drew bows, training them on him.

"The assassin…"

"Marelle…" Bertus noted Yusa's shrug. "Alanna, Marelle, whatever she calls herself now. I knew her when she was good for him."

"Bonesage tea," Yusa offered. "She thought she was helping him."

Bertus shuddered. "I've seen what it can do. It's outlawed everywhere I've been, and for good reason."

"I don't like it either," Yusa shook his head. "Nor do I allow it on my ship. But it kept him moving for days while we trekked up to meet the elves, and who knows how long before that?"

Marelle, or her memory, drove Kevon to become the Hero that we needed, Bertus thought as they followed the path inland. He shook his head and tried not to worry about it anymore.

"Mirsa?" he asked. "How does she fare?"

"Sick also, at times," Yusa chuckled.

"Well, how…" A flash of white and a crush of snapping undergrowth turned Bertus's attention off the path. "Was that?"

"Unicorn. Yes," Yusa laughed. "Welcome to the Glimmering Isle."

"*Bertus*?" Kevon asked, trying to blink away his bleary vision. "And… more… dwarves."

"I didn't even bring them all," Bertus grumbled. "Left most of them on the ship."

"Carlo? He's not with you? And Alma?"

“Alma and your brother-in-law, Martin, are with Carlo.” Bertus placed a hand on Kevon’s chest to keep him from struggling up into a sitting position. “And several other dwarves…” he added, smirking.

“Martin and Alma?”

“I approved,” Bertus shrugged. “You’ll just have to wait.”

Kevon settled back on the bed, breaths deepening and slowing. “So tired… I just want to sleep…”

“Rest, then. We’re here. We’re safe. Carlo and Alma are well on their way to us.” Bertus moved toward the doorway. “I still need to speak with the others.”

Bertus led the dwarves out of the room into the custody of their Elven escort. “Take us to our friends,” he said, turning his head and swiveling his gaze to meet that of the silently approaching Huntmistress. “Please?”

Bertus followed the eldest elf, taking care not to stare so openly at the incongruity that the inked shadows on her legs posed as she strode shadowless along the woven branch pathways that led from building to building.

“The others are staying here,” the younger huntress gestured toward the doorway of a dwelling that stretched between two of the larger trees in the vast network of suspended buildings. “We will begin preparing another across the way. I trust you will not cause any trouble if we take our leave?”

“I can’t speak for my companions, but I’ll be good.”

The Huntress wrinkled her nose at Bertus’s jest, but the elves continued upward into the higher tiers of the aerial city’s structure.

“Kylgren-Wode!” Bertus cried as the dwarf answered the knock at the door. The two clasped arms in greeting before Bertus moved clear of the doorway to reveal his companions.

“Aye. Yusa said ye’d be along,” the ambassador grumbled.

“Don’t act so grumpy,” Bertus admonished him. “We’re all here for the same reason.”

“We need te get word back te Bargthar-Stoun as soon as possible,” Kylgren-Wode said, shaking his head. “I have reason te believe Kevon is…"

"The Mage from the tapestry in the throne room?" Bertus interrupted. "So do we. The Dwarven King is the one that showed it to us."

"Kylgren-Wode." Britger-Stoun stepped into the room, barely hiding the sneer in his voice.

The Dwarven ambassador shrank back for a moment in the full glare of his superior, a reminder of the dwarf he'd been during his time in the Hold. The moment passed, and he stepped forward to offer a hand in greeting the Noble. "So yer uncle has sent ye te retrieve the Hero?"

"Te protect, not retrieve," Britger-Stoun corrected. "If he is the Hero, he'll return on his own."

"Well, he's yet te stand on his own in more than a week," Kylgren-Wode shrugged.

"He should be better after he sleeps a little," Mirsa said, entering from a side room. "Bertus."

Bertus drew his Dwarven-forged blade and handed it hilt-first to the nearest Stoneguard. He pulled the dagger at his belt from its sheath and dropped it behind him. Casting a downward glance to check for other metal, he stepped forward to meet the Mage's rushing embrace.

"Don't leave again," she said, pushing him back after she'd finished squeezing.

"I missed you, too." Bertus laughed. "I'll do my best."

"Ugh! *Bura*?" The Stoneguard in the doorway shifted to the side. Rhysabeth-Dane slipped in beside and past him, aiming the business end of her walking stick at the other burly dwarf's ribs.

"*Zarre…*" the other Stoneguard tiptoed aside, Bertus's sword held concealed behind his back.

"Aelion and I have finished translating the second set of symbols," Rhysabeth-Dane announced. "He's not certain what the other three languages are, but says one might be Myrnar."

"Ye speak Common?" Britger-Stoun blurted.

"Aye, and yer as dahft as yer uncle," the librarian retorted, mocking his accent. "The Elder also wishes to discuss another possibility with us, as soon as Kevon is feeling a little better."

"Listen, you!" Britger-Stoun griped, stepping toward Rhysabeth-Dane.

Bertus tore his gaze from Mirsa, and turned to place a hand on the Dwarven Noble's chest. "No, you listen. We're grateful for your help. Our goals are the same. Kylgren and Rhysabeth are a vital part of what we are trying to accomplish here. Don't try and make this about who is more important. You won't like the answer."

"If ye were any other Man, I'd have yer tongue cut out," Britger-Stoun whispered in the sudden silence of the room. He sighed. "But I yield te yer judgment on this."

"Good," Bertus asserted. "So, then, we wait?"

CHAPTER 20

"I'd wager that's more smoke than the Blacksmith's district should be sending up," Martin commented as they rounded the hill and Navlia came into view.

"It's not the palace, but very nearly," Carlo squinted to get a more precise read on the smoke plume's origin. "Looks like we're riding straight through." He held up a hand to signal a stop. "Pass the rations!" he shouted. "We move again in five!"

"At least the moon is nearly full," Martin whispered to Alma, who glanced at the sun that was just touching the western horizon.

"Take heart, tonight we dine with royalty," Alma laughed, moving around to the dwarves to finish parceling out the evening meal.

"Or die with them," Martin muttered to himself. The dry, dense bread lost all taste in his mouth, and he tossed the crust away from the wagon.

"Does it look bad?" Alma asked as she bundled up the rest of the provisions and handed Carlo his portion.

"The column thickens in the middle," he answered, pointing to the middle of the smoky plume. "It could be the wind, or it might have been the worst of the fire is hours past. Either way, it still looks bad now, and we're not stopping again until we get there."

Carlo's mounted soldiers milled around ahead of the wagon, watering their mounts from their own skins. The commander chewed mechanically, finishing his meal in short order, and calling out to begin the frantic dash toward their destination.

The miles flew by, and in under two hours the light of the risen moon had seen them halfway to the base of the eerily lit cloud of smoke.

"The team needs to rest!" Martin shouted as Carlo dropped back from the head of the formation.

"We'll go on ahead," Carlo shouted back. "Be on your guard!" He dropped back further, and signaled for the two soldiers following the wagon to move up and flank it. Spurring the stallion back up to speed, he motioned to the riders ahead to break away, and by the time Martin had slowed the wagon to a stop, Carlo and his men were out of sight over the next hill.

The two remaining soldiers tethered their steeds to the back of the wagon, jumping down to help wipe down the draft horses before the chill of the evening could turn their sweat cold enough to endanger them. As they turned back to their own horses, the Dwarven regulars were at the ready, watering and graining just enough to refresh the animals without slowing them down.

"It's been a few minutes since the team stopped breathing hard," Alma observed.

"Right." Martin glanced around. The dwarves were settled back into the bed of the wagon, and Carlo's men were checking their saddles, preparing to ride again. "Let's go to town."

Carlo and his soldiers galloped single file through the opening gate, his relic shield held high as identification. He turned out of formation at the inner gatehouse, while his men surged ahead and secured the intersection. "What burns?" he demanded of the emerging watchman.

"A section of the palace wall!" the Guardsman saluted, averting his gaze. "The Court Circle has been battling the Dark Brotherhood!"

"Why have the Guildsmen not put down these rogue

Magi?"

"Sir! The Guildhall has been razed... The Dark ones hunt down those with the brand. Many seek refuge behind the palace walls, but most of the Blademasters are dead."

"Marco?"

"I'm... sorry."

"Others follow us. A wagon and more troops. Escort them to the palace when they arrive. Protect them with your lives." Carlo headed down toward the market square, his men spreading out in a defensive ring around him. The Blademaster pried his eyes away from the rooftops long enough to unlimber his crossbow and make sure it was ready to fire.

When they turned south from the square to head to the palace, Carlo could see that they had nearly circled the fire. The fire had been on the western side of the palace wall, near the stables and barracks, far from where the royals were housed. Remembering how completely this Dark Brotherhood had invaded the last time he was here, Carlo wondered if the attack was truly over. "Eyes open!" He called, and began the advance toward the palace gates.

The occasional eye peeking through a shuttered window was all that greeted them on their way up to the gates. The iron-bound portal started to creak open, accompanied with shouts of encouragement, as Carlo and his men approached.

"To arms!" Carlo shouted, spotting the Dark portal forming in the middle of the street off to the left of the gate. As he backed the stallion away, he noticed the Magi emerging from an alleyway in the opposite direction. "There!" he shouted, spinning around to face the new threat.

Two of the Magi stepped out to either side of the third, flaming spheres building between their contorted hands. Carlo swung his crossbow around, steadied it a moment, and squeezed the trigger. He tossed the empty bow to a nearby rider, and slid off his horse, sword drawn and iron-banded shield hefted defensively.

"You could run," Carlo called out to the two remaining

attackers as he stepped to the front of the formation. He swatted down a launched fireball with his shield, the impact softer than a lobbed sack of bread as the magic nullified on contact. His sword flicked out to cut through a blast of flame directed at one of the men behind him, and the magic faltered. A second Mage fell, struck by an arrow from the troops on the palace wall. "Or, I'll be with you in a moment." Carlo sprinted toward the remaining Mage, shield half-extended before him, ready to block or ram as needed.

Carlo was almost to the backpedaling Mage when the screaming started. He'd already slapped aside two more fireballs, and blocked the signboard that had ripped itself from the front of the nearby apothecary's shop to hurtle at him.

Concern about the rest of the battle only magnified the mild contempt the Blademaster felt for the Mage before him. As Carlo turned his head to see what was happening, the retreating Mage spun around to flee down the alleyway.

"Blast it! If you can't handle a few of those Leapers..." Carlo abandoned the chase and turned back to see what was happening in front of the palace gates. Over half of his escort lay dead or dying. The remaining three were backed into the corner of the gate and palace wall. The creature they faced was similar in size to a leaper, but that was where the similarities ended.

The lower half of the summoned beast was that of a twisted, demonic grasshopper, backward jointed legs flanking a shiny ebony segmented abdomen. The insectoid body flared upward into a broad, triangular chest that terminated in what appeared to be a glittering onyx helmet. Segmented upper arms with sickle-blade ends scythed at the cornered men, deflecting off of swords and shield as the soldiers mounted a valiant defense.

Eyes open for other potential dangers, Carlo circled around behind the nightmarish creature, and began looking for a weakness. The shinier carapace segments looked like they would be more difficult to pierce than leaper armor. The rough leathery splotches around its joints seemed to stretch and flex as it moved, suggesting a possible vulnerability.

Another of Carlo's men fell, one of the beast's sickle-tipped forelegs speared through his thigh. Sensing his chance, the Blademaster leaned forward to strike at one of the demon's lower leg joints.

The demon's leg twitched, and using a fraction of its potential, spun itself to the left. Its left sickle stabbed into Carlo's shield and flicked it from the Blademaster's grasp, across the street, and through a shuttered window. It continued its spin, and bludgeoned Carlo in the side with his screaming comrade, still skewered on its other forearm. The creature's mouth, that Carlo had been unable to see from behind, screeched and snapped near the top of its thorax.

Following their commander's lead, the remaining two men sprang at the flailing menace. One of the guardsmen's swords bit into a lower leg joint, and the monster's stance shifted. The other soldier slammed into the creature's back with his shield, and it tottered forward.

Carlo rolled aside, and the carapace sickle meant for him cracked against the cobblestone. Another twist, and he was back on his feet, whirling his broadsword to sever the beast's head from its shoulders.

The demon convulsed, throwing the stricken soldier free, and keening in pain. It leapt over Carlo, nearly to the alleyway the Mage had fled down, and turned back toward the gate again. It rocked back and forth, favoring its injured joint. Its sickle-arms traced opposing circles as it swayed in a slowing rhythm.

"It's blinded..." Carlo kicked the faceted bud that had been atop the demon moments ago.

The creature squared off, focusing on Carlo as he spoke, taking a halting step forward.

"It can hear us well enough. Spread out, move slowly. It's still dangerous," Carlo rumbled. "But it's time we sent it back where it came from, our way." He pulled a second sword from the hand of one of his fallen men, and began advancing. "Focus on the left, it's weakened..."

The demon crouched and sprang in one fluid movement. Trusting that it knew what it was doing, Carlo leapt forward into a roll, and slipped under the beast's lunge.

Something clattered near the gate. As Carlo rolled to his feet and turned, he saw a hand poking from the top of the wall, dropping rocks to the street below. The Blademaster started running as soon as the creature turned to face the new noise.

The demon's next leap was stopped short by the solid stone wall that surrounded the palace grounds. Shaken, stunned, it rolled backward, screeching.

Carlo rushed forward, swinging his sword down and reversing his grip. He leapt the last few feet, casting aside the second blade to use both hands to ram the broadsword dead center, straight into the thing's mouth. He scrambled clear before it could react, flailing at the offending weapon with sickled forearms.

One of the beast's swipes caught the crosspiece of Carlo's sword, prying the weapon loose and flinging it aside. Its legs scrabbled against the stones for purchase, and it pushed down with its right arm to roll toward an upright position. Its angry shrieks faded to a weak mewling, and it slumped back down onto its back.

Carlo recovered his sword as the demon twitched its last. "Open up!" he called up to the figures poking their heads over the wall. "Form a burial detail! Go get my shield!" He found his crossbow near the body of the soldier he'd thrown it to, and picked it up after closing the man's eyes.

"A handful of Magi, striking from behind buildings. Just fire though. We haven't heard anything in the last few minutes," one of the soldiers from inside the wall reported.

The Blademaster stuck two fingers in his mouth and whistled. His horse peeked around the corner of a building down the street to the east, and trotted over. "Still more sense than most men," he scratched the stallion's forehead, and picked the reins up to hand to one of the milling guardsmen. "Take him to the stables. Get the hands to come move these bodies out of the street. Tell them to be ready for a wagon team and two more saddle horses." He patted the stallion's nose once more before turning toward the opened gates. "Send the others directly to the prince."

A dozen mounted guards met the wagon before it was even halfway from the market square to the palace gate.

"Look alive, there's been an attack!" the detail split and flanked the wagon. Martin let the team speed up to match the escort's pace, his teeth rattling as the sturdy transport jounced along the darkened cobble street. The gates spread wide open to receive them. Martin almost did not see the single-horse cart off to the side of the street, and the crowd of men gathered around something that glinted darkly in the torchlight next to it. He shifted his attention back to the slowing troop complement before him.

Four guardsmen peeled off as they entered the compound and the gates began to close. The remaining newcomers guided the wagon to the front steps of the palace.

"Welcome to Navlia," the guard leading the half dozen servants offered Alma a hand down from the wagon while the dwarves piled out of the back end. Their belongings and supplies were offloaded in seconds, and hustled into the palace alongside them. "It's not safe here," the guard cautioned, leading the way toward the residences. "But it's safer than out there. Come. The others are waiting."

"Sister of the Hero," Alacrit clasped Alma's hands as she entered the room. "Yes, I can see it clearly. Please, be at ease here. Anything you require is yours."

"Thank you," Alma frowned, extricating her fingers from the unexpected grasp. "And how do you know Kevon?"

"He and his friends saved my kingdom, and continue to work toward that end."

"Oh!" Alma noticed the jeweled circlet that was mostly

concealed by the prince's hair, and backed into a curtsey.

Alacrit waved the gesture off. "Nonsense. Civility is sufficient. Certainly from citizens of the outer provinces. To you, I am little more than an occasional tax, and someone to curse at."

"Well, you can't be expected to travel just everywhere..."

"Correct. Few understand, and fewer still appreciate that fact. I wish more would..." The prince chuckled. "But I forget myself. This is Martin, I assume, and the Dwarven delegation?"

"Sire," Martin shook the monarch's outstretched hand and nodded. "Commander Carlo has delivered our message, then?"

Alacrit shook his head. "It has been only minutes since he arrived, and the assault on the walls has been foremost in our conversation."

"Walls?" Alma peered at the prince. "Who is attacking the walls?"

"We think it is some of the same forces that infiltrated the palace a season ago," Alacrit explained. "Increased security has prevented them from gaining entrance, but the attacks all seem to be connected, similar. They're mostly magical, almost exclusively using fire and darkness."

"Why have they not used magic to get in?" Martin asked. "A few Magi sent Bertus across the realm to us, getting across a wall should be easier than that."

"Though far removed from the War of the Magi, my ancestors built the palace grounds carefully, fearfully." Alacrit smiled. "Every brick, every cobble, are ensorcelled to resist manipulation by the forces of Earth and Movement. We now have other measures in place to assure that no portals can be made in or out of the palace grounds."

"I shall rest easy tonight, knowing my Alma is safe," Martin said, nodding to Alacrit. "Such peace is a luxury since our departure from home."

"Extra guards will patrol for the duration of your stay," Alacrit announced. "Barring a second War of the Magi, or unfathomable treason, you are safe within these halls. Now, to business."

We are safe here? The guard's warning replayed through Alma's mind, in blatant opposition to the prince's reassurances. Her mind raced as the Dwarven translator introduced himself and the others in his group. *Perhaps I should speak more with that guard, learn more about...*

"What brings such a formidable group of your people to my home?" Alacrit asked after the introductions were completed.

"A prophecy of their people, involving my brother-in-law," Martin began. "They seem..."

"A truth we were not prepared to reveal before," Carlo interrupted, "Must now come to light."

"Your secret?" Alacrit asked, grinning. "The one I was *not ready* to hear a season ago? Let us think. A secret kept from me by a handful of heroes. Whisperings of heresy from Eastport. A Dwarven prophecy, the focus of which... one of those very same heroes?"

"Sire..."

"Commander," Alacrit interrupted Carlo. "I've had my suspicions for weeks, tonight has done nothing but point toward the verification of those suspicions. Should they be proven correct, I may have to stand against the Guilds, or against my Heroes. But please, by all means, continue."

"I thought it was bad when I found out," Carlo muttered. "All I had to do was try and kill him."

"You?!" Alma's hand moved to the skinning knife at her belt. Martin wrapped his arm around her, staying her hand on the weapon's hilt.

"Do not blame Carlo," Alacrit reassured Alma. "Things are changing, power is shifting as never before in recorded history."

Minutes passed in silence.

"Kevon is..." Carlo continued, "A Mage."

Prince Alacrit exhaled, nodding. "As I suspected. First, he shows up here with Bertus, and now this. Portents abound..."

"Bertus?" Carlo's face scrunched in disbelief as he questioned the monarch. "What does the boy have to do with any of this? Portents? What are you..."

"You believe you are the only ones allowed secrets?" Alacrit countered. "What you know of the world is but a shadow, *Hero*. Perhaps, in time, you will glimpse a portion of the knowledge my family has collected throughout the ages." The prince glowered a few moments longer at the Blademaster before speaking again. "For now, I must consult with my advisors, decide the best stand to take on this matter. Personally, I will not forsake any of my Heroes. Publically..." Alacrit sighed. "I shall try my best. Lady Alma?"

"Hmm?" Alma startled at the mention of her name amid the tense revelations.

"Would you humor me by speaking with the Court Historian tomorrow?" Alacrit asked. "I would ask Kevon..."

"Of course."

"Thank you. Thank you all." Alacrit turned to the dwarves, who waited in silence in a corner of the room. "I shall speak with you at length, in the following days. For now, eat, drink, refresh yourselves, and relax."

CHAPTER 21

Light spilled into the room and pooled on the blanket covering Kevon. He arched his back against the new warmth, neck popping as he stretched.

"Promising," Alanna remarked from a shadowed corner of the room. "The first morning in a week you haven't whimpered yourself awake."

"The ache is still there, but it's not the only thing I feel, or even the first thing," Kevon answered. "I haven't hurt this good since Elburg."

Alanna said nothing, leaning further back into her darkened corner.

"I'm sorry." Kevon sat up, pushing aside the blankets and retrieving his clothes from the bedside table. "I'm still not quite myself."

"Who of us is?" Alanna asked. "The dwarves are all out of their element, even more so since more of their countrymen have gathered. Yusa and his pet Mage have been acting more strangely since we arrived. Mirsa's 'situation', your sickness. Bertus is the only one who seems all right, but he's only been here half a day."

"Mirsa? She's been sick from the voyage... Keeping the pull of the sea at bay is a strain at the very least." Kevon pulled his tunic on, and glanced at the sword that leaned against the table.

"She's been sick since we left Eastport, and before that, if my guess is right. The herbs she's been taking to hide it are obvious. You... really don't know, do you?"

Realization stabbed through Kevon's being, and he cursed himself for not spotting it sooner. "But whose? Waine?"

Alanna tightened the straps on her braces of daggers, and shrugged. "Not my business. Her pet dwarves and the returning hero seem to have matters well in hand."

"Bertus? I don't think..." Kevon frowned. He'd gotten no indication of a relationship between the young Warrior and the Mage in Eastport, but they'd had less than a day before being forced to part ways. "I don't think..."

"You've said that already," the assassin chided. "Finish putting your pants on, and let's take a walk."

"The Realm be damned. I'm not leaving your side again."

"This is why I didn't tell you before," Mirsa sighed. "There are things more important than any one of us, things that need doing."

"We've got the others. We've got the dwarves behind Kevon now, Carlo and the royal army, for all we know. Plus whatever help the elves will be." Bertus clasped Mirsa's hands together between his own. "The world will be fine, we need to take care of you."

"Who do I have to speak with to get a fried trout for breakfast around here?" Kevon's voice drifted through the sheer curtained window from a tree away.

"We do have to deal with that, and soon." Bertus gave Mirsa's hands another squeeze before standing and moving to the door. "Coming?"

"There he is!" Kevon shouted as he spotted Bertus coming out of the doorway. He threaded his way across the branch bridge, holding on to the railing and wheezing by the time he reached the landing.

"You're in no shape to be out and about," Bertus admonished Kevon. "Go back to bed."

"No. I need. To do this," Kevon gasped. "Too much time.

Lying down. Already."

Alanna glowered sideways at Kevon. "How is the Mage? Still sick?"

"She's staying here, and I'm staying with her," Bertus announced. "For as long as it takes."

"I understand. And agree. You've both done so much already. It's time I took more responsibility for this task," Kevon admitted.

"Aelion asked us to meet him before noon, further up in the city," Alanna announced. "With Kevon in this state, we should leave now."

"You two go ahead, I'll get Mirsa, and we'll catch up with you."

"We'll see you up the mountain, then," Alanna nodded to Bertus, and took Kevon's arm to steer him past the doorway and onto the next bridge of branches.

They ascended along the branching paths, skirting around residences and avoiding obvious dead-ends. The mid-air city varied in height from as low as twenty feet above the steepening mountain, to rarely more than fifty feet above ground at the bottom level of bridges. More houses were layered above. Stopping regularly to rest and drink from water-collection pools, Kevon and Alanna were in sight of a woven wall of branches pierced by a single wooden door when Bertus called to them from an adjacent pathway.

"There?" The young Warrior called, pointing to the door, at least a half a dozen trees distant, and a hundred feet or more above them.

"He said we couldn't miss it," Alanna shouted back, dragging Kevon to his feet again.

Two bridges later, and the four met back up, continuing their upward trek in relative silence.

"What?" Bertus asked as he topped the last ascent to their target. "You guys are already here?"

"The Elder asked *us*..." Rhysabeth-Dane motioned to Kylgren-Wode.

"You've been sailing on my boat," Captain Yusa grumbled. "I'll follow where I want to."

"I'm sure it will be fine," Kevon said, slumping against the weave of vines and branches near the door. "Does anyone know what this is all about yet?"

"Aelion has finished helping me translate the Elven portion of the book," Rhysabeth-Dane mentioned. "He said there might be something else he could do to help, but was very secretive about it."

"Reko's not so sure about..."

The door creaked open a few feet, and Relaniel stepped out. She glanced around, frowning at Yusa, before speaking. "The Elder awaits you. Come."

The group filed in through the opening, and Relaniel pulled the door shut behind them.

"Everything today reminds me of Elburg," Kevon whispered, surveying the garden that lay below them and past the vine curtain ahead.

"This way," their Elven guide led them down a spiral ramp that hugged a nearby tree, and stretched all the way to the manicured meadow below. She gestured to the flower-lined stone path that snaked up the hill before them. "He awaits you at the top."

"It's much stronger here," Mirsa commented, as they began their way up the slope. "The Light. I can feel it... radiant, yet constrained."

"I feel it too," Kevon labored for his next breath. "The power is like a wet fish, slipping from your grasp as you reach for it."

"I don't feel well," Bertus clutched at his stomach. "I haven't eaten today though." He waved the others ahead, doubling over, bracing his hands on his knees. His vision swam, and for a moment the shadows flickered. Shaking his head, he straightened up and followed the others.

The crown of the hill rose above the trees that surrounded it, giving a breathtaking view of the ocean behind and around them. Kevon shaded his eyes and looked upward, noticing two imperfections in the light above them near the peak.

"The ocean is my life," Yusa growled, "But this is not how man was meant to see it. I feel like I'm going to fall straight up into the sky."

"I doubt men have seen this before," Rhysabeth-Dane snapped. "And you're not the only one who is uncomfortable right now."

"I meant no disrespect, little sister," Yusa laughed. "It's the land-sickness getting the better of me."

Rhysabeth-Dane huffed, and continued up the hill, Kylgren-Wode scrambling to keep up with her.

"Thank you for agreeing to this," Aelion called from up the path, strolling down to meet them.

"I didn't agree to anything," Bertus muttered, resting his hand on the hilt of the ancient sword he'd reclaimed his first day on the island.

"Nor I," Kevon reaffirmed, scowling as the Elder met them on the path. "We're merely here at your request."

"Not prepared? Relaniel..." Aelion smiled. "I forget my Apprentice is not always as comfortable around others as I am. No matter. I believe you are ready enough."

"Ready for what?" Alanna asked after the elf, who was already headed back toward the summit.

Kevon shrugged, took two deep breaths, and resumed his upward climb.

The focus of the power on the hilltop was evident well before Kevon reached the summit. A high-backed throne, double the size of Alacrit's in Navlia, sat dead center on the hilltop. The nearly flattened area around the throne stretched barely a dozen feet from it in all directions.

"Close your eyes," Kevon whispered to Mirsa.

"I know..." she answered. "I can still see it, too."

Kevon advanced toward the source of the power, stretching his hand out toward the arm of the throne, marveling at the way different roots had entwined to form the near perfectly smooth artifact.

"No being has touched the throne since M'lani's exodus," Aelion announced, stepping in front of Kevon. "And none shall, until her return."

"Well then, it's been fun to look at," Alanna grumbled. "Can we go now?"

"Amuse me for a moment."

Yusa's barking laughter echoed over the hilltop, as Alanna's face contorted in confusion.

"Amu… *Humor* you?"

"Ahh. Yes. Now you have done both?" Aelion smiled.

"That was actually funny in three languages," Rhysabeth-Dane chuckled.

"I would have you rest longer," Aelion continued, "But time, and light, are a factor."

"Of course," Kevon nodded.

"You've been healed as much as I can manage in so short a time, but there remain some weaknesses that I'm unable to even approach. Time and rest, I'm afraid, might not be the answer."

Perhaps the Guilds are right to forbid the mingling of sword and sorcery, Kevon winced. *For more reasons than we thought before.*

"Since the arrival of the second ship, and the revelation of the Dwarven prophecy, I'm convinced that you need to be made whole, so that your journey may continue."

"You've already said that you can't heal him," Alanna protested, glaring at Aelion.

"Yes. *I* cannot. We may be able to open the way to one who can."

"A portal…" Mirsa whispered. "A portal that you would open here could only lead…"

"You disapprove?" Aelion asked.

"No…" Mirsa shook her head. "I've opened many Dark portals, with only the failing light as a focus. Four of my classmates and I could not even begin to open a Light portal at noontime."

"With my help, you'll do just that. Are you ready to begin?"

Seeing Mirsa nod, Aelion motioned for her to step closer to the throne. "Who will accompany Kevon?"

Alanna's fingers twined around Kevon's.

"I'll be seeing these new horizons for myself," Yusa mused.

"Well done. Three should suffice." The Elder stood to one side of the throne, and knelt, facing it. Mirsa watched him, and stepped to the other side, mirroring his actions.

The bound light infusing the throne and surrounding hill-side shifted, concentrating, purifying itself even further, twisting and braiding into a form before the throne that Kevon could see with open eyes, without concentration. The arched framework seemed to glitter, waves of power spreading outward from each sparkle, washing over the semi-transparent construct.

"Now."

Kevon saw the Light rune form in Mirsa's mind, and with the sun overhead providing the initial push, the portal spell expanded within the Elder's guidelines. Soft warm light radiated from the doorway between Mirsa and Aelion, bright enough to obscure the view beyond, but soft enough to gaze into.

"I don't need to remind you of the..."

"The light. We get it." Alanna squeezed Kevon's hand. "Ready?"

Kevon gazed into her eye for a moment, and turned to face the portal. "Let's go."

Kevon and Alanna stepped through together, melting into the warm light. Yusa grimaced, edged through sideways, and was gone.

CHAPTER 22

"We've camped here two nights, and still no sign of the ship," Carlo complained, gazing out over the waves toward the northeastern horizon. "I would have preferred riding to Eastport."

"It would have taken weeks longer, and I don't fancy a path through dark woods, after what we've been through," Alma retorted. "The prince sent Magi to Eastport to charter passage on a ship that meets us here. This is closer to Navlia, and closer to the Glimmering Isle than Eastport is. Have a little patience."

"We haven't been attacked in a week or better," Martin offered, "And the troops Alacrit assigned to us have been the only thing keeping us alive."

Carlo frowned, and poked at the fire with a stick. "They slowed us down, at first. It took half of the infantry dying, and two of the archers, before they could keep our pace. And that last battle... four of those Obsidian Reapers?"

"We lost a Mage in that fight, too," Alma reminded him. "The other three have been on edge since then, not sleeping for a day or more at a time."

"It's possible he was a traitor," Carlo spat into the fire. "No sign of the enemy since he died? Good riddance."

"If there was a traitor, let us pray he is no longer with us," Alma agreed. "The damage he could do aboard ship might be more than on land, and we'll be shipbound soon enough." She pointed to the triangle of sail to the north that caught the last rays of evening light.

◆ ◆ ◆

"The three Magi are quartered in one of the upper cabins. We have infantry and Stoneguard rotating watches on that cabin, inside and out. Dwarven regulars and our archers patrolling the decks. More watching over cannon in the hold. The sailors are nervous. If this were a commercial vessel, we'd be over the side already."

"Thank you, Lieutenant." Carlo turned to Alma. "Anything further on the Magi?"

"They're drained from yesterday, pushing the ship to the edge of the shallows. Fighting to keep their sanity while we sail over the depths."

"The crew says that we should be able to follow a nearby island chain most of the way, they estimate nearing them in less than a day," Martin reported. "It's a longer route, but given our capabilities,"

"Longer is faster, direct is dangerous," Carlo muttered. "Nothing is ever simple with them, is it? Supplies?"

"More than enough," Alma assured him. "We had provisions for nearly twice as many mouths, plus the extra on the ship. Three weeks or more, for a trip that should take four more days?"

"Only four, eh?"

"Depending on the Magi. You saw what the three of them together did our first day aboard." Alma shuddered. "I don't even like to think about it."

Carlo nodded, remembering where, in the shallowest parts of the sea, the wake of their passage had exposed the ocean floor. The thundering of the torn seas colliding behind them, and the trail of dead fish that surged around them when the Magi slowed their mad rush still echoed in his dreams, and tainted his nostrils. "Let's say *five* days."

"I'll let them know, as soon as they're coherent," Alma reassured Carlo. "Will there be anything else?"

"You three are free to go," Carlo waved them toward the door. "*You...*" he said, pointing toward the Dwarven translator, "I have more questions for."

The translator spoke a few words in his native tongue, and his Stoneguard companion followed the others out of the room. "What do ye need te know?"

"Sending so many of your people to help Kevon, there must be more to it than an old picture."

The dwarf fidgeted.

"Your work alongside us so far has been a great stride in relations between us," Carlo warned, "Do not let secrets kept from us prevent the possibility of a deeper alliance."

"There's been little said, even since we left the Hold," he admitted. "Whispers of ancient lore... Britger-Stoun may know more."

Carlo waited, his eyes never moving from the dwarf's face.

"Ah. One more thing..." the dwarf's eyes shifted aside under Carlo's gaze. "Every dwarf that left the Hold fer this mission... swore a blood oath te protect the Blademage with their lives."

"I see." Carlo thought a moment. "Your boys take that kind of thing seriously?"

"They do. Oathbreakers are killed or banished from the Hold. Their family names are marred by shame fer generations."

"I suppose that will have to do until we rejoin the others." Carlo nodded to the dwarf. "Unless you remember something else?"

"Aye. Ye'll be the first te know."

"Remember that," Carlo cautioned, gesturing to the cabin door.

As the door closed, Carlo moved to the bunk in the corner of the room, to rest his eyes for the first time in over two days.

The wave assisted Carlo's roll to his feet instants after the knock at the cabin door. His sword was in his hand before his eyes were open and adjusted to the dim light from the porthole.

"What is it?" he called, lowering his weapon once he realized the room was clear.

"Islands ahead, sir!" The Lieutenant's voice distorted through the thick mahogany door. "The Magi are ready!"

Carlo glanced at the burnt out candle stump, and realized he'd slept for five hours, at the very least. "Tell them to start slowly!" he shouted back to his officer. The Blademaster sheathed his sword, and stretched, joints protesting the denial of rest they'd been promised.

The cabin shifted, and Carlo grasped the edge of the desk that was bolted down in the center of the room. "I told him *slow*." he grumbled. Carlo waited for the initial swell to pass, and then opened the door to the hallway outside. He passed two closed doors, then took the stairs up, two at a time, to emerge through the already opened door to the main deck. A few steps forward, and Carlo could see one of the Magi over his shoulder, on the upper deck near the railing to starboard. He shifted his gaze over his other shoulder to see the Mage stationed on the port side.

"I don't know why we bother steering while they're up there," the captain shook his head as Carlo neared.

"Control," Carlo answered, stepping around the man as he made his way to the stairway beyond. "Or its appearance."

The Blademaster made his way to the top deck, passing the younger Mage he'd spotted to starboard, and headed toward the silver-haired Wizard who stood near the back railing.

"Rough journey, lately," Carlo remarked as he closed in on the blue-cloaked figure.

"Some of us have lesser tolerances for the elements," he laughed, turning to face Carlo. "Weaving together three minds of such differing abilities is a tricky thing."

"Only one Mage I'm interested in right now," Carlo stated flatly. "How fast can you get me to him?"

"The *heretic*?" The Wizard's lip curled in disdain.

"That heretic slew an Orclord, and instead of suckling at the teat of fame, *went about his business*." Carlo shook his head. "The Orclord was only a sign of the darkness that has fallen over our lands. He searches for the cause, and the means to correct it. I'd advise you to do as much for the Realm, before you stand against him in judgment."

"The laws have been in place..."

"For as long as anyone can remember," Carlo finished the Wizard's sentence, and laughed. "Who among *you* remembers an Orclord? Think on that. Move the ship. Obey your prince."

Defiant eyes tracked the back of Carlo's head as he moved to the lower deck, and out of sight. The Wizard calmed himself before reaching out again to touch the minds of his fellow Magi. Marshalling their focused energy, drawing from the sea below, and wrapping his guidance around it all, the waters below surged upward and onward.

Hours beyond the effort that should have been attempted, the Wizard felt the lure of the sea lessen. He extended his awareness, and felt the island ahead, not more than a handful of hours at their current pace. He began to withdraw his rigid control of the spell that he had held for nearly half the day, and felt one of the other Magi retaking that responsibility.

He staggered across the upper deck to the Mage's cabin, passing by Carlo's perch near the wheel. "Perhaps you find my service acceptable?"

"The sailors told me when we passed into the depths," Carlo nodded. "You risked all our lives to prove your point, and we're further along because of it. Well done."

"Only hours to go," the Wizard agreed. "Wake me when it's over."

CHAPTER 23

Kevon blinked, but the brilliance that surrounded him did not even blur, and his eyes reopened. The tang of Light magic that had enveloped him as he passed through the gateway slipped away, fleeing to the furthest reaches of his mind, but not vanishing completely.

"I'll assume it's not just me, then," he laughed, watching his companions wave their hands in front of their eyes.

Alanna frowned, steadying herself on the ivory-shaded replica of the throne they'd left on the other side of the vanished gateway. "It's gone… they were supposed to hold it open?"

Yusa whistled. "Not such a loss, if you ask me." The ship captain pointed down the path to a meadow below, where a herd of unicorn chased whirling bits of light.

"We're not staying," Kevon reminded Yusa, glancing upward to the sky. A smooth light, as bright as the sun, filled everything above the horizon. "We don't belong here." He patted the sword at his belt, took Alanna's hand in his, and started down the path.

"They're not eating," Yusa observed, as they neared the meadow at the bottom of the hill. Sections of the unicorn herd wheeled about the meadow like flocks of birds, leaping and turning in waves that defied explanation. Others lay basking in the brilliant glow from overhead, but not one in the herd of several hundred had taken a bite of grass, that they could recall seeing.

"Well," Kevon shrugged. "I'm not tired, or thirsty. It's been a good hour since we crossed over…"

"I would have said half that," Alanna argued.

"It's been three if it's been a minute," Yusa declared. "But I'm not tired, either. This... place..."

"I'm not fearful," Kevon commented, "But suggest we all remain on guard."

"Agreed," Yusa took a step away from the thundering brilliance of the unicorn herd that passed no more than an arm's length from them.

"There!" Alanna pointed to the lights that swirled in the wake of the herd, which slipped away to dance around the three of them.

The gleaming bits of light crisscrossed in and around the group, evading contact by as little as inches, sliding across the periphery of Kevon's consciousness like distant enchantments. "Amazing," he laughed.

"See?" Alanna pointed to the only thing even resembling a building in the distance, almost out of view in the ambient brilliance. The lights spun and leapt between the group and what seemed to be their destination.

"It'll take us a day to get there," Kevon shrugged.

"Or a few hours," Alanna tugged at his arm, the lights separating as she pushed into their midst, framing her against the glowing landscape.

"That's a week afoot," Yusa grumbled, "At least. But there's nowhere else to go."

"And no need to rest," Kevon laughed as the light-spirits jangled noiselessly about him in Alanna's wake.

The path up wound through brightly colored fields and valleys, each twist exposing another canvas painted with brilliant flowers and twirling fauna.

"Have the two of you been seeing elves?" Kevon asked, squinting, to absolutely no effect, at the horizon.

"A few, at the edge of my vision," Alanna confirmed.

"Not so bold as these fellows behind us," Yusa said, pointing a thumb over his shoulder at the dozen frolicking Unicorn behind them, the holdouts from the group of fifty or more that had started following them out of the lower valley.

A cloud of lantern-bugs swirled by, blinking and buzzing to a tune Kevon felt he should know. He could not tell if the melody that he felt pulsating through his mind was because of the glittering insects, or if they were performing to music that they heard as he did. After a moment, he stopped wondering, and just enjoyed.

◆ ◆ ◆

"Kevon..."

"Yes?" he answered, looking up at Alanna, who crouched over him.

"You're awake. Open your eyes."

Kevon struggled to raise his heavy lids, succeeding after a few moments, to Alanna's benefit. The brilliance of his surroundings was already full and clear behind his closed eyes. "I was asleep?"

"I don't know if that would be called sleep, or not," Yusa muttered, stepping into view. "I think after more than a day, it's called something else."

"More than a..." Kevon stretched, used the tree trunk he was leaned back against to climb to his feet.

"Just a few hours," Alanna corrected. "We were worried, all the same."

"I was watching the lantern-bugs..." he mumbled.

"And you collapsed. Yusa wanted to strap you on a unicorn and haul you up the hill."

"If I'd brought any rope..." the ship captain grumbled.

"If he was in a hurry, he could have carried me," Kevon laughed. "We haven't gotten tired here yet."

"We hadn't passed out, either," Yusa retorted.

Kevon glanced around, and pointed to the upward-winding path. "Still headed that way? No sense in waiting around." He hurried to the path, striking out in front, letting his eyelids close again once neither of his companions could see.

The path continued for what seemed like ages before they

even got another glimpse of their destination. Freed from the bonds of normal fatigue, Kevon kept up a brisk pace, faster than he would have gone on the other side of the portal. Even so, a weariness of spirit crept up on him, his eyes closing involuntarily more and more as the journey wore on.

"Elves," Yusa called from behind Alanna, back down the path. "More, and closer."

Kevon turned to see what the sailor was talking about, only half managing to open his eyes before Alanna saw his face.

"You're still not well!" She rushed to his side, wrapping an arm around him for support.

"That's why we're here," Kevon inhaled sharply as Alanna's supporting arm tightened around him.

"Just being here cures a handful of ails," Yusa noted. "My left knee, both my wrists, have not ached since we crossed over." He rubbed at the back of his neck. "Some things are beyond help."

"Take his other side," Alanna ordered Yusa, sliding her neck and shoulders under Kevon's left arm. "Time is anyone's guess in this place, but it still passes. We should hurry."

Kevon grunted as Yusa maneuvered under his right arm, then stooped to balance out with Alanna on the other side.

"Let's do so," the captain said, taking a tentative step forward, waiting for Alanna to match up with his stride. "The fact I can carry him all day, does not mean I wish to."

"I know we have no rope," Yusa griped, "but still, I am tempted to throw him astride one of these pale beasts, and hope for the best."

"We're in view of the..." Alanna slowed, and readjusted Kevon's arm around her neck. "Building? Whatever it is."

"Aye. And the natives are... thickening." Yusa swept his gaze from the trio of unicorn that still followed them, across the broad field to the side, and the sprinkling of elves that danced through it. "Not much for talking, not that I'm complaining."

"Not much for clothing, either," Alanna focused on the structure ahead, as an ageless Elven maiden spun across the path in front of them, a floral wreath about her head, and budding vines coiled and draped in lieu of other vestments.

"No tattoos, these folk," Yusa observed. "Maybe the Hunters..."

"I doubt there are Hunters here," Kevon whispered. "The Light... sustains."

"I wish it would sustain you a little better," Yusa teased, "or that a bevy of these nymphs would bear you up..."

Both Alanna and Yusa shouted in surprise as they found themselves twirled away from Kevon, who rose up on a dozen hands, settled eyes closed, staring up at the glowing sky.

The Elven male who had spun Alanna away, as though they were dancing, grinned and offered her his hand.

No tattoos, indeed. She sheathed her dagger, and turned her attention to the group bearing Kevon, and hastened to catch up with them, escort in tow.

They reached the building ahead in what seemed like minutes. The closer they came, the more translucent the blocks of the structure became, never quite achieving transparency. Shadows composed of color, rather than darkness, flickered frenzied motion from inside as they approached. The inside appeared brighter than the outside, as viewed through the golden-hued archway they drew nearer to.

The crowd of elves bearing Kevon, now more than a dozen in number, began turning and lowering him as they passed through the portal into the brilliance of the cathedral. They tipped him up onto his feet, facing forward toward the pool of light in the center of the large room. The Elven maidens moved away as they concluded their support of Kevon, their final caresses lingering long enough to crease Alanna's brow.

The assassin nodded to the Elven men at her elbows as they released her arms, and she moved up to Kevon's side. Yusa chattered with the crowd of maidens that had conveyed him along, unconcerned that they were not answering him, as they slipped away to join the others ringing the inside of the building.

"Ah." Yusa cleared his throat. "We're here." He settled into his place alongside Kevon. "What is here, exactly?"

"Power..." Kevon breathed, sensing the energy in the pool of light that lay just feet from where they stood. Light from the circular hole in the ceiling funneled into the pool, which fairly pulsed with a life of its own. "There's more... there's something here..."

As if in response, the light in the pool contracted, gathered to the center, and drew itself upward. It stretched and writhed, growing in brilliance until Kevon looked away in anticipation of pain. He saw Alanna do the same, and heard Yusa swear on his other side.

Be welcome, children.

Kevon felt the words in his mind, and saw runes, pictures, as the being before them spoke. Yusa swore again, then apologized.

Step forward, let me see you.

Kevon took a breath, stepped forward, and turned to look up into the face of divinity. The light had coalesced into the form of utter perfection that stood before him, a woman of Elven build towered twelve feet tall, smiling down on them. Stylish, translucent garments shifted design as she moved, ranging from matronly to suggestive.

You're not...

The figure of light stooped to get a better look at the three, and Kevon nearly fainted from the shift in magic.

Men! But Men were destroyed, along with the rest of...

The goddess stood, smoothing her shifting garments.

The Plane of Enchantment endures?

"Our realm survives, a darker, harsher one than this, to be sure," Yusa affirmed.

And you know me...

"A thousand pardons, ma'am," Yusa sputtered. "I don't..."

This one does. My name is imprinted on his heart.

"M'lani..." Kevon coughed. "Are you M'lani?"

M'lani leaned down, extending a perfect hand to brush against Kevon's cheek. Inches away, she recoiled, and the light flickered.

WHAT IS THAT?

The ground rumbled at her question, the elves surrounding them wailing in confusion. Kevon followed her gaze to the weapon that hung at his side.

"It's a sword," Kevon answered. M'lani convulsed as he touched the hilt, and his magic drained away. "It is an instrument of death, and I apologize for bringing it."

I fail to see how even my brother could use so vile an object.

"It can be used to prevent evil, as well as cause it," Kevon explained, flush with embarrassment.

Bring you... news of my children?

"Your..." Alanna began. "The elves! They sent us."

They prepare for my return. Their faithfulness shall not go unrewarded.

"Y-Yes... your majesty," Yusa stammered. "But they also sent us to see if Kevon could be healed."

They have lost... It has been so long. Come closer, child.

Kevon took a few steps further into M'lani's light, and she knelt, taking his head in her hands.

The evil at your side destroys you from within, yet you believe it to be your greatest strength.

"I'll do whatever it takes to protect my friends, my family... my realm, from the darkness that threatens it."

Darkness.

Memories of the portal beneath the ruins of Gurlin's tower flooded to the forefront of Kevon's mind, the breaking of the enchantment, and the malevolence of the being that attempted to use Kevon to pull itself across into the world. The memories slowed and played over and over, until Kevon screamed.

Peace, child. I'm sorry.

Light flooded Kevon's mind, banishing the darkness of the memory, scouring away the despair that had come with it.

M'lani scooped Kevon up, and cradled him to her bosom, humming a soothing lullaby. Runes he could not grasp flickered at the edge of his mind, and his pain and fatigue began to fade. Her song finished, she kissed him atop his head, and placed him back between his friends.

Such pain.

The goddess stroked Alanna's hair, pausing after a minute, then running her finger from the bridge of Alanna's nose, to the tip.

Some things I can heal, others merely take time.

She turned her attention to Yusa, and tilted her head, grinning.

The most beautiful of things can sometimes spring from the most horrific events. You are far too lovely to fix.

"I've often said so," Yusa said, taking M'lani's hand, and kissing it.

M'lani's laughter thundered through Kevon's brain. He could almost see the runes, as if mirth and joy were spells that could be cast. After a moment, she grew quiet.

Now that the plea of my children has been answered, we must set about truly saving them.

CHAPTER 24

"If he's not here, everyone else in the realm surely is." Carlo nodded to the ship's captain, who shouted the order to drop anchor.

Soldiers crowded below, gathering last minute supplies before boarding the longboats. The men and dwarves that were staying behind on the ship helped the others into the large rowboats, and aided the crew in lowering the craft to the water below.

"Thoughts?" Carlo asked as the sailors crewing the boat began to row toward shore.

"Much as I hate the sea, I'd rather return home on it than set foot on this island," the senior Mage admitted. "Something feels wrong about it. No..." he corrected himself. "Something feels *too right.*"

"There's something I've never..." Carlo grunted. "Well, there was this one lass... I..." The commander shook his head. "So, let's just be ready for anything."

"Someone ashore!" one of the soldiers called from the front of the boat.

"Bertus," Alma announced, shading her eyes to get a better look.

"Odd that he should be the only one of the bunch here..." Carlo remarked. "Then again, who's to say what is odd for this company?"

Martin forced a smile, and craned his neck to look over his shoulder toward the shore once more.

The sun neared its apex as the boats reached shore.

"Took you long enough!" Bertus shouted over the rumbling surf.

"Demons," Carlo answered with a shrug.

"Mirsa felt the disturbance in the sea earlier, sent me down to meet you." Bertus squinted at the blazing orb in the sky. "She's on top of the mountain, hoping Kevon will come back today. It..." the young hero looked into his mentor's eyes. "It has been weeks now."

The commander handed Bertus a rucksack of supplies. "We'll get settled in, then, and decide what to do at our leisure."

Letting the waterfall that fed the small basin hammer down upon his shoulders a few moments more, Carlo frowned at the absurdity of the whole situation. Kevon, vanished from the top of the mountain above, along with his troubled lady-friend, and the captain of one of the ships anchored below. For the first time in ages, Carlo could turn his head and not lay eyes on a dwarf. It would not last. Outside the glade he bathed in, the homeland of the elves stretched over half the island. He was no stranger to the Elven people, having dealt with their kind often in Eastport, and more recently in Navlia. Having their lilting, breathy speech as the background noise of a city... was another thing entirely.

Carlo climbed ashore, standing in the sun to dry, and pitched rocks at the unicorn that poked their heads through the treeline. He changed into his military dress uniform, the only clean outfit he still had, gathered the rest of his things, and went to find the others.

"Mirsa has returned to her quarters," Bertus told Carlo as he entered the central square. "She's staying further up in the city, because of Kevon, and her..." The young Warrior's face reddened. "We'll have to hike up to see her, and the Elder."

"The four of you, stay here." His two soldiers snapped

salutes Carlo's way, and the Dwarven translator jabbered at the lone Stoneguard that had accompanied the group into the city. "Understood?"

"Stood!" The armored dwarf mimed a salute, his arm joint creaking and preventing the full motion.

Carlo patted the ferocious dwarf on the helmet. "Lead on, then."

"Standard escort, the last few weeks," Bertus murmured, noting Carlo's attention to the huntress that led them up through the winding pathways of the city. "Since Kevon's departure."

"I've no particular issue with it," Carlo answered, studying the hypnotic movements of the bark-tattoos across the twisted branch walkways, through the splotchy shade of the jungle canopy.

"We're here," Bertus announced half an hour and a mile or so later, as their escorting huntress slid to the side of a doorway and stood at a relaxed attention. He opened the door and walked in.

Carlo followed, but the huntress's unstrung bowstaff caught him under the chin and to the right side of his face, steering his gaze into her eyes. He stared for a long moment into her grey irises, and the weapon was again at her side. She turned her head forward, surveying the trees ahead.

"Huh," he chuckled, and followed Bertus into the building.

"He still has not returned?" Bertus asked Mirsa.

"No," the Mage answered. "Several elves have volunteered to make the trip across to investigate, but Aelion and I both agree that it is not safe. We will continue opening the portal daily, and hoping."

"Why did they cross over in the first place?"

"Kevon's… illness was beyond what Aelion could heal, with either potions or magic," Mirsa answered.

"Elves can heal with magic?" Carlo asked, turning from Bertus to Mirsa, and back. "Since when?"

"Aelion is Elder here, and his skill, combined with this place, make it possible, to a degree." Mirsa explained. "It wasn't enough, and they sent him somewhere that he could be healed, completely."

Carlo gritted his teeth, fists clenched. "I don't know why you people think magic is always the answer. Rest! Decent meals! He would have been fine!"

"The way he was using magic, the volume of power he was controlling," Mirsa shook her head. "It was eating away at him from inside. Burning him up. Nothing was working."

"So you sent him into the unknown," Carlo scoffed. "With others. Brilliant."

"Come with us to the Seat tomorrow. You'll see what we've been trying."

"Enough talking," Bertus helped Mirsa over to a cushioned bench. "You need your rest."

"Easy there, boy," Carlo laughed. "You're treating her like she's..."

Bertus met Carlo's gaze without comment.

"By the gods! Is she?"

"I won't be leaving the island for at least two more seasons," Mirsa replied, smiling.

"How can you endure the strain of what you've been doing?" Carlo glared at Mirsa. "Let me bring along the Magi that accompanied me here. Maybe between the lot of you..."

"Yes, perhaps that will help," Mirsa sighed. "Bring them up the mountain before noon."

"His sister, and brother-in-law, as well," Carlo added. "I'll have to return to the beach camp to fetch the Magi, of course." He opened the door, winked at the huntress, and began following her down the mountain.

CHAPTER 25

Blinking his eyes from habit, Kevon shrank back from the bubble of retreating light that had engulfed the three of them, and was reforming into M'lani. "Save them?" he asked, catching the armrest of the throne for balance. "What do you mean by that? What do you know? You didn't even think we existed until a few moments ago."

M'lani's form resolved, sharpened into the breathtaking beauty she'd been at the temple, but smaller, now only a foot taller than Kevon. As she returned to her true shape, Kevon could have sworn he saw the faces of his sister, his mother, and at least one elf he recognized, before the goddess resumed her otherworldly façade.

Your memories showed my brother attempting to enter your world. Should he manage, he could terrorize you as he has the rest of us, but to greater effect.

"That was..."

It is. He has harried my other brothers and sisters from our home on the Plane of Magic, forced a retreat into our personal realms. His power grows, as ours weakens.

"So if we bring you back with us..." Alanna began, "You could help us against him?"

I would do my best. Let us begin.

M'lani stretched, growing tall enough to sit on the throne where they'd first entered her realm. The illuminated sky dimmed fractionally, and the goddess swelled to her original height, skin glowing with amassed Light energy. When she fit the throne perfectly, her radiance blossomed further, the surrounding countryside fading in comparison. She stood up to her full height, and gestured to the spot the portal had been.

Curious.

The amassed power dancing about her calmed, sank beneath her skin, where it still glowed.

"What's wrong?"

I still cannot open a gateway to your world. Something interferes. You try.

Kevon formed the runes it had taken to open the portal to this place. He forced his will into them...

No, child. Enchantment. Your Plane is Enchantment.

M'lani's thought-runes showed the difference between spell-forms, and Kevon adjusted his efforts to match.

"Nothing..." Kevon could feel M'lani's magic pressing up against a barrier, and going no further.

This is why we feared your realm was lost. Why we had not returned.

Alanna's eyes, wide with fear, locked onto Kevon's. "How are we going to get back home?"

Kevon tried again, visualizing the hilltop on the Glimmering Isle, sharpening his runes to crystal clarity. His senses wrenched, and M'lani stumbled before him.

The portal flickered open.

Children!

M'lani's stored magic burst to the surface, and the portal widened.

I'm coming, children!

The goddess stepped forward, extending a hand into the grayness before her. With an arm halfway through, her face contorted into an expression of disbelief. She pushed a few inches further through, and the portal began shrinking.

No!

The anguishing thought was more than Kevon could bear. His world spun, and he collapsed.

Kevon snapped to awareness, gazing into an angelic face through closed eyes.

Surprisingly fragile.

"What happened?"

The portal only allowed a fraction of my being through. There is a curious resistance, something that prevents my passage.

"Like when the Dark one could not force his way through," Kevon opened his eyes and sat up. "He made it further through."

Your memories make more sense, now. My brother is much more powerful than I.

"That portal had been there for some time, and the destruction of the enchantment did things I've never seen before."

How long had the portal been open?

"Years. Many years. Enough for the Orclord to grow large enough to..." Kevon paused. "Many dark creatures spilled from it before it was destroyed."

He's gained more influence over your Plane.

"These are dark times, milady," Yusa remarked.

The force that bars me from your realm, I can sense it more clearly. Part of it is here.

Kevon followed M'lani's gaze to the sword at his side.

I must see this evil firsthand, try and understand it.

Most of Kevon's mind was paralyzed with fear, huddled within itself, mumbling. His body moved as if of its own accord, drawing the sword, and holding it out to the goddess for inspection.

A memory from the furthest reaches of his mind collided with the scene unfolding before him. A woman's perfect hand curling about the blade, closing on its sharp edges. The anguished cry that echoed throughout his being at the contact might have been hers, or his own, but Kevon recoiled, and the blade slid, slicing the insides of her knuckles, as well as the flesh between her thumb and forefinger. The awareness of pain blossomed, a saturating empathy, and Yusa cried out to the side.

Hold fast.

Kevon looked away, unable to shut out the spectacle before him in any other manner.

The pain stopped.

Look here, child.

Edging his view toward M'lani, Kevon could see her hand still grasping the blade in a far too familiar manner. The blood that had dripped down the blade oozed back upward, and into her wounds, which closed up. The droplets that had hit the ground bloomed into miniature roses at her feet.

The goddess pulled the sword free from Kevon's grasp. Holding it hilt upward, looking at it as though it held the answers she sought, she began to smile.

I see. This is part of the...

The blade just past the handle flashed. The afterimage of a Light rune floated dark on Kevon's vision against the backdrop of M'lani's neck, a ghostly birthmark on her perfect, lustrous skin.

Well. This changes things.

"How?" Kevon sighed, more exhausted than this place should allow. "What is happening?"

The denial of our entrance to your Plane. It may be insurmountable. But... perhaps we can help each other.

"You've already helped us, saved Kevon. What can we do?" Alanna asked.

My brothers and sisters are trapped, as I am. They have no knowledge of the Plane of Enchantment, or L'mort's designs on it. Travel to them, as you have come to me. Take the weapon. They will know what to do with it, as will you, in time. Hasten, before my brother's power grows, and he is able to enter your realm, or mine.

M'lani handed the sword back to Kevon, who looked at it for a minute before placing it back in its scabbard.

"I can't open the portal yet," he began.

No need. I feel the pattern now, and... there.

The portal formed of its own accord, and M'lani's light flowed into it, widening and stabilizing it.

Go, my children. Your friends await you.

CHAPTER 26

Kevon followed Yusa and Alanna through the portal, into the dim noonday sun. He raised his hand to shield his eyes from the dull orb, grateful that his eyelids worked once again.

"They're through!" Bertus called out, and Kevon felt the portal collapse behind him.

"Carlo?" Kevon asked, blinking until his vision cleared.

"It's about time," the Blademaster grumbled. "I've been here four days."

"Four days?" Kevon shook his head. "We were there two, at the most."

"A week, at least," Yusa corrected.

"Not even a day," Alanna argued.

"You were gone three weeks, to be precise," Aelion moved to Kevon's side. The Elder placed his hands on Kevon's temple, and over his heart. "Fully healed. You'll still need to rest a few days."

"It is so much darker here than... Wait..." Alanna fumbled at her eye patch. She tore the covering free, and waved her hand in front of her face with a hysterical laugh. "It's still darker... but She..."

"She said I was too pretty to fix," Yusa interrupted, "And I'm starting to feel pretty hungry."

"So what have you learned in the last four days?" Kevon asked Carlo as they began the trek back down the hill.

"Your friends have deciphered two out of the five languages in your book, and still have no solid idea of its value. Unicorn are a *pain* in the backside, and Elven women are not as fragile as they appear. You just came out of a shiny hole in the air, I'm more interested in what *you* know."

"As you should be," Kevon nodded. "It's just that..." He whirled to the side, taking Alanna by the hand, and peered into her startled face. Her rejuvenated eye was its natural, vibrant green, but streaked throughout with golden lines. "There is so much to tell."

The assassin turned her wrist and captured Kevon's, extending his right arm to her right, sliding to her left as he turned with the force. "You might have asked," she whispered in his ear, constricting his neck with one arm, pressing the heel of her other palm between his ear and jawline.

"Not a bit sorry," Kevon rasped, gurgling as Alanna's grip shifted.

"I really shouldn't break you, as it was so much trouble to have you repaired," Alanna mused. "Will you behave?"

"Within reason."

"That will have to do."

Kevon staggered forward as Alanna relaxed her grip, and rubbed at his throat. He twitched only somewhat when her stride brought her even with him, she took his hand then twined her fingers with his.

"You spoke with the Elven goddess?" Carlo sputtered, bread crumbs launching from the corners of his mouth. "What... was she like?"

"She was big," Kevon began. "And bright, and kind..."

"And afraid," Yusa added. "Family troubles, it seemed."

"I don't like the man," Alanna murmured to Kevon, "But he's not easily shaken. We may need that."

"She wants you to visit the others?" Mirsa pushed her plate aside and brushed at her robe.

"That's what she said," Yusa affirmed. "And you're welcome to use my ship to get anywhere to that end. I'd volunteer to visit the other realms in a heartbeat."

"Knowing that light is the most pleasant of all the elements?" Mirsa asked. "I, for one, am relieved to have to stay here for a time, though returning to the Seat of Earth is not an unwelcome prospect."

"It is a known destination, but does not further our understanding of the book," Kevon spoke carefully, his mind full of memories and possibilities. Images of a vast expanse of waving grasses moved to the forefront of his thoughts. "Where is the Seat of Wind?"

"Lore on such things is unreliable, at best," Mirsa shook her head. "Based on where Light and Earth reside, the most likely place is in the Highplain of Kelanoth."

"Yes, far to the south, where the air grows cooler," Aelion agreed. "Not a journey to be undertaken lightly."

"Fewer things are these days," Kevon shrugged. "As dangerous as the journey there will be, the crossing will be more so, and the waiting... doubtful there is a place so pleasant to pass the time as there was here."

"You said before..." Aelion began in a low tone, as the room grew quiet. "She mentioned us?"

"She wished to know how you fared, and that you awaited her return," Kevon answered. "But..." he searched for the correct phrasing. "She seemed surprised that any of us were alive at all. She thought our realm, our *plane*, had been destroyed. They all thought it. They've tried to return here, with no luck, and thought we were no more."

"She did not forsake us..." Relaniel whispered.

"I told you not to despair, child," Aelion chided his student. "Perhaps, with Mirsa's continued help, we can send groups through to..."

"I will go with Kevon," Relaniel stood from her place by Aelion, and crossed the floor between them in three quick strides. She sat by the Warrior, and peered at him. "If he'll allow it."

"I... uh..." Kevon looked at Alanna, who shrugged, smirking. "Why do you want to do that?

"You have spoken with M'lani, received her blessing. She cannot cross to be with us, but bids you speak with her family. I would love to see her," The elf's eyes glistened with half formed tears. "But you would be gone before the first group returned. I would see your journey to its successful conclusion before satisfying my own desires."

"We would value your help on our journey, but…" Kevon smiled. "We welcome your friendship even more."

"We'll recruit a band of Hunters for each of your ships before you leave," Aelion announced. "Until then, we celebrate."

CHAPTER 27

"Seems more natural…" Carlo scratched his chin, and squinted into the sun creeping over the horizon. "But I'll no doubt regret saying that, before too long."

"Your Court Wizard was the one to suggest it," Kevon countered. "But it makes sense. Focusing on the wind instead of the water could help with the sickness, and besides, there is no telling how much more difficult keeping two ships balanced like that would have been."

"It'll keep the crews in sailing shape," Yusa offered, throwing the last bag of provisions onto his longboat. "That's the reason we sent the ship Bertus and the dwarves brought back to Eastport. It was smaller, would outpace either of these in the same wind."

"The cannon on my ship was another factor… You heard the captain," Carlo grumbled, stepping into his own boat. "No time to waste."

Kevon climbed into the boat next to Yusa, and both craft shoved off toward their ships.

"The tide's wrong," Yusa muttered. "If that accursed Reko would show his…"

"No need," Kevon smiled, and focused his Art to propel the craft onward, the rowers lifting their oars clear of the sea with murmurs of appreciation.

"See me at once in your cabin," Reko commanded as Yusa

and Kevon climbed the rope ladder to the deck. The Mage scowled and vanished after he delivered his message.

"We're going to set a few things straight," Yusa barked after the disappeared Mage, turning to offer Kevon a hand up.

After the rest of the crew was aboard, and the longboat hoisted and lashed into place, Yusa marched to his cabin, Kevon scurrying on unsteady legs to keep up.

"Out of my chair!" Yusa shouted as he threw open the door.

"I'm not in your chair," Reko smiled, and his image flickered, he reappeared lounging on the captain's bunk.

"Don't test me, Wizard!" Yusa growled, hand on the wooden baton at his side.

"I'm not testing, I'm showing," Reko laughed, flickering to a spot right before Yusa. "Before I tell."

"All Illusion," Kevon whispered. "I can feel it."

"Yes," the Reko-image bowed his head slightly to Kevon. "Always Illusion. And I'm tired of hiding it."

Kevon closed his eyes and extended his senses, but could not detect anything out of the ordinary. "So where are you, really?"

"I'll get to that in a moment," Reko was back in Yusa's chair. "But first things first. *She* said *I* was *beautiful*."

"You've not been with us around any women save Alanna and Mirsa," Kevon mused. "The elves would have mentioned you. Who..."

"You were there..." Yusa's jaw hung open.

"I am always there," Reko's form blinked to its spot before Yusa, and pointed between the captain's eyes. "I am always *there*."

"Explain yourself!" Yusa roared, reaching for the Mage's chest.

Reko's form wisped away, but his voice continued. "There were so many times I considered ending it, killing us both. The years of helplessness, never being my own man, tied to your whims. But that's over. She said I was beautiful. Too beautiful to fix."

"She was healing injuries," Kevon scowled at Yusa. "What..."

"I..." Yusa's hand moved to the base of his skull, and he rubbed at the indentation. "I think I know."

"Yes." Reko's voice whispered. "We were never the same after that."

"I was so young. I was climbing in the barn, and fell, hit my head."

"Our brother was there, ran for help," Reko's voice added.

"There was so much blood. We had two healing potions in the house..."

"It took ten in total," Reko amended. "Rufus rode the province begging them from neighbors."

"I was never the same," Yusa frowned. "Had to relearn everything. Walking, talking,"

"I railed against the prison behind your eyes for years, trying to get you to hear me, to lift a finger. It wasn't until..."

"You studied magic," Kevon whispered. "You told me that you studied the Arts for a time, but couldn't make sense of it."

"But I could," Reko laughed. "Being nothing but an imprisoned mind, magic was something I could feel, something that I could do, my connection to the world outside. But I couldn't really talk to you until I mastered Illusion."

"Things got strange when I started studying the Arts, it was part of the reason I left," Yusa shook his head. "That was you?"

"Before I knew what I was doing," Reko affirmed. "I started out small, forming obstacles for you to avoid, working up to strangers in a crowd. I made things glimmer to catch your eye, direct you places I wanted to go. It was years before I perfected this form, and began to really talk with you."

"You had me buy books for you," Yusa chuckled. "You always had me check the pages to make sure they were worth buying."

"I had to read them somehow," Reko's form appeared once

again, behind Yusa's desk. "I'd love to reread some of them."

Reko turned to Kevon. "I want to help, as much as Yusa does. I hope we can work through..."

"Make the other cabin available for the other Mage and I, these are the highest rooms on the ship. You choose how or whether to reveal this to your crew, but I would. People are more trusting than we assume." Kevon looked over to Yusa. "So, you can touch metal?"

"I'd rather not. It makes me uneasy."

"I'd rather he didn't, it hurts like nothing else," Reko added. "I used to black out for days."

"And now?" Kevon asked.

"Pain. Confusion." Reko shuddered. "Shall I go on?"

"And your magic?"

"Limited, afterward," the illusion answered. "Like all of my magic had been stolen. The worst part, though, is not being able to concentrate."

"Interesting." Kevon scratched his chin. "Perhaps we should discuss this more at length, before Carlo finds out. He tried to kill me when he found out I was a Mage. He's mellowed some in the past few seasons, but..."

"I understand. An angry Blademaster is not something one looks forward to."

The ship rocked as the Magi aboard both ships linked minds to call the wind.

"Maybe you'll take a shift?" Kevon asked Reko.

"I'll rest now, while you bring my books in from the other cabin," Reko suggested. "I can do this in his sleep."

CHAPTER 28

The days roiled by, darkness and daylight blending into a froth of time separated into six hour shifts.

Wake. Link with the other ship's Mage. Call the wind. Hold until the end of your shift. Eat. Clean. Cook. Mend rope. Sew sails. Sleep.

The routine was not a full day, but lent itself to the resources at hand. The Magi could recover from six hours of sorcery in twelve hours with relative ease. After the first shift, Reko had insisted on taking his time alone, and had not faltered or thrown them off course. He was quick to take over when it was his turn, and slow to relinquish the duty to his relief, often taking an extra hour so that they could eat and relax.

"Two more days at this pace, we should reach the southern trade lanes," Yusa pointed to the chart on his desk. "It'll be slower, but the Magi will have a chance to really rest. Reko has been... irritable."

"I would welcome a break," Kevon admitted. "My Wind magic has never been so focused as it is now, but some of my other training has suffered."

"The crew should be able to resume all of the ship's duties when we reach the lanes, natural winds will mean less breakage of the rigging." Yusa said, rolling the chart and placing it in its holder. "We'll ride those winds as close as we can to Kelanoth, but we'll have to use the Magi again for the last leg of the journey."

"I'll cross over to the other ship, and let Carlo know." Kevon slipped out of the cabin, and made his way across the deck to the longboat.

Kevon climbed aboard the craft, and using a pair of Movement runes, turned the handles on the winches that held the landing vessel in place. Shifting his focus to a Water rune, and battling to keep the power at a mental arm's length, he caused the sea below to swell the last few feet, releasing the hooks that held the boat aloft. Kevon released the Movement rune, and wrestled with the water magic, sliding the boat swiftly over to the side of Carlo's ship. He secured the lift-lines that were thrown down to him, and waited for the crew to pull him up.

"I could see that this was wearing on everyone," Carlo grunted. "A fine thing, my being concerned about the Magi."

"You took the news about Yusa and Reko surprisingly well," Kevon laughed.

"He doesn't wear a sword, has no traffic with any Guild," Carlo corrected his student. "Yusa didn't know any better, Reko still makes me uneasy. Our Magi say he's at least as powerful as both of them together."

"Yusa has handled every physical aspect of their lives," Kevon mused. "Reko has been trapped, but free to focus his mind as he wished for years on end. It's a wonder he's sane. How are the dwarves holding up? This prophecy of theirs has been awkward for most of us."

"Most of them, excepting the Stoneguard, have kept below for the bulk of the journey," Carlo shrugged. "Rarely a day goes by when one of them nearly goes over the railing. They play like Novices, but there's something about them, something dangerous, just under the surface."

"That's the same impression I had of them," Kevon admitted. "Bertus said that the Ambassador, Kylgren-Wode, was a fierce warrior, but the Stoneguard were more so, and very demanding trainers."

"The two Stoneguard that remained on the Isle with them will keep his skills sharp," Carlo chuckled. "If we didn't need Rhysabeth-Dane with us, I'd have liked her to stay with Mirsa, also."

"Agreed. Those three, and Kylgren-Wode, have become quite the family this past season."

"And your family?"

"Alma is… Alma. We've always been different. She's glad the Dwarven translator is aboard your ship, and not trying to talk her into an Ambassadorship. Martin… I'd begun to think of him as almost a brother, as we worked with Holten, far before it was official. He's been a good friend, but…" Kevon shook his head. "He's not had the years I have to wrestle with Holten's betrayal. That, too, will take time."

"Your burnt friend?"

"Pholos…" Kevon shrugged. "Hunting for signs of Holten, on two Planes. We have no way of knowing where he is, how he fares. Mirsa showed me how to look for him, but every time I try, I feel nothing. He's either shielded, *elsewhere*, or dead."

"An odd ally, to say the least." Carlo shifted in his chair. "I'll be glad to set foot on land again, even though it's going to be Kelanoth. Waine would have dragged us around the Highplain until he bagged a lion."

"The Elven Hunters aboard our ship have been cagey about the whole trip, more so than usual." Kevon fidgeted before speaking again. "I know they're our allies, but it seems there is something they're not telling us."

"How's the girl?"

"She's…" Kevon fumbled for words. "Withdrawn. Since the return of her eye, it's confusing. Even as an assassin, she was straightforward, most times. Now…"

"I've seen it, from the war," Carlo shook his head. "Something changes in them, things they keep seeing. Not everyone is suited for the lives we lead. Fewer still understand when things… go wrong."

"I have nightmares," Kevon whispered. "But she'll be awake, and *somewhere else*."

"Give it time."

"I don't want to wait," Kevon blurted. "There are things that..."

"Things happen as they will," Carlo corrected Kevon. "Was I happy about leaving Bertus and Mirsa back on the Isle? We need them. But we'll do what we can, what we must." The Blademaster shook his head. "She'd only just made her peace with being broken. Magic can't heal everything, time is what she..."

"M'lani said something like that!" Kevon interrupted.

"Then listen to her, if you won't listen to me!" Carlo roared. "It'll save me having to beat some sense into you."

"I'll try," Kevon relented. "It's just..." He sighed.

"Why don't you start trying back on your own ship?"

CHAPTER 29

"Wind's still holding, another day at least before we split from the lanes."

Kevon nodded at Yusa's report, verifying by extending his senses outside the cabin, into the upper atmosphere. A picture of the air currents formed in his mind, dulled only by the seas below them, and the cliffs rising far to the east.

"Keeping in constant touch with these winds, using their power to fuel our progress, handing off the connection to our relief?" Kevon asked Yusa and the other Mage seated next to him, across from the captain.

"I think that drawing power from the trades and pushing it elsewhere could shift things," Reko interjected. "Unfavorably."

I know he's an illusion, projected from Yusa's mind, Kevon thought as he recovered from the suddenness of the Mage's appearance. *But I can't help being startled when he appears.*

"I tend to agree," Kaleb shifted in his chair. "Rearranged air in the doldrums will settle as soon as we pass through, but keeping linked to an active windstream... I dare not think of the damage we did when we used Water magic to force our way across the sea."

"I..." Kevon touched the shells that hung at his neck. "I should contact the Myrnar as soon as this leg of our journey is complete. They deserve to know what has happened."

"As a sailor, I'd not want to risk changing the trade lanes," Yusa agreed. "But our journey is not simple, nor trivial. Completing it swiftly is not without merit."

"We can manage without tapping into the trade winds," Kaleb waved off Yusa's concern. "We're well rested, the crew is practiced by now for the rigors of our Wind magic. A week or less will not be too taxing."

"Working the Magi hard until we hit land?" Yusa scowled. "Our mission is of the utmost importance. *She* sends us to..."

"I like having magic ready to use..." Kevon agreed with Yusa. "But if we run into something that two squads of Elven Hunters, over a dozen Dwarven Stoneguard, and Carlo's complement of guardsmen can't handle..."

"Amusing that *he* is the one to become overly dependent on magic," Reko commented from his corner of the cabin. "I vote we rely on local Wind magic as we go along."

"I'm not sure how I feel about him having two votes," Alanna scowled at the dark illusion in the corner. "His power must be fading, at any rate. I can see right through his image."

The others turned to look at Alanna.

"His Illusion magic is at least as good as mine," Kevon countered. "I can't see any flaw in his..." The Mage trailed off as he saw Alanna squinting and blinking at the projected image of Yusa's alter-ego.

"Oh. It's..." Alanna quieted. "Nothing."

"We'll be tearing at the fabric between worlds soon enough," Kevon assented. "Disturbing the local energies as little as possible with our passage seems to be the best course of action. Are we agreed?"

"Seeing no objections, I'll draft up a message to Carlo, and have Reko send it over to the other ship," Yusa thumped the heel of his palm on the weathered top of the desk the others were gathered around. "Now, if you would all kindly... get out."

"We haven't really had a chance... lately..." Kevon stepped up to the foredeck railing beside Alanna, who was gazing into the distance. "I was hoping that..."

“I’ve had a shift in perspective.” Alanna’s terse response cut through Kevon’s mumble like a rigging knife through rope. “Sometimes we’re forced to look at things differently.”

“We’ve all been forced to re-evaluate our places in the world…” Kevon put his hand on Alanna’s as it rested on the railing. “Now that we see this is not just a struggle between nations, or political factions, but a battle that spans realms, and lifetimes. We can’t see the world the way we used to…”

“No.” Alanna spun her wrist and brought Kevon’s captured hand up to the cheek by her gold-laced eye. “I *see* things differently.”

Kevon looked around, and saw only the Elven Huntmistress even remotely in earshot. “I think we should discuss this in private.”

“Five. Two. Three. Stop changing so fast!”

Kevon felt Alanna slap his hand. He called up a flame, and relit two candles and a hanging lantern before releasing the hold on his Art.

“Amazing. I think there’s a spell one can do to be able to see in the darkness, but you…” Kevon shook his head. “You just see like that normally?”

“No, it’s different than that,” Alanna sighed. “It doesn’t work at night, or nearly as well. The darker it is outside, the darker it would be in here without light. I don’t know how I would sleep if it didn’t work that way.”

“Light…” Kevon breathed. “Manipulation of light. Like the elves.”

“The shadows?”

“Well, no shadows, but… yes…” Kevon sat forward on his bunk and stuck his hand between the nearest candle and Alanna. “Do you see my hand, or the light?”

“Both, plain as day. And it disturbs me that it’s not…” Alanna squawked in frustration. “More disturbing,” she finished, glaring tight-lipped at Kevon.

"Right. The training... or talent... that the elves have to conceal their shadows, to let light pass through themselves, it's the same principle your eye uses to capture light from beyond obstacles." Kevon stood and began pacing. "I don't know if M'lani meant this to happen, or if she repaired your eye to see the way she knew vision to work, but this is amazing."

"Full moon is in a week," Alanna countered. "We'll see how amazing it is when I can't sleep for three days."

"Oh." Kevon sat, his exuberance deflating. "Sorry, I... don't always see..."

"What's in front of you?" Alanna smiled, candlelight dancing unevenly in her eyes. "I've noticed."

"Give me a day. I'll talk with Kaleb, see if we can devise something to ease the effects..." He stood to follow Alanna to the door. "Give me a day."

"I'll give you a day," Alanna stopped in the doorway, leaned back through to look up into his eyes. "But you'll owe me a night."

Kevon spat over the side of the ship, holding the railing to remain upright. "I'm sorry to have involved you in this, Kaleb. You've done nothing to deserve it."

The other Mage staggered and grabbed the railing himself. "I've held the Dark rune before," he gasped. "Never for so long."

The vile symbol still lurked in Kevon's mind, anchored there by the patch he clutched in his hand. The deepening dusk pushed inward, eager to power the enchantment through him.

"No," Kevon croaked, addressing the night as much as his flagging assistant. He shoved the scrap of cloth in a pocket, and wiped his hands on his tunic. "Nor have I. That was the second worst experience I've had with the Dark rune. Thank you." *You'd have nightmares if I even told you about the first,* he added silently.

"I pray it is my worst," Kaleb took a deep breath, stood up

straight, and sighed. "And I bid you a good night."

Memories of L'mort's attempted entry into the Plane of Enchantment under the ruins of Gurlin's tower flashed through Kevon's mind. He blinked them away, and bowed to the Court-Mage as Kaleb walked back toward the cabins.

"Thank you, too, Reko," Kevon whispered, twisting an illusion into invisible representations of the words as he spoke them, powering it for a few seconds.

"Not at all," the words drifted in Reko's voice from somewhere near Kevon's ear. "I felt you working, thought I would help."

"I didn't know how it would affect you and Yusa," Kevon messaged back.

"He woke up in a cold sweat, halfway through," Reko allowed himself a dry chuckle at his 'partner's' expense. "He's just settling back in now, none the wiser. I doubt he'd have approved of binding M'lani's gift in such a fashion. I am grateful she did not *fix* us, but am not as taken with her as he is."

"Well, with your help, it took only one evening, instead of the two I feared it would."

"See to your lady," the disembodied voice whispered. "Let me know if you need any more help."

The hushed sound of nearby deckhands returned to its normal volume, and Kevon looked up to see the first smattering of stars, unfamiliar yet this far south. "I will," he said softly, not enhancing the speech with Illusion for Reko's benefit. "And, I will."

"This may help your condition," Kevon winced as he held the enchanted eye-patch through the partially opened doorway to Alanna's cabin. "It was the first thing I could think of. If we need to try something else..."

"Two things," Alanna chuckled from the shadows beyond the threshold. "First, it works, well enough."

"And second?" Kevon asked.

"We need to try something else."

Her hand reached out into the torchlit hallway, and grasped Kevon by the collar. She pulled him into the darkened cabin, and closed the door.

CHAPTER 30

The sounds of increased activity from the morning crew goaded Kevon awake, and he called up a glowing sphere to find the candles to light.

"Ahh..." as he turned his head to look to the bedside table, the aches and pains accumulated throughout the night wakened as well. Rolling his head back to its original position, he spotted Alanna, eye-patch off, head propped up, watching him. Her tousled half-blonde, half-dark hair gave her a decidedly feline aura. The stinging sensations that prickled trails along his back seemed to echo that sentiment.

"You're awake."

"Yes, I..."

Alanna's finger pressed into his lips, silencing him.

"Good."

The assassin maneuvered through the tangled blankets. With each advance, Kevon's aching muscles protested, but only just. Dangling locks of hair tickled his ears, and she traced a finger slowly from the tip of his chin to the center of his stomach, arching herself upward as she went, framed exquisitely in the soothing Mage-light.

Her other hand produced a dagger.

Kevon's mind convulsed. The light flickered, and his chest tightened, his heart racing faster than it had already been. He remained still, enthralled only by the continued tracing of her finger from his lower stomach to the center of hers, and beyond. The tracing slowed, and the knife shifted, pushing him to the brink of panic.

The flat of the blade touched his side, plunging the room

into abrupt darkness. She dragged the knife slowly across his abdomen. With a slight shift, and a sudden *swish* of air, it was gone. A sharp *thunk* at the cabin door audible proof the blade was no longer a threat.

Alanna crouched, molding her body to his, nibbling at his ears, then his neck.

"Well," Kevon whispered. "That's... something else."

Kevon emerged into the midday light battered, bruised, and elated beyond anything he'd thought possible. His first encounter with Marelle had been one of innocence and exploration. This had been a brutal combination of frustration, acceptance, and reunion. He was not completely sure what footing Alanna and he were on after last night, but he felt like it was a two day march in the right direction.

"Been looking for you!" Yusa called from the upper deck.

"I told him not to look too hard," Reko whispered in Kevon's ear. "You're welcome."

"We're turning, and Kaleb says we're reaching the edge of the trade winds." Yusa waited until Kevon was beside him to continue. "Hours, at the most. He volunteered for the first shift. You... been sparring with the Stoneguard again?"

"No, Captain. Thank you for your concern," Kevon smiled. "I'll take the second shift."

"Reko claims he's going to take every other shift, to save everyone else the strain," Yusa scowled. "Says he'll sleep when we get there."

"That's a generous offer," Kevon frowned. "And no small task. Let us know if you need any relief at all."

"Aye, we will," Yusa slapped Kevon on the back. "I'll send for you just before third shift."

Kevon closed his eyes and nodded, keeping the renewed pain in check. Opening his eyes, he maneuvered around sailors and barrels, piles of coiled rope, to the aft railing. He peered down into the wake behind the ship, contemplating the swirling blue-green water they churned steadily through. He turned his face upward, savoring the contrast between the hot sun overhead, the warm breeze following, and the cool spray that churned from below.

Something touched his arm, and he turned to see Alanna holding a bowl of gruel.

"They're done with breakfast. This is cold, but it'll have to do." Alanna handed him the bowl, then sat, back to the railing, looking over the bustle of the ship's crew.

"Thanks for bringing… me… this…" Kevon slumped to a seated position by Alanna, eyeing the apple she'd pulled from a pocket and was crunching into. He spooned a few bites of the mixture into his mouth, chewing absently.

Alanna stood, pitching the core of her meal over the side. She stretched her arms, yawned, and turned toward the steps to the main deck.

"Alanna," Kevon spoke just above the churning ocean sounds behind them, "Are we…"

"Together?" She turned to stare at Kevon, her golden eye twinkling the sun's reflection. "Yes. Betrothed? No." She reached into a pocket for another apple, and tossed it to him. "Pay a little attention, you'll never have to ask stupid questions." She tilted her head and smiled. "Kaleb mentioned something about you being free until third shift?"

CHAPTER 31

"You're sure this is the best place to land?" Kevon asked, peering at the sheer cliff face that stretched for miles on either side of the sandy beach ahead.

"Another week of hard sailing to the south, there is another port, but it's far from the Highplain." Yusa scratched his head. "I think."

"A hidden town, and a winding path to the plateau above?" Martin asked.

"If Reko remembers his research correctly," Alma shrugged. "I'll be glad to be on land of any type, after the trip we've had."

"As will I," Kevon nodded, recalling the unseasonable storm that had tossed the ships about for the better part of three days, breaking only the night before. "And I'm sure the dwarves could use a smaller slice of sky."

The two nearby Stoneguard turned at their mention, but laughed and made the fluttering hand gesture Kevon had come to recognize as meaning 'too much talk'.

"The crew will remain aboard, the Mage Kaleb, two Stoneguard, and two Hunters." Yusa announced. "There will be a similar crew complement on the other ship, but its Captain shall be in charge of both vessels in my absence. Have your gear ready. We'll drop anchor in about ten minutes, longboats ten after that."

◆ ◆ ◆

"About time!" Carlo taunted, hauling on the line tossed to him, dragging one of Yusa's longboats up on shore.

Kevon nodded, eyeing the tents set up beyond the high tide mark, and Carlo's second in command barking orders to the scrambling soldiers.

"Second load's coming ashore," Carlo observed as he held open the door to the Command tent. "Mostly dwarves, and the last of our soldiers. Anneliese and her Hunters are scouting the perimeter."

"Anneliese?" Kevon asked, stepping into the candlelit room.

"Near as I can pronounce it," Carlo answered. "The Elder Huntmistress."

"They've already reported in once," Relaniel corrected, scratching additional detail onto the rough map lying on the small table in the center of the room. "No one for over a mile in any direction, the road is clear for two miles toward town, and it's only an additional half mile to reach it."

"They're back, and gone again?" Carlo asked.

"They were scouting," the Elven Noble answered. "Now they're hunting."

"Inform the mess crew," Carlo tapped a soldier on the shoulder. "Shift them to digging cook-pits. No fish tonight."

"You sound fairly sure of their success," Kevon observed.

"Anneliese is many things," Carlo replied. "Inexperienced… is not one of them,"

"Those elves are no slouches," Yusa's entrance trampled over the unasked question on Kevon's lips. "They hopped out of the boat and disappeared, and by the time we unloaded it, they're strolling back into camp with the others, and two fat deer-things."

"The Elder Huntmistress is an artist with a blade," Alanna added, following on Yusa's heels. "It would seem as though she's skinned thousands of those. I didn't think any of them even ate meat."

"Many elves hold to our diet even off the Isle," Relaniel

offered. "There, it is law. We sometimes eat fish if at sea for long enough. Hunters, though, often indulge in many different foods when away from home."

"Interesting appetites, they have," Carlo mused. "Aligned closely enough with our own, I suppose."

Kevon's brow furrowed as he tried to read Carlo's expression.

"Cheer up, boy." Carlo gave the map one last look, and shifted over to open the case that held his crossbow. He inspected the weapon, checking the tension and alignment, making sure the firing groove was smooth and unobstructed before returning it to the case. "First game we'll have had in near a season."

Still feeling the tug of the sea, Kevon excused himself and exited the command tent. He walked around the canvas structure, and away from shore until he felt the mental *slosh* of insistent Water magic wedge against the Earth magic that loomed in the cliffs ahead and to the north. A detachment of Carlo's men were busy setting up another tent not far from him.

"Tent for the Magi?" he asked, moving over to the half-built structure.

"Yes, sir!" one of the soldiers snapped, bracing one of the poles with his foot as the others threaded it through the canvas tabs, and snapped the locking end into two of the other converging poles.

Kevon nodded, and walked back toward the main part of camp. *Quite the setup for the one Mage that will be using it. Reko and I are the only others that would even need to sleep that far out. Reko is not one to complain, Yusa would not allow it. Neither would Marelle, in my case.*

He stopped in his tracks. *Alanna. Alanna would not allow it.*

Kevon spotted his assassin talking with the Elder Huntmistress, Annaliese, as the Elven Hunters were finishing carving up their catch near the mess tent. Shallow cooking pits ablaze with driftwood circled the seaward quarter of the structure. Low hanging spits attended by soldiers were already turning slowly, the smoke and flesh smell fading in and out of the base odor of the sea.

"Yes, Carlo *is* a fine specimen of a man," Alanna raised her voice as Kevon walked within earshot. "Though my tastes tend to run a bit younger."

"Here is my preference," Alanna commented, snatching Kevon's hand and pulling him to her side as he approached. "Oh, the stories we could trade..."

"I'd rather not, dear," Kevon's face flushed with embarrassment. "Annaliese? Good to see you again. Carlo speaks highly of you."

"It is well that he does. Few men hold my interest." Anneliese's blade flashed two more times, and she handed the two remaining portions of meat to the waiting soldiers. "My interest in you is born of my respect for Aelion, and deepened by the curious way that Carlo views you. A threat to his ingrained values, but an example of responsible power."

"He told you that?" Kevon's embarrassment shifted to confusion.

"Not with words," Anneliese scoffed. "He's too... male."

"As wise as she is beautiful, don't you think, Kevon?" Without waiting for an answer, Alanna reached a hand out to the Huntmistress's woven hair. "Will you teach me to do this?"

"I will adjust the plait for the Highplain just before dawn," Anneliese answered. "You may observe, if you wish."

"We'll have to see what the morning brings," Alanna withdrew her hand and pressed in closer to Kevon. "It'll take us all day to reach the top, we'll need our rest."

"Two days, at least, with this group," Anneliese corrected. "Three, if there is the usual amount of *talking*."

"All the more reason for a good start," Alanna laughed. "You'll see to our accommodations, then, and I'll bring along dinner?"

Kevon nodded, glad to be free of the elf's piercing eyes. He turned and marched off to find the crew that had been putting up tents.

CHAPTER 32

"Dawn's coming."

The whisper was followed by a sharp nibble on Kevon's ear.

"I can see the light through the plateau."

"I don't see anything," Kevon groaned, opening eyes to nothingness.

"The elves are getting up. I'm going to go play with Anneliese."

An inappropriate squeeze, a rustling of blankets and canvas, and she was gone.

After a few long breaths, Kevon sat up and lit the interior of the tent with his Art. His sleep had been better than any since the Glimmering Isle, away from the crush of Water magic, on unmoving ground. He'd spent all night wrapped around Alanna, disturbed only when a soft cry or dream-induced spasm was loud or large enough to wake him from the sanctuary that was the curve of her neck.

"Are you ready for what today brings?" Carlo called as Kevon pushed through the tent flap into the pre-dawn bustle of camp.

"That depends on what the day decides to bring," Kevon scowled, accepting the mug of steaming tea one of the cook staff handed him as he approached the campfire where Carlo sat. "Are you?"

"I don't have to squeeze myself through a magic door and play hide and seek with one of the creators," Carlo countered. "My question is the important one."

Kevon nodded, sipping the bitter drink, taking a seat

across the fire from the commander.

“Anneliese and the other Hunters seem to think they can get us past the town ahead, if we want,” Carlo continued. “They don’t seem to think there is much of a threat there, we’d just as well walk through.”

“I’d like a local perspective on what lies above, if it’s no more dangerous than passing the town by,” Kevon shrugged. “These folk have less reason to dislike us than their neighbors to the north do.”

“We’ll leave most of our people here,” Carlo explained, handing off his empty mug to a passing soldier. “Anneliese and one of her Hunters we’ll take to handle scouting. Relaniel will insist on coming along. You, Alanna, and Yusa will be crossing over, as before. The librarian will need to come along with her books. A single Stoneguard will be enough extra muscle, but will likely not take direction from Rhysabeth-Dane.”

“Kylgren-Wode, then? He’ll help with translation, packing Rhysabeth-Dane’s research, and is no slouch with an axe.” Kevon continued after Carlo’s confirming nod. “We’ll need another Mage to reopen the portal from this side, if last time is any indication.”

“Jacek?”

“I was thinking he would be the best candidate,” Kevon nodded. “Aside from Reko, he’s the strongest Mage we have. If we could spare both him and Kaleb…”

“We can’t. My second in command will remain here, and run the camp in my absence,” Carlo added. “I’d like to take two others to help with general duties, cooking, and such. That will bring us to twelve when traveling, and nine when you are *elsewhere*.”

“I would almost suggest Alma and Martin,” Kevon hesitated. “I’ve not spent as much time with them as I’d like since they rejoined us. For such a small group, though…”

“We’d be safer with soldiers?” Carlo asked.

“As they would be here at camp, or back aboard ship,” Kevon agreed.

"It's the same call I would make," Carlo cleared his throat. "If we knew more about the road ahead, we might risk taking them instead. We don't, and we won't. If you are the one the dwarves seem to think you are, you'll need to start making decisions like this more and more often. It's a good start."

Kevon stared into the fire for a few moments longer, before shuddering at the last swallow of the bitter tea.

"The Hunters collected some eggs this morning," Carlo said, pointing toward the mess tent. "If you hurry, there might be some left."

"We'll gather our gear after that, then?" Kevon asked, shaking the last few drops from his mug into the fire. He looked to where the sun's rays lit the ocean to the west, throwing a small amount of light back against the cliffs that rose to the east.

"We'll try to reach the village by the time it lights up," Carlo shrugged. "I can't see us reaching the Highplain today. Tomorrow at the earliest. Then we'll have to look for your throne?"

"The Seat of Wind," Kevon corrected. "I wish Mirsa had been able to come with us. She's the only one to have felt the energy of both the Seat of Earth, and the Seat of Light. Reko and I will have to try and locate it by ourselves, as Jacek has no experience with them."

"Well, you can tell your sister," Carlo smirked. "I'll tell everyone else."

"Visitors from below!"

The cry came as soon as the group rounded the last curve in the path before the village. Curious children hid behind the legs of their parents, peering out to see the newcomers. No weapons were produced, but the shifting grips on long-handled gardening tools were unmistakable.

"What is your business here?" A man built much like

Carlo, but younger, a full head shorter, with a circular patch of vertical rust-red hair slipped from between two other onlookers. His light jacket of hardened leather sported small, thin riveted plates of gleaming metal across his shoulders, forearms, neckline, and other targets that Kevon would imagine could use a little extra protection. The braided joints moved with the wearer, rather than against him, showcasing his deadly grace instead of concealing it.

"Is it our concern, Rowyn?"

The onlookers parted, and the speaker appeared. Waves of flaming red hair spilled over armor that was somewhat like the man's, with smaller, darker metal plates, closer in appearance to noble riding garb in the Inner Cities.

"Ashera," the man chuckled as she reached his side. "What concerns our neighbors today, may concern us tomorrow. I'm not that patient."

"*Please. No fighting...*" Ashera strained through clenched teeth, her crooked smile eliciting a barking laugh from Yusa.

"Griffinsworn, may your winds be fair." Anneliese stepped forward, inclining her head as she spoke. "We mean you no harm, and ask to accompany you to the Highplain."

"Fair winds to you, Child of Light. Your people have not visited in more than a generation." Ashera swept forward to clasp palms with the Huntmistress.

"Were fondness in itself reason enough..." Anneliese smiled and released Ashera's hands. "Supplies for your village?"

"Salt, and fish," Ashera nodded. "Two things the Plain cannot provide."

"Any help you require is yours." Anneliese glanced sideways to Carlo, who could only whisper "*Griffinsworn?*"

CHAPTER 33

"I don't like our company being this burdened," Carlo growled under his breath to Anneliese. He shifted his grip on the burlap sack over his left shoulder, and adjusted the angle of his scabbarded sword with his free hand.

"Four bags," the Huntmistress teased. "Tripling the amount the Griffinsworn can bring back to their villages will be an ideal show of friendship toward their people."

Carlo sighed. "If anyone knows where this wind chair is..."

"Seat of Wind," Kevon corrected, dropping his burden and rolling his strained shoulder. "It will likely be them."

"Jacek and Rhysabeth-Dane, at least, are not weighed down by this task..." Yusa chuckled, then tilted his head as if listening to something. "Or Reko," he added with a snort.

"Half our number was already carrying supplies," Anneliese lectured. "It won't take much to drop a sack and draw a sword, if it comes to that."

"It appears we're to stop for the evening," Alanna shifted her load to her other shoulder and pressed ahead of the others, pointing to the switchback in the trail ahead where Ashera and Rowyn had paused and were setting their cargo down.

"We should press on," Rowyn complained, pacing back and forth as the others reached where Ashera had stopped.

"The two of us, without supplies, would make it to the Plain before twilight," Ashera shrugged. "The others are not what slows us down. Calm yourself."

"There is not enough sky here," Rowyn complained. "I don't like it."

"Sit down. Look to the south." Ashera rolled her eyes. "*Be silent.*"

"How far is your village, once we reach the top?" Carlo asked, depositing his sack with the others.

"Three days walking, perhaps," Ashera assured him. "The supplies will be picked up by other Riders as soon as we reach the Highplain. That will make our way easier."

"Riders on the Plain, yet they use us as pack animals?" Alanna whispered to Kevon as he joined her at the outer edge of the gathering.

Kevon shrugged, slumping down at the assassin's feet, leaning against his bundled cloak. "Closer to our goal. It's all that matters."

"I have not been able to discern which one of them is in charge," Alanna complained. "Both ask and order, at turns. It's frustrating."

"Could it have anything to do with them being brother and sister?" Kevon laughed. "Alma and I were often in disagreements of similar nature."

"You're both correct," Anneliese sat by Kevon, motioning for Alanna to do the same. "Much of their conflict is familial, though they do represent two of the three factions of their society. If I'm not mistaken, they are leaders in those factions."

"They're barely our ages!" Alanna scowled at the news. "How could they be in charge of two-thirds of their society?"

"Life on the Highplain is harsh, the old and the weak do not survive long." Anneliese shuddered. "These two do seem young for their stations. They must be truly skilled, to be Fist, and Claw."

The Elder Huntmistress took to her feet. "You should join the others, build trust with our hosts. It is the surest route to our goals."

"I still don't…" Alanna continued mumbling as she stood and waited for Kevon.

"No sense in being difficult," Kevon shrugged as he pushed himself up to a standing position.

"You don't know me at all," Alanna whispered, eyes flashing wider in exaggerated paranoia.

Kevon fought the urge to laugh, and gave Alanna a shove in the direction the others were clustering.

Rowyn sat away from the fire, talking with Carlo, Kylgren-Wode, and the Stoneguard that had accompanied them.

He surrounds himself with strength, Kevon thought, glancing back across the fire to where Anneliese sat speaking with Ashera. Beyond the lilting laughter and the animated storytelling that reminded Kevon far too much of Waine, he felt her hawk-like gaze settling on him more than he felt comfortable with. The occasional coinciding squeeze of Alanna's hand on his leg only reinforced his discomfort. *She looks beyond it.*

As if sensing his discomfort, Ashera spoke.

"Military commanders. Dwarven warriors. Immortal Hunters. Assassins." She stood, and circled the fire to sit near Kevon, turning her sky-blue eyes to glare at him. "Why do I get the feeling you're the one everyone is concerned about?"

"Why, indeed?" Kevon smiled, placing his hand over Alanna's, squeezing gently to soften her vise-like grip on his leg.

"You wear the rank of your Guild openly, but do not carry yourself like a soldier. You're built like a miner, one who has not swung a pick in a season or two, but would still know how. You walk like a would-be assassin, as if she has begun to rub off on you... and your eyes hold enough secrets for two lifetimes."

"Blacksmith."

Ashera craned her neck, gazing at Kevon and his terse response.

"Not miner. Blacksmith. Everything else is fairly accurate." Kevon frowned. "And I've been swinging the hammer a lot lately."

"And the secrets remain hidden?" Ashera smiled, shaking her head. "Very well. You have no great reason to trust us, beyond our history with the elves. That will change soon."

"You seem sure of yourself," Alanna sneered.

"Bonds that form in life and death battles overcome many things. Once…"

"Battles?" Kevon interrupted. "What battles?"

Ashera looked at Kevon, then to Anneliese. "Oh. The troubles have increased since the Children of Light last visited. I had assumed you knew, as heavily armed as you are."

"Troubles?" Anneliese moved closer, concern lining her features. "Other than the occasional chimaera, the Highplain has always been hospitable. Are the tribes at war?"

"The tribes are more united than ever," Ashera shook her head. "The chimaera are the problem. They have overtaken most of the Highplain. Our villages have been under attack since before Rowyn was born."

"We had no idea," Anneliese bowed her head. "We would have come, had you sent word."

"Your aid is welcome," Ashera frowned. "The tribes have chosen not to involve others. The Highplain is vulnerable to invasion. Our strength has long been the only thing preventing the Lowlanders from moving against us."

"How has this not spilled over to the lowlands?" Anneliese peered at the Griffinsworn, confused.

"Garrisons at each of the three paths to the lower lands keep outsiders away, and the chimaera contained," she explained. "Each of the four tribes pledge five Griffinsworn, two Riders, two Striders, and a Meek, to each garrison."

Anneliese hung her head in dismay. "There were five tribes when I visited last."

"There are many of the Meek from Seacliff that are scattered amongst the rest," Ashera continued. "All of their warriors perished trying to retake the village."

"The fortifications are mostly intact," Rowyn added, joining the group. "The village spring and defensive perimeter help the chimaera nearly as much as they did the clan. There has been talk of burning them out, to take their safe haven from them." He shook his head. "The rebuilding would be too costly, the greater numbers of chimaera on the Highplain would overwhelm incomplete defenses."

"Rowyn has been leading the spring and autumn hunts," Ashera threw an arm around her brother. "The greatest Fist in three generations."

"Some would disagree," the Strider grumbled. "The looks some of the Hiders give me..."

"Meek," Ashera corrected. "The Seacliff Meek are alive because of you."

"We should have joined the others in defense of the walls."

"And lost everyone?" Ashera shook her head. "This is not a game we play once we return to the Highplain. Your decision is beyond question."

"The law prevents others from questioning, not me." Rowyn sighed.

"What would you need to retake the village?" Kevon asked. "We'll need your help once we reach the Plain, I see no better way to earn it."

"If I had a dozen more Striders," Rowyn chortled. "I could do something with that. Warriors who had faced chimaera before."

"I'll train them."

Every head turned to look at Anneliese.

"I have fought chimaera here, on occasion," the Huntmistress shrugged. "Give us a week, we will meet you at Stonespire Camp."

CHAPTER 34

Kevon braced his foot against the spasming corpse of the chimaera, shoving and pulling his blade free from his defeated enemy's body. He circled the thrashing carcass, staying clear of the powerful forelegs. A carelessly defended swipe had set his training back two days at the beginning of the week, the fever from the infected wound finally yielding to a healing potion.

"No arrows," he called, finishing his examination of the creature. "So this one counts?"

"Expertly done," Anneliese called from her position near the garrison wall. "Two more, and we'll all be ready to journey to Stonespire."

"Nice move, that," Reko's voice whispered in his ear. "Taking a wing and the tail in one slash."

"Unintentional," Kevon whispered, unable to force the Illusion-speech he normally used to converse with Reko at a distance. He took a stoppered wooden vial from his cloak, and splashed the contents on the fallen chimaera, careful to avoid the liquid himself.

Two more chimaera, two more doses of poison... he thought. *Easy, right?*

A telltale ripple in the waving grasses caught Kevon's eye an instant before the chimaera leapt from cover. He rolled forward and away from his last kill, slashing upward as he regained his feet.

The beast spread its wings and flapped, checking its momentum enough that Kevon's attack missed the soft, wooly underbelly and chipped into its right rear hoof.

"Hah!" Kevon twisted, transferring the momentum from his swing into a tighter arc around his body, slashing again between himself and the chimaera before his foe even touched down.

The pull of the blade and the roar of pain brought a smile to his face as he arched his back and threw out his free hand to complete the backward roll to his feet, and pivot to face the enemy.

The chimaera hissed, flicks of what remained of its tail spattering blood on the grass behind and to the side of it.

You bring it here, Kevon thought, smirking. *I can wait until you bleed ou…*

The ground quivered, and Kevon leapt to the side, dodging the tumbling mass that flopped past where he'd just been. He caught a glimpse of feathered shafts protruding from the eye and chest of the newer chimaera, and shuddered as *his* crouched for another leap.

"Oh, no, no," the Warsmith lectured as the remaining chimaera leapt wide, faking a wing strike, and turning, trying to drive Kevon toward the lashing tail-fangs of its fallen companion. Seeing no movement other than the tail spasms from behind him, Kevon dove backward, lopping half of the thrashing appendage from the otherwise still form, and stooping to retrieve the 'safe' end with his free hand.

He swung the whip experimentally, an errant twitch flopping the curved spikes closer to Kevon's legs than he liked.

The chimaera stalked closer, the large, human-looking eyes pleading at him from the contorted feline face.

Kevon backed past the Elven-slain monstrosity, and away from both of the fallen obstacles. He swung the tail-whip slowly, deliberately away from his body.

The remaining chimaera reached the unpoisoned carcass, and licked the face of its companion.

Kevon used the pause to swing his gaze around and behind him, checking for more of the beasts.

The roar that accompanied the lunge was the loudest he'd

heard, and it stunned Kevon for a split second. A twirl and a flick of his left arm, and the severed tail-fangs were lunging to intercept the leaping chimaera. Kevon released the makeshift weapon, unable to trust it as he did his sword. He rolled forward and to the right, hoping for the technique to work with the added distraction.

The chimaera flicked its wing out, batting away the flung tail, but altering its passage through the air.

Kevon spun as he rolled to his feet, slashing the creature's abdomen on the side where the goat-wool began the transition to the reptilian scales that covered its back and base of its tail. The drag of the blade's deep passage slowed Kevon's turn, and wrenched him back around to the left.

The creature's hind hoof lashed out, hammering Kevon below the ear, squarely on the jaw.

The world spun. The sword pulled free from fingers that were suddenly not answering to Kevon, and the chimaera twisted and flipped, advancing toward him on three legs.

A jet of flame spewed past Kevon, spraying across the creature's face and mane, as arrows blossomed from half a dozen points in its head and neck.

Still... two... more... Kevon thought, as darkness enveloped him.

"Ten more," Kevon wheezed, falling to his knees as he staggered clear of the quivering, poisoned carcass. "Done."

"That was nine," Anneliese called, strolling out to meet him, eyes sweeping over the terrain. "We shot the second to last one." She kicked the carcass, turning it to expose the arrow in its neck.

"Doesn't count," Kevon gasped. "It was already dead."

The Huntmistress allowed a shadow of a smile to creep onto her face. "Good. It's late enough we need to stop, regardless." She poured poison on the latest kill, and helped Kevon to his feet. "The garrison is expecting a new batch of supplies tomorrow. They're low on poison, we'd have to burn the carcasses if we killed any more this evening. Filthy cannibals."

Kevon nodded. The Meek from the garrison were already filtering out, under the guard of the other Griffinsworn, Carlo, and the Dwarven Stoneguard. They worked swiftly, collecting the oversized canine teeth from the mouths, and the venom sacs and spikes from the tails of the carcasses.

"Just another day for them…" Kevon shook his head. "How do they do it?"

"It was not always this way," the elf straightened, stepping away from Kevon. "When I was here last, the chimaera were something to be hunted twice a year, as a rite of passage. The constant press we've seen is unheard of. Unnatural. The tribes have hardened into something capable of withstanding it, but only just."

Not our first encounter with hordes of unnatural creatures, Kevon thought, pressing on toward the garrison walls without the elf's help. *But eerily similar.*

Kevon walked through the entrance to the garrison wall, staggered, and was caught by Alanna.

"Hasn't he done enough?" the assassin asked Anneliese.

"Quite." The elf nodded. "Though I expect more from him than anyone else here. He's dispatched nearly twice as many beasts as even Carlo. We'll need them all to be in top form before we attempt the crossing to Stonespire Camp."

"It's all right," Kevon sighed. "I'm just tired, that's all…"

"And you need to be more careful." Alanna touched a scratch near Kevon's left elbow, smudging the glistening fluid near it away from the crusted-over wound. "You're lucky we've all been drinking that tea."

"Luck has nothing to do with it," Anneliese corrected, stepping aside as the Griffinsworn barred the door after closing it behind the last of the Meek to reenter the structure. "Anyone old enough to lift a sword or a bow drinks cups of it a day. The Striders drink nothing else."

“I know it is supposed to help you endure the poison better,” Alanna made a face. “But it smells like an outhouse.”

“A week ago, that scratch would have put him down in under a minute,” Anneliese shrugged. “He got that fighting his second beast of the afternoon.”

A keening shriek sounded through the layers of wood and stone above.

“Sounds like Ashera’s back,” Anneliese grinned. “She may be wondering why we haven’t left yet.”

“Attacks are intensifying,” Ashera reported, after drinking two mugs of tea, and appearing to relax somewhat. “We’ve lost a Rider and three Striders this week alone.”

“Our training has lasted longer than anticipated,” Anneliese frowned. “I’ve been pushing them hard, knowing what lies before us.”

“We spotted what may be a new den, a day’s march to the east of our camp. We cannot spare the Striders from the fortifications, and do not have enough Riders for a decisive strike.” The hand holding her mug of tea shook noticeably. “We are losing.”

“We’ll attack the den, before we meet at your camp,” Kevon declared. “We should be able to clear it out, give your people the advantage again.”

“I’ll take Rhysabeth-Dane to my camp, and meet you there with a Wing of Riders in seven days,” Ashera nodded. She turned to the Dwarven librarian, grinning. “It’s… kind of like riding a horse.”

CHAPTER 35

"Stormclaw! Behave!"

The griffin snapped once more at Rhysabeth-Dane, then gave in to Ashera's demands, bowing its head and relaxing its ruffled neck feathers.

"Beautiful," the dwarf murmured, running her hand along the griffin's beak, curving down under to scratch at the beast's neck feathers. She startled as Stormclaw opened his beak and uttered a low hiss, but continued scratching, watching the griffin's closed eye.

"Oh, well, we don't have time for that," Ashera groaned, patting the leonine flanks of her steed. "You, little lady, have made a friend."

"I petted housecats in Eastport," Rhysabeth-Dane giggled, fending off nudges and squawks with quick ruffles of feathers and dodging back to where Ashera waited.

"Stormclaw! Down."

The griffin clicked his front talons against the stone slab atop the garrison-wall, then sat, and leaned forward, spreading his wings as he did.

"You'll have to hold on to me," Ashera beckoned for Rhysabeth-Dane to follow her around the outstretched wing closest them, and slipped a leg over Stormclaw's back, grabbing on to the wooden handle that was the focal point of the simple rope harness around the griffin's neck and shoulders. "The transport harness would have been too heavy, not to mention awkward. A combat saddle would have been a little better, but there is not a spare here. You can do this."

"May I sketch him when we get there?"

“I don’t know that he would stand still long enough for that,” Ashera laughed, giving the dwarf a hand up. “You’re welcome to try. Hold on.”

Ashera whistled a sharp note, and Stormclaw stood, wings flexing. Three practice flaps, a half-second crouch…

Rhysabeth-Dane squeaked and buried her face in Ashera’s hair, fingers digging at the armor-plates on the Rider’s sides. There was a momentary feeling of falling, and then she could feel the rippling of Stormclaw’s muscles as the griffin’s wings beat harder, climbing ever higher in the sky.

“Look,” Ashera called over the whistling of the wind past them. “Your friends!”

Rhysabeth-Dane turned her head to the right, and opened her eyes a crack, squinting down through the whipping strands of hair. She spotted the organized dots inching along the mid-morning plain below, and the scattered blotches of brown surrounding them, wandering chimaera. She shook her head and closed her eyes again.

“You might want to relax a little!” Ashera laughed. “We’re hours away from camp!”

“That them?” Kevon asked, shading his eyes to look at the newest speck wheeling through the sky.

“Yes,” Anneliese confirmed. “It does look like it.”

“Why couldn’t we all ride griffins?” Jacek grumbled. “I could have controlled one of them easily enough.”

“For three hours?” Anneliese scoffed. “And how would you have defended yourself from it once you stopped? No, Riders are chosen by griffin once a year, and will not take the harness from anyone else. Ever.”

“So there aren’t enough griffin for everyone?” Alanna asked, eyes still sweeping the surrounding grasslands for chimaera.

“Most griffin are unbound, and stay near the hatching

grounds," Anneliese explained. "They lie beyond the ruins of Seacliff Camp to the west."

"Where the chimaera have taken over?" Carlo groaned. "Are they in danger of being overrun?"

"The griffin nests are where chimaera cannot follow," Relaniel assured. "The Seacliff Hollows may be where our quest is leading us. One of few possibilities in our search."

"They may not be able to follow, but are still an obstacle." Anneliese frowned. "Not an impassable one, but inconvenient."

"We don't even know if our path lies that direction," Kevon pointed into a clump of high grass, and Anneliese buried two arrow shafts in the lurking chimaera taking shelter there. "If Jacek and I could journey about the Highplain freely, and search out the Seat..."

"It may be possible," the Huntmistress conceded, scanning the area around the fallen chimaera for others. "Depending on the griffin and the Rider. "You'd be more difficult, but the Court-Wizard..."

The color drained from Jacek's face.

"You said you wanted to fly," Alanna smirked.

"Not enough poison, no time for fire," Kevon remarked, pulling the arrows from the fallen beast and laying them aside. He knelt, placing a palm on the ground near the dead chimaera. Forming an Earth rune, he tapped into the weak sympathetic magic from below, and forced his own energy into a spell that lowered the carcass into the ground, covering it over with freshly turned soil. "Hope there aren't too many of those," he stood slowly, and returned Anneliese's arrows.

"Agreed," Carlo grunted. "Let's move."

CHAPTER 36

"It's been five days."

"I'll sleep when we get to Stonespire," Anneliese assured Carlo. "We've needed the extra eyes at night."

"We'll need you fresh when we reach the nest," the Blademaster lectured. "I'll readjust the watch schedule, you will sleep the entire night."

The Huntmistress chuckled. "At my age, a day or ten without sleep is not such a burden. You'll learn that, in time."

"Until I do, you will sleep," Carlo growled.

"Given the exposed nature of the sleeping arrangements, having you force me to sleep would be inappropriate," Anneliese pouted.

"Sleep the next two nights," Carlo rumbled, glancing over to where the others were finishing up breakfast and striking camp. "And I'll be as inappropriate as you like."

"Mmm." Anneliese shrugged. "You're not as fragile as I feared. We have a bargain."

"Fragile?" Carlo whispered, squinting at the grinning elf. He shook his head and smiled at the faint ache he'd been masking from a pulled hamstring nearly two weeks prior. "We'll see about fragile."

"Incoming!"

Carlo's head swiveled to Kevon's shout from camp, then to where the Mage was looking, a growing figure in the sky to the northwest.

"Mark out that clearing!" the Blademaster shouted, sprinting to the nearby patch of low grass and turning outward to watch all of the surrounding terrain that could hide a chimaera or even a lion. "Circle it up! Press out!"

The circle around the clearing stretched out to about fifty feet in diameter before Carlo called a halt. He gave one final glance, and stepped back to the inside. "Kevon!" he barked. "Fall out! Shift to cover!"

The routine was familiar enough that the Stoneguard did not need Kylgren-Wode to translate. The remaining eight shuffled to maintain the perimeter as the griffin and its two passengers landed.

"Three to the northeast!" Ashera called as Jacek scrambled off Stormclaw's back. "Clumped together. They might be trouble later."

"Thanks for the warning," Carlo replied. "We'll head that direction first. Then directly north?"

"That's correct," Ashera nodded, straightening her hair and smoothing the creases from the light tunic she wore. "It'll be good to be back in my armor, and we're all looking forward to a fight that will make a difference."

"Not." Jacek gasped. "Like riding. A horse."

Ashera shrugged. "Well, I've never ridden a horse. How was I to know?"

Alanna laughed at the Mage's responding glare before turning back to watch her section of the surrounding plain.

"I'll have some of my Riders deliver water before nightfall," Ashera whistled to Stormclaw. "Save you the time you'd have spent digging for water-bulbs."

The griffin sprang back into the air, and within moments was nothing more than a distant smudge in the sky.

"Well?" Kevon asked the still-trembling Mage.

"All four camps..." Jacek whispered. "The other two garrisons. Circled and crossed the entire Plain."

"And?" Carlo prodded.

"Felt it. Where we thought it might be. Past the Seacliff Camp. It gets stronger near the Hollows, but we had to turn back." Jacek stood a bit straighter and licked his lips. "I've never felt so glad to be surrounded by chimaera."

"Surrounded..." Carlo scrunched his face and shook his head. "Three to the northeast. Let's go."

"Ahead, just beyond the tall grass," Kevon let go of the Wind rune in his mind, and the extra senses it had granted drained away.

"We haven't had to fight three at once," Carlo frowned. "Two, more than a few times. But three?"

"Let's not fight three, then."

Kevon felt Jacek's Control rune form at the same time he heard the Mage speak. A strangled roar drifted up from ahead, and the others tensed.

"A little help?" The Court Wizard staggered, and Kevon reached to steady him as he offered power to the spell.

"Swing to the right," Kevon suggested. "We've got the one on the left."

Anneliese and the other Hunter were to the edge of the tall grass before the others could react. Bow drawn, the Huntmistress shook her head as she looked back at Kevon.

"Try now," Kevon suggested as Carlo and the dwarves reached where the elves had stopped. He took control of the other Mage's spell, and focused a feeling of panic, rather than the confining, imprisoning focus that Jacek was using.

Another roar, and the elves shifted aim toward the sound. The grass churned, and rippled in arcs curving either way to flank the clearing where the party stood.

Anneliese backed toward the Mages, bow leading the grass-rippling passage of the chimaera on the right. The Hunter at her side split off to the left, tracking the other.

"Now hold..." Kevon whispered to Jacek, easing the spell back to its original focus.

The chimaera to the left sprang first, soaring high and batting aside the Hunter's arrow with a flip of its wing. It landed in a roll, lashing its tail-fangs out at Kylgren-Wode and his Stoneguard companion. It emerged from the roll in a leap that took even the Hunter by surprise. The beast's powerful ram haunches, aided by a backward swoop of its wings, launched it straight toward the recovering elf.

The Hunter's arrow was nocked, but not drawn. A step and a half back from where he'd loosed the last shaft, the elf grunted and whirled as the chimaera's left paw raked his right arm, claws catching, twisting, and tearing flesh and bow alike.

The Hunter's knife was in his left hand before he finished his first revolution, slashing backhanded at the foreleg that continued to rend his right arm. He leaned into the stroke, shifting the angle of the knife as it slid around the bone, neatly severing the thick tendons beneath a coarse layer of fur.

The claws went slack, releasing the Hunter's arm, and the elf turned further, his blade slipping free from the beast's leg, head tilting back to see his target more clearly, narrowly avoiding a forward swing of a leathery wing.

The Hunter jabbed the point of his blade at the side of the chimaera's neck, slicing an instant too late into the thick mane. It carved a trail up the monster's shoulder before wrenching free from the elf's grasp as it sunk up to the hilt in the base of the chimaera's left wing.

Anneliese loosed three arrows, half-seconds apart, into the grass where the other chimaera still hid. She twisted, and sank two more into the one that tumbled past her kinsman. Quiver emptied, she cast aside the bow, and an instant later, leapt between the other Hunter and the wounded chimaera, sword and dagger at the ready.

Whooping with glee, the Stoneguard with Kylgren-Wode advanced on the limping creature, axe held almost casually. A shrugged shoulder deflected the strike of the beast's tail fangs. The chimaera roared, and hopped on its wounded left foreleg to swipe at the oncoming dwarf.

Stepping to the right, the Stoneguard switched to a two-handed grip, swinging the flat of the axe to smash into the oncoming claw. He shifted his left foot back, guiding the continued momentum, letting the handle of the axe slip through his fingers until they reached the extra wrap of leather around the end. The dwarf's follow-through stroke severed most of the chimaera's head from its body, leaving the loosely connected parts to flop to the ground together.

"See to him!" Carlo called to Anneliese. He motioned to groups of the others, directing them forward or to the right, leading the charge forward himself.

Carlo and Kylgren-Wode reached the controlled chimaera as the spell collapsed. The beast's rigor dissolved, and it swiped a paw at Carlo, and at the same time whipped its tail at the Dwarven Ambassador.

Kylgren-Wode slashed with his axe, severing the creature's tail as it curled most of the way around him, burying both glistening spikes solidly into the back of his right shoulder. The dwarf cried out, and reached for the wound, slapping his back several times before catching hold of the amputated limb, pulling it free, and casting it aside.

Carlo rolled under the chimaera's attack, missing a slash at the beast's neck as it whirled and convulsed at the loss of its tail. Taking a cue from the Stoneguard's attack, Carlo extended and redoubled the momentum from the missed attack, bringing it full circle as he stepped closer to the chimaera's side. The glance he took to direct the stroke showed a raised right paw, poised to descend on Kylgren-Wode, who was still staggering from the wound in his back. Carlo fine-tuned his aim, and leaned into the attack, face contorting, eyes closing from the extra effort he forced his body to generate.

The longsword caught the chimaera between the foreleg and ribcage, the blade squealing into bone as Carlo levered the tip of the sword forward and stepped back, slicing the monster's side open. As the blade pulled free, Carlo shifted his weight, and kicked the chimaera squarely in the split shoulder. He shook off the flailing strikes of the creature's wing, shifted his grip on the weapon, and raised his sword to plunge it into the slowing beast's back.

The chimaera toppled toward Carlo, and the Blademaster jumped aside. Ivory handled throwing daggers protruded from both its eye-sockets, and its tongue lolled lifelessly from its mouth. Carlo nodded to Alanna, and moved to help Kylgren-Wode.

The Stoneguard poked at the holes in Kylgren-Wode's tunic, and laughed. He poked *through* the holes, and the ambassador yelped. Raising an eyebrow at a few snarled curses in his native tongue, the armored dwarf shrugged and wandered over to where Anneliese and the others tended to the fallen Hunter.

"Are you all right?" Carlo asked, watching as Kylgren-Wode worked his injured shoulder in circles, wincing.

"It hurts," the dwarf admitted. "Yon elf is bound te be in worse shape than I," he said, motioning to the group gathering back in the clearing.

A breeze stirred, and Kevon clutched at it with his mind, using the faint trickle of energy funneled into a Wind rune to reach higher. His awareness drifted upward, and he felt the griffin circling to the west, above Stonespire Camp. Dizzied at the reach of the spell, he focused back in on the surrounding area.

Leaping, flapping, crawling, breath stinking of carrion... the wind seemed to say of the dozen or more forms that surrounded the sunken nest some two miles further north. The breeze gusted around Kevon and the others as he centered the detection spell on their location and expanded it. Feeling no other large beings closer than the nest, Kevon released the magic, and rushed to where the others were gathered.

"His wounds will need rinsed, dressed, and bound," Anneliese declared, turning to Kevon. "A week's rest, minimum. Is it safe to set camp here?"

"The nearest threat is the nest," Kevon replied. "But we can't afford a week's rest. We'll need his bow tomorrow."

"Ruined," the Hunter whispered, closing his eyes tighter against the pain as Alanna poured water from a canteen over the jagged tears in his flesh.

"You can use another. Someone else's, maybe the Riders can spare one," Kevon sighed. "We can't spare you." He opened his pack and brought out a gourd-flask. "The last one I have, courtesy of Alacrit's armoury."

"I'll heal well enough..."

"Not in time." Anneliese chastised her subordinate. "This lesson will serve you better than years of training on the Glimmering Isle. You are an elf. You are not infallible."

The Hunter nodded, and opened his mouth to the milky liquid. When the large potion was empty, he relaxed somewhat, wincing as the last bandages were snugged around his forearm.

"A dozen?" Carlo grunted. "It was all we could do to handle three."

"She said she'll bring a Wing of Riders," Kevon offered. "That could be... I don't know, half a dozen?"

"Six to ten," Anneliese clarified. "The number of Riders is always changing, so Wings reorganize as needed."

"Their number could change today, as may ours." Carlo glanced around at the others striking what was left of the sparse campsite. "We move out in ten minutes."

Kevon nodded, and edged away from the others, facing into the light morning breeze. He let the rune form, and his awareness wheeled into the sky. He again felt griffin circling toward the west, riding warm air currents up to dizzying heights before soaring eastward. He pulled his attention back toward their objective, the nest only hours to the north.

They've split... he thought. *Fortunate, but will it be enough?*

He pulled away from the magic and returned to where Carlo was still speaking with the others. "I can see seven at the nest right now, the rest are scattered to the west and southeast."

"We'll head northwest, then angle back, to avoid the smaller groups," Carlo decided. "If we can overrun them there, we'll hold the location and take on the stragglers as they return."

The elves led the assault on the nest, Anneliese and the recovered Hunter standing at the edge of the tall grass and downing the two nearest chimaera with one arrow apiece. Annelieses's second target tumbled forward, but rolled back to its feet, and leapt behind the mound of stone slabs at the center of the clearing. The Hunter's next arrow barely penetrated the hide of a larger chimaera, hanging loosely in the beast's front shoulder and mane.

"Now!" Carlo shouted, and the others stepped forward as one, emerging from cover, weapons drawn.

Crossbow bolts from two of Carlo's subordinates struck the wounded chimaera in the neck and chest, and it toppled over, convulsing.

Two of the remaining beasts leapt for cover in the tall grass to the left, another diving to the right.

Oh. Kevon thought. *They weren't supposed to do that.*

"Move in!" Carlo bellowed. "Form up!"

"*Fiiight.*" The Stoneguard jostled Kevon with a mailed elbow. "Har har!"

Kevon forced a smile as he recovered from the jolt. *His common is improving, but I'll have to make sure Kylgren-Wode explains things a little better.* Relieved of his magic, the Seeker drew his sword and took his place in the forming circle.

"Where are those Riders?" Carlo complained, looking to Kevon.

"I can't tell right now. Jacek?" Kevon turned toward the center of the circle.

The Court-Mage nodded, releasing the tongue of flame suspended above his outstretched palm.

Kevon turned back to scan the grass for lurking chimaera.

"There!" Jacek called almost immediately, pointing to

the 'V' formation of specks growing in the western sky.

"Kevon, Anneliese, with me!" Carlo ordered, looking at the approaching Riders. "Circle east, the nest should be vulnerable!"

"Sword already?" Carlo asked as they broke ranks and neared the rock formation. "Should I take the Stoneguard instead?"

"If it would keep him from bumping into me, please," Kevon retorted. "That's the third time since we left the garrison." He smiled. "He's worth more than his trouble, though. I thought Kylgren-Wode could swing an axe… but him?"

"Careful," Anneliese cautioned, as they came around the curve of the rock pile and saw the opening to the large burrow beneath it.

"It did go in," Carlo pointed to the spattered blood near the entrance. "Let's go get it out."

Carlo and Kevon led the way into the passage that was barely large enough for them to walk, stooped, with weapons drawn. The Blademaster walked a step ahead, leading with the shield he'd begun to use more since they'd reached the Highplain.

Thunk!

Carlo's shield spun away, impaled on the tail-fangs of the wounded chimaera. The Blademaster pivoted toward the direction his shield had gone, and shifted grip on his sword. Kevon slid two steps past his friend into a wider section of the burrow where he could stand upright, and there was room to swing his sword.

A muted glint in the dank gloom was the only warning.

Kevon turned his left shoulder in and rolled forward, swinging his sword backhand as he did. The blade sparked against the iron banding of Carlo's shield, missing the intended target, the chimaera's tail that swung it.

Carlo kicked out to his right, pinning the shield against the tunnel wall, and hacked at the straining tail.

The chimaera roared, its fury amplified in the enclosed

space.

"Kevon, back!" Carlo shouted as the tail-fangs pried loose from the captive shield and whipped back into the near-darkness.

Kevon scrambled back as a claw raked through where he'd just been.

An arrow whizzed by Kevon's head, answered with a snarl from the moving darkness that lay beyond.

The passageway dimmed further, then seemed to erupt into a cacophony of shifting light and sound. Jacek's newly formed orb of light hovered behind him, throwing dancing shadows down into the pit beyond. Anneliese fired another arrow into the stricken beast.

Jacek stepped forward and aside, releasing a scorching bolt of flame that lanced between Kevon and the others, knocking the already mortally wounded chimaera against the cave wall. Its claws scrabbled against the rough stone floor, and it mewled twice before settling to stillness.

"Watch where you're slinging that!" Carlo grouched, stooping to recover his shield. "Why are you...?"

"The Riders have arrived, and are helping the others hunt the few that remain above," Jacek explained.

"Then we finish this," Kevon nodded, motioning for the others to follow him deeper into the cave. He froze as the still form of the fallen chimaera mewled yet again. "Wait... That's not..."

The four crept toward the sound, keeping tight against the wall to the right. Anneliese slid away from the others, bow drawn, for a better angle. She prodded the fallen chimaera with a foot as she passed it, then returned her full attention to the unknown around the bend that lay ahead.

Carlo stopped as they reached a point where the passage narrowed again, signaling Jacek to move the light forward.

"It's stopped," Kevon observed as the light spilled around the corner, out of sight.

"There!" Anneliese held the drawn arrow at the corner

of her mouth, sidestepping to get a better view of the motion ahead.

The chimaera leapt around the corner, hissing. It stumbled, somersaulted three times, and landed on its back, oversized paws and hooves lashing out at random angles.

Anneliese relaxed to a half-draw. Three more chimaera cubs romped into the light, tackling and biting the first, slapping at each other with spike-less tails.

"This is it," Carlo announced, moving forward, to peer around the corner where the cubs had come from. "The nest, more eggs. A lot more."

One of the cubs sank his fangs into Carlo's trouser-leg, shaking it from side to side as furiously as it could manage.

"We can't allow them to grow up," Carlo shrugged, raising his sword. "No more than we can allow these eggs to hatch."

"Wait," Anneliese countered. "The clans may have use for captured young. Training griffin not to panic at their scent. Harvesting venom when they are older."

"We'll leave it to them, then." Carlo agreed. "Jacek, want to take care of the eggs?" The Blademaster sheathed his sword, slung his shield, and scooped up a cub in each arm.

Kevon put away his weapon, and gathered the other two cubs as Jacek unleashed a torrent of flames into the nest, destroying the remaining piles of eggs in a matter of seconds. The fumes burned Kevon's eyes, and he lurched toward the exit, his charges squirming and kicking as he went.

Leaving the Mage-light provided by Jacek, half-blinded by the smoke, Kevon tripped over a stone formation jutting out from the floor. He fell forward, dropping the cubs, landing palms down in a sandy depression. As he pushed himself upward, his hand slipped, uncovering a smooth curve of stone buried near the obstacle he'd tripped over. In the dim haze, he could not see the stone clearly, but he pushed more sand away. His fingers brushed against the cool surfaces, encountering a chip or a crack here and there. One of the cubs mewled, pawing at the sand beside him.

Kevon reached a fragmented end of the object he'd begun to uncover, narrowly avoiding cutting himself on the sharp edge of the stone. He pushed more sand away, revealing the end to be just wider than an outstretched hand, and nearly half as thick.

"What have you got there?" Jacek asked, shifting the light closer. He scratched the ears of the other cub Kevon had dropped, quieting the squirming chimaera he held in his arms.

"I'm not sure. I…" Kevon's words slid away as his hand touched the carved sigil and the twisted image of the Dark rune entered his mind. "Another broken portal?" His eyes moved to the object he'd tripped over, a smooth formation rising from the floor, broken off inches above it. "There." Kevon pointed to a dirt mound three feet further away. "What's under that?"

Carlo kicked at the mound, uncovering a similar fractured protrusion. "Your Mage friend was busy, wasn't he? Before you killed him?"

"This portal must have been broken years ago, for the pieces to be buried this deep." Kevon stood, brushing himself off before collecting the cub who was still digging at his feet. "Gurlin, Holten, any of their brotherhood may have done this. There are no orcs or imps here, though. What was the purpose?"

"It's broken, anyhow. Let's just get out of here." Carlo led the way out of the cave, bouncing as he walked to entertain the cubs curled under each arm.

"We'd suspected this to be a breeding pit," Ashera nodded at Carlo as he emerged from the tunnel and surrounding mound of stones. "It's a rarity to have the forces to spare on offense."

"The nest has been destroyed," Carlo assured her. "We found something else, something we've seen before, a cause for great concern."

"Grave enough that all your leaders should know," Kevon added, shushing the squirming cub in his arms. "Oh. Um. What would you like us to do with these?"

CHAPTER 37

"Get up."

Carlo's muffled order floated into Kevon's awareness, and he willed himself awake. He nibbled at Alanna's ear for a moment before untangling himself from her and the blankets. Stretching muscles aching and weary from battle and travel, he stumbled to the hide-flap door of the small wood and stone structure, and accepted the two mugs of warm tea that Carlo offered.

"The leaders of the other tribes are beginning to arrive," Carlo announced. "The High Council will convene after the midday meal."

"We'll take another shift at the wall between breakfast and midday," Kevon shrugged. "It'll be mostly talk after that, I assume."

"Might be," Carlo grunted. "Decisions here are much like those on the Southern Frontier, I'd imagine. Bad ones cost lives, and quickly. They've lived like this a long time. They should know what to do."

"They snatched up the chimaera cubs quickly enough, flying one to each camp," Kevon observed. "Relaniel said they were going to raise the males to use as mounts for some of the Striders, and the female will lay eggs for extra food at the camp in the north, where they have trouble growing crops."

"They waste nothing here," Carlo nodded. "There's little to have, much less squander."

"We'll eat, and hurry to the wall," Kevon lowered the leather curtain. "See you at midday.

◆ ◆ ◆

“Don’t know that I could ever really get used to this,” Kevon rubbed at the sore spot on his ribs where a chimaera had caught him with a hind hoof. Alanna dabbed at the gash on his left forearm with a damp cloth.

“Fortunate there was not venom from this tail strike,” she consoled the bleeding Warsmith.

“No, there was,” Kevon corrected her, blinking widened eyes and steadying himself against the lowered rope ladder that led back up to their watch-post. “If there is another attack before midday, I may have to just work the ladders.” He fumbled at the swaying rungs with fingers that were starting to numb.

“Let’s get you up to safety while you can still climb,” Alanna suggested, pulling at the bottom rung to steady the ladder.

“Go,” Kevon told the fretting Meek that had pulled him up the last few steps to the small semi-enclosed platform atop the walls. “Send back a Strider to replace you.”

The white-robed man nodded, taking a yellow flag from its holder, and waving it so that his counterparts in the neighboring posts could see it. He scanned the landscape outside for a few seconds, and repeated the motions with a light blue colored flag. “You know the colors?”

“Brown, chimaera attack,” Kevon answered, pointing at the first flag in the sequence. He moved down the order. “Red, serious injury. Yellow, Striders returned safely. Light blue, no visible threats. Dark blue, activity out beyond the perimeter. White, Riders inbound.” He paused. “I haven’t seen black used.”

“No one has died since you arrived,” the man smiled. “Pray we will not have to use it.”

Kevon slumped onto the low bench near the doorway as the Meek exited to find a replacement. “I should have had him bring back some tea.”

“You’re not a Strider,” Alanna chastised. “The tea helps

you get used to the venom. It's not a good idea to add more when you've just been injured."

"I forgot..." Kevon yawned. "You're good with poisons, right?"

"Better than I'd like to remember." Her icy glare was wasted on Kevon's heavy-lidded, vacant gaze. "Are you sure you're all right to finish the shift? It's only another hour, I'm sure one of the Meek would come watch for you. Elster would come back, certainly."

"S'only an hour," Kevon agreed, thick-feeling lips slurring his response. "M'okay to watch."

Alanna shook her head and moved to the outer railing of the watch-post. After several minutes of catching no variation in the wind-blown grasses around the crop plots and the surrounding cleared area, she returned to sit by Kevon.

"Feeling any better?"

"Mmmblmm..." he mumbled, pinching his tongue.

Alanna snapped her fingers in front of Kevon's face rapidly, and he wobbled in his seat. "Yeah. That's helpful."

"What's wrong with him?" Rowyn asked, walking up the stairs into the watch-post.

"Stubborn," Alanna sighed. "Will you be all right here for a few minutes until I get him some help?"

Rowyn surveyed the landscape for a few seconds, scanned the other posts for waving flags. "Of course," he smiled. "Send Elster and Semal."

"Thanks," Alanna said, helping Kevon to his feet. "See you at the Council gathering."

"S'yoo!" Kevon waved at the Strider with his right hand, using the arm Alanna did not have draped over her shoulders to support him.

"Chimaeraddled," the Meek in the medical tent remarked as soon as he saw Alanna dragging Kevon through the door-flap. "Water," she directed her young assistant. "Lots of it."

"Chimaer..."

"Chimaeraddled," the Meek repeated. "Far too much

venom. He's used to it enough that it doesn't paralyze him completely, but it's still a problem. Water will push it out of him. Let's see to that arm, though."

The wound was slicked with salve, covered with leaves, and wrapped and tied with cloth by the time the young helper returned with a pitcher of water. The Meek helped Alanna steer Kevon to another bench to one side of the tent, and handed her a carved wooden cup.

"Get as much of this down him as you can," she advised, taking the pitcher from her assistant and setting it on the bench beside Kevon. "He'll be fine in an hour or so."

"We discovered something while destroying the chimaera nest to the east," Carlo addressed the gathered heads of the four tribes. "Something disturbing. Something only some of us have seen before, and only once. The remains of a portal, a broken gateway that leads to and from a realm of darkness."

The Elders conferred amongst themselves, and Ashera spoke.

"What harm can these gateways visit upon us?"

"In previous cases, permanent gates have let orcs, imps, and other demons into our Realm," Carlo answered. "Temporary ones have done much worse."

"We have seen no such evidence of these threats on the Highplain," the Claw of one of the other tribes rebutted.

"Have you not?" Relaniel stood. "Chimaera are twisted enough to be creations of L'mort. They do not cling to the darkness as many of his others, but could be born there. Are the numbers that have risen against your people in recent years natural?"

"The tide that rose against us two generations ago..." the Claw answered, "Was anything but natural. Many lives were lost, and it took the cooperation of all five tribes to construct the garrison walls that protect the lower lands from the dangers we face daily."

"Evil Magi," Kevon began, taking measured breaths between sentences. "Magi that we knew were on Purlon, to the west. We suspect they were near Alcron, far to the north. Now we know they were here."

"What are we to do with this knowledge?" Ashera asked.

"The portal arch we discovered had been destroyed, on accident, or on purpose, years ago." Kevon stood straighter, shaking off the last of the venom-haze. "We sealed that nest, it will not be a safe haven for chimaera any longer. But there may be others."

"Nesting sites seem a likely place for there to be portals," Carlo continued. "The objective our group seeks lies near the western edge of your territory. When ready, we will march toward it, emptying nests, searching for portals as we go. Any support you can lend is appreciated. The fewer chimaera there are to hinder us at our goal, the better."

The Elders whispered furiously for minutes.

"Enough." Ashera growled. "I'll just ask them."

"Ask us what?" Yusa wondered aloud, as Reko paced at the edge of the firelight.

"Two of the nests on your path are very near the remains of Seacliff Camp. If there is any chance of retaking it..."

"We'll need your help, but we will make the attempt." Anneliese stopped Carlo's response before it left his mouth, a sharp glare silencing the Blademaster. "Saving the Realm is no use if we allow parts of it to be destroyed while we pass by."

"I was going to say..." Carlo stared at the Huntmistress, "That a recovered Seacliff Camp would be a better base of operations than this, once we near the Seat."

Murmurs of agreement ran through the gathered elders, spilling into the others assembled around the meeting-place.

"You will have the help you need," Ashera announced as the Council settled into silence. "Every spare Rider, and the fastest of the Striders will gather here within five days."

CHAPTER 38

"Hold on tighter!" Carlo suggested.

"Grip with your legs!" Ashera shouted, "Relax your arms some. Don't suffocate him!"

"I've got it! I..." The child's triumphant cry stopped short as his grey-feathered mount banked near the top of the enclosure, kicked at the nearest crosspiece, and launched itself back toward the straw-littered ground.

"Not a..."

Folding one wing back, sweeping the other in a powerful downbeat that rolled it completely over, the akembi freed itself from its unwelcome passenger. Snapping the folded wing back to full extension, it skimmed the outer edge of the cage, making two passes before landing near the heap of Rider in the center of the straw-padded arena.

"Again," the boy finished, as his rogue steed snuffled at the bits of dried apple stuffed deep into his pockets. "No!" he admonished. "You have to let me..."

"The training is for you, not him," Ashera corrected. "Before the season is out, you'll have outgrown him, and your only chance at the sky will be on a griffin."

"I know," the boy grumbled, crawling to his feet and digging in his pocket for a strip of dried fruit. "Good boy..." he muttered, pressing his forehead to the downy tuft between the akembi's wide-set eyes, scratching the winged horse's ears as it chewed the leathery treat. "Are you ready to go back to the barn?"

The akembi stopped chewing, and threw its head, rocking the boy back on his heels. It trotted around in tight circles, folded wings twitching in anticipation as the boy neared the chute-gate that led back into the nearby building.

"All right. Here you..."

The boy was left holding the gate in a swirl of dust motes and horse-feathers.

"You start them young," Carlo observed, following Ashera toward the center of the camp.

"Anyone who wants to be a Rider has to learn early," she shrugged. "Training with akembi is the closest thing the young ones have. It toughens them up. They need to be confident in their ability before the young griffin leave their nests each year."

"Do you choose and capture the griffin, break them to the saddle?"

Ashera's choking laughter stopped Carlo in his tracks. "There are five times as many Unbound as there are Riders. Enough to scour the tribes from the Highplain." She shook her head. "The griffin choose us."

"With Spring drawing to a close, we may get to witness the Choosing?" Anneliese asked, approaching from one of the walkways to the upper walls.

"It is our hope that this expedition clears a path to the nesting grounds, at the very least. Flynn, back there, and the other Aspirants will leave for the nesting cavern ten days from now." Ashera frowned. "The timing is *almost* perfect."

"Almost?" Carlo asked.

"The path we clear will not take the Aspirants directly to the cavern," Ashera explained. "It will be safer, but they will have fewer dedicated escorts from Seacliff Camp onward. They may miss the first few flights, and there are only ten nesting pairs this year."

"You said there were only seven potential new Riders this year," Carlo shrugged. "You still might get them all."

"About one in four choose Riders," Ashera frowned. "It is unlikely that all of our Aspirants will succeed this year."

"All that fuss for two new Riders?" Carlo could not mask

the disbelief in his face. "How...?"

Ashera shook her head. "The fledgling griffin do not choose. The parents do, as soon as their offspring leave the nest."

"Oh. That... Okay," Carlo nodded. "Makes sense." The commander rubbed the stubble that was beginning to show again on his chin. "So how do we get them there sooner?"

"Delicious," Kevon scraped the last of the savory *naota* from the stone dish with a torn bit of the soft flat bread they'd been given. "But..."

"There is more to come," Ashera reassured him from several feet away.

Kevon nodded. Most of his group sat in the loose circle around the fire, their number less than a tenth of those in attendance. Heads of the three factions from the other camps and their officers sat in clusters, laughing and conversing in low tones.

"Thank... you..." he managed, as the empty *naota* dish and wicker bread basket were collected by a Meek that disappeared back into the shadows without a word. "About our departure tomorrow,"

"No." Rowyn's voice cut through the music that came from all directions. He sat between Kevon and Carlo, handing each a fresh cup of fruit-laden wine. "During the *Hariya*, the meal and festivities are the only focus. This is our concession to the Meek."

"It's so difficult to let go of..."

"Not so much as one might think," Rowyn corrected Kevon as he took a cup from a veiled dancer that spun through the crowd, delivering drinks from a swaying platter. The Fist's eyes traced her path until she was out of sight.

"I suppose..."

"He feels he needs permission to enjoy anything more than the meal," Anneliese laughed, reaching down to take

Alanna's hands. Her steps were a combination of stagger and sway in time with one of the threads of music that Kevon could only discern because of the lurch and tilt of her body. "Let's make sure he enjoys this."

Alanna sprang up with the elf's help, and mimicked the Huntmistress's moves, easing into the relaxed sway a bit more with each measure of accompaniment. The pair worked their way around the fire, passing out of Kevon's sight for longer than he liked. Howls of approval echoed from the far side of the circle, and both women reappeared wearing the colorful shawls that had replaced the drab ones worn by the Meek on any other day.

The multicolored fringe of the garments magnified every movement in the firelight. Alanna's gleeful undulation under the guiding hand of the Elven elder was tantalizing torture for Kevon. As she drew nearer, she locked eyes with him, her movements becoming more deliberate and direct as the music intensified. Her smile widened as she detected his paralysis, and altered the angle of her leading hip toward him with almost possessive accuracy.

"This is..." Kevon breathed through the flush of the wine, breath catching as the various instruments gave way to the accelerating fervor of the drums.

"It certainly is," Carlo rumbled, lost in the dance that was meant for him.

Five staccato drumbeats, and all of the music stopped. Alanna stumbled into Anneliese, and laughing, they helped each other the remaining few steps back to their seats.

Service of the next course of the meal resumed with light accompaniment, and dance by a few of the more elaborately costumed Meek. Portions of boiled, spiced tubers in small divided plates played unfamiliar tastes against each other, confusing and delighting senses at turns. These dishes were whisked away as soon as they emptied, and Kevon could see the next course being passed out across the circle.

"What?" Kevon tilted his head back in response to the

gentle tap on his forehead. His mouth snapped shut as the slice of marinated heartmelon touched his tongue. The preserving brine brought a sharp bite to the otherwise sweet fruit, shocking his palate as much as the unexpected touch of the Meek standing over him. He shuddered, and accepted the delicate pastry the next server handed him as they moved past to Alanna.

Kevon licked his lips, contemplating the flavors that faded into memory.

"Carefully, with this," Rowyn cautioned, biting into his pastry with a deliberate air the Strider usually reserved for combat.

"Hmm." Kevon crunched into the crisp, slender treat, and bitter spices swirled about his throat and nose. He coughed, cracking much of the remaining crust in his hand. After calming himself, he took another hesitant bite.

"Chicken and egg from Highspring, saffron from Burntrock, milled sugar from Fallenlake. Flour from our grain here at Stonespire." Rowyn finished chewing his last bite. "This dish represents the unity of the camps, of all our tribes."

"And Seacliff?" Kevon asked, breathing in the aroma of the remainder of his broken pastry.

"Salt. There are few other places to get it here. We've had to buy it from the lowlanders in recent seasons."

Kevon nodded, appreciating both the flavor and the deeper meaning of the dish.

"But this... is a real treat," Rowyn grinned as he accepted the skewer of roasted meat and potatoes from the serving Meek. He waited until the others had been served. "After you," he gestured.

"Is this..." Kevon thought back to the season he'd set out on his adventure, before he'd reached Eastport, shortly after he'd met Alanna. *Marelle*, he corrected himself. "Lamb?"

Rowyn grinned, shaking his head. "Chimaera."

"You eat them?" Alanna sputtered, holding her skewer at arm's length, but only slowing her chewing of the bite she'd already taken.

Rowyn shrugged, smiling as he finished chewing. "The flank is the only edible part, small, and not the easiest to harvest. It's easier to poison or burn the whole carcass in most cases. For special occasions, we take the time."

"Anneliese is probably pretty good at that," Kevon laughed.

"She carved about half of the chimaera for this meal," Rowyn agreed. "Like she'd been doing it for a lifetime."

"And she didn't warn us!" Alanna squeaked, lobbing a chunk of apple fished from her cup at the giggling elf.

Anneliese parried the hurled fruit with her skewer. "Hah!" she shouted, louder than she normally would in combat.

Heads turned, and the Huntmistress leaned into Carlo's side, giggling. "*Don't eat too much of the fruit!*" she whispered, wide eyed.

"We leave in the morning," Carlo announced after the evening meal.

"There are still three days before the others get here," Kevon mentioned. "We're barely rested from the trip here."

"With similar support from Ashera's Wing, we should be able to destroy the two nests with relative ease," Carlo explained. "Clearing the way, the others should catch up with us as we reach Seacliff Camp. That's where we'll need the help, anyway. It'll buy us two days. It'll keep us moving. It puts their new Riders in a much better position."

"If you think we can do it," Kevon shrugged.

"I'd rather not have the other troops underfoot until we absolutely need them," Carlo grunted. "We have the training and experience to clear the nests out, and you have the know-how to shut the portals down if we find them. We'll need fighters that know the layout of the Camp when we reach it, but not really until then. Besides, the more we do for them, the more help we'll get when we need it."

"Agreed." Kevon nodded. "Holding the location once we find the Seat of Wind may be costly."

"You should really get some sleep," Alanna whispered, snuggling in closer under the blanket. "It's the last night we'll be this safe."

Kevon felt the press of her form against his back, still dulled by the subsiding venom of the chimaera sting. He shivered as the words floated through his mind, their passage punctuated by the tickle of her lips on his earlobe. Kevon smiled and clasped her draped arm tighter to his chest. His breath and pulse slowed and aligned with hers, each heartbeat a lunge toward unconsciousness.

CHAPTER 39

"To arms!"

Kevon slipped free of the bedroll, scrambling to his feet, cursing his impulsiveness as his magic drained into the hilt of his sword. The others were up, blinking into the pre-dawn gloom, searching for the danger Carlo's voice had warned of.

"Really?" Jacek grumbled, as his Mage-light brightened the campsite, exposing Kevon's drawn sword.

Kevon shrugged, and bolted after Kylgren-Wode and the Stoneguard.

Carlo stood near the corpse of one chimaera, and sidestepped to keep in front of the one that remained. Anneliese circled, trying to get a clear shot, but the wary creature kept Carlo between them.

"*Pah!*"

Kevon watched as the Stoneguard hurled his battleaxe, the unwieldy weapon spinning end over end, slicing through an outstretched wing to embed in the beast's shoulder.

The chimaera roared, turning toward the new threat. Its tail lashed forward, curling around the axe-handle, prying it backward for an instant before releasing it.

Carlo leapt at the chance, hacking at the chimaera's other outstretched wing, then at its tail. He blocked a backhanded swing from the creature's massive paw, rocking back on his heels from the impact. Recovering from the blow, Carlo stepped further inside, first batting aside a wing-strike with his shield, then severed the already tattered wing with a counter-stroke.

The Stoneguard punched the chimaera in its leonine jaw

with a mailed fist as he marched into range on the beast's stricken side. He wrenched his axe free, whirling with the same motion to bury it back in the chimaera's throat.

Raptor-calls sounded from above, the Riders stationed in camp already in the air, searching for more assailants.

"Clear," Carlo shrugged, wiping his blade on the fallen beast's hide. "Time to get up anyway."

"We knew the risk, staging so close to this nest," Kevon shrugged. "That's two we know won't be there later."

"The last nest was nothing," Carlo grunted. "Five adults and a dozen eggs. Talk is that this next one is the largest nest on the Highplain."

"Ashera says the Striders will catch up with us by noon," Kevon offered. "If we want to wait."

The Blademaster sniffed. "Two more Wings of Riders due here just after dawn. That covers scouting. The dwarves and I can draw them out. Anneliese and her Hunter covering the flanks, my guys with crossbows. You, Jacek, Yusa, and Alanna in reserve. We'll need the Magi fresh if there is a portal, and she's the best mid-range fighter we have if something breaks through."

"With a plan like that..."

"I've done more with less," Carlo interrupted. "But nothing goes exactly to plan."

Kevon nodded, recalling the fiery cataclysms two of his plans had erupted into over the last few years.

"Breakfast done and camp struck before the other Riders arrive," Carlo barked. "Go."

"Focus your bow-fire on outliers," Carlo directed Ashera, sweeping his pointer-stick in wide circles to either side of the dirt map between them. "Leave the rest for our ground forces, try to funnel them toward us."

"I'll assign a wing to either side," she agreed, nodding. "My wing will drive them to you, though I can't promise they'll all make it to your lines."

"I'd hate for you to make a promise you couldn't keep," Carlo grimaced. "Have one Rider hold station over the nest. No surprises. If we move now, we should be there in less than an hour."

"Commander." Ashera nodded slowly, still not used to taking orders from anyone, much less an outlander.

"Sense anything?" Carlo asked, turning to Kevon.

"No," Kevon frowned. "Approaching the Seat of Wind, the magic in the area is... distracting. I can see how Jacek could feel it from the air."

"As long as it won't interfere with what you need to do," Carlo turned to address Kevon directly. "Slip-ups like this morning are dangerous. We could have used an extra Mage. If we're going to protect you from two Guilds, you've got to work at least twice as hard at this as anyone else." He glanced back at Ashera. "As soon as your Riders are in the air, we'll form up and move out."

Kevon clenched at the Movement rune in his mind, and the chimaera directly ahead lifted its face to the sky, paws stretching downward in an attempt to gain purchase in the turf below. Two arrows struck the beast in the throat and chest. Kevon relaxed his focus and scanned for his next target.

Sensing the similar rune projecting from Yusa beside him, Kevon offered power to Reko. The grasses ahead writhed, and parted. Tall greenish-brown stalks coiled around feline forepaws and ram hindquarters, pulling the now revealed chimaera down to splay flat against the ground. Additional stalks caught the fanged tail, reducing the lashing motion to a quivering strain.

The magical outflow subsided as the Stoneguard scampered forward and severed most of the beast's head with his axe.

The Riders in the wing to the south spiraled downward, loosing arrows at stray chimaera that sought to circle the ground forces. The northern Wing held a long oval pattern higher up, seeing nothing in the shorter grasses to the main group's right flank. Extra riderless griffin, the Unbound, criss-crossed the skies above the battlefield, dropping arrow-fast at random intervals to harass or maim the surrounded chimaera.

Rowyn and a handful of Striders charged forward, greatswords flashing, into a tangle of chimaera on the left flank.

"Good to see you!" Carlo bellowed, directing the rest of the forces to shift to the right.

Kevon stumbled on a rock protruding from the dirt, then stepped back to put a hand on the stone. He sensed the outline of the formation running deep into the plateau, to where the latent magic was separate from the distracting lattice of Wind energy that poked at his awareness.

The grass ahead rustled, and Kevon directed the energy from below into a spear of stone that hurtled from the ground, through the hidden chimaera's chest, and out its back. The beast, lifted above the height of the surrounding grass, shuddered for a few seconds, and fell still.

Roars of enraged chimaera, screeches of swooping Unbound, and the near joyful cries of the Striders and the lone Stoneguard melded into a frantic melody, lives ending with each refrain.

Kevon's magic trickled to nothing, helping Reko divert the murderous leap of a large chimaera toward Carlo. Reaching deeper, but finding nothing left, he gritted his teeth, and drew his sword.

The spiral formation to the left lifted and flattened, the Wing had cleared out all of the outlying chimaera, and retreated to a suitable viewing distance.

Ashera's Wing pressed toward the ground forces, driving the last wave of chimaera before them, crowding the Unbound out of the skies above the battlefield.

"Hold fast!" Carlo commanded, edging forward as he motioned the archers back.

Projectiles from the archers and crossbowmen whizzed in a curious rhythm as the menacing shapes continued their advance.

Forced from the higher grass, the remnants of the advancing pride roiled into the open. Lacking the speed of their younger counterparts, the older chimaera more than compensated with their size and experience.

"They're shifting to the left!" Kevon called, directing Carlo's attention to the knot of chaos the Striders were about to engage. He and the Blademaster broke formation, and the archers spread to cover the gaps.

One of the elder chimaera leapt toward the Striders, flapping wings and twisting its body to land on one side of the group. A backhanded strike knocked a greatsword aside, the reverse stroke crumpling its bearer to the ground. The beast roared, rearing back on its hind legs, wings spread.

Rowyn shifted his advance toward the attacker, his sword flashing at angles that played reflected light across the chimaera's face. The beast waved a paw between itself and the advancing Strider, then dropped back to all fours.

Half a breath later, Rowyn was charging at full speed. The greatsword completed another revolution and a half, steadying as the Strider shifted his grip to balance the blade straight forward, braced at his side.

The chimaera flapped its left wing, and spun to the right, tail whipping out to coil around Rowyn's leg. The Strider stepped over the tail with his free leg, planting his foot sideways to arrest his forward momentum. Before Rowyn could shift his blade to attack the imprisoning tail, the chimaera continued its spin, pulling the trapped leg forward, and lashing out with a powerful hooved hind leg of its own. The strike caught Rowyn squarely in the side, below the ribs. The Strider flopped to the ground, dropping his sword.

Two of Rowyn's companions charged. A volley of crossbow bolts and arrows struck the chimaera, but the distance and thicker hide deflected all of the projectiles.

The chimaera completed its turn, dragging Rowyn's limp form to bounce twice across clumps of Highplain grasses before releasing it to tumble into a heap off to one side.

The two Striders continued to close the distance between themselves and their target, stepping apart to split its attention. They defended strikes from the fanged tail, lacerating the envenomed appendage as they kept it from themselves.

Each breath brought the archers closer. An outstretched wing turned aside most of the next volley, but one arrow managed to sink into the beast's lower right ribcage. The chimaera snarled and snapped at the feathered shaft, craning its neck as far as it could, to no avail. It straightened to roar at the nearest Strider, tensing its legs for the leap that would overwhelm the lightly armored attacker.

Griffin cries sounded from close above, and a handful of arrows rained down on the chimaera from the sky. One shaft fell true, burying itself in the creature's scaly back, just below where its left wing sprouted.

The chimaera looked up, swiping first one paw, then the other, at the Riders that were pulling out of their dives to regroup. Ashera and Stormclaw veered off at the last second, and the chimaera returned its attention to the remaining Striders, who had maneuvered closer.

Rowyn leapt over the chimaera's twitching tail, bounded off of the creature's rear haunch, and plunged his twin shortswords into its back, just above its wing-sockets. The chimaera bucked and flapped its wings in an attempt to dislodge the Strider, but Rowyn gripped the sword hilts tighter, twisting as hard as he could, crying out from the effort.

The chimaera turned from the Striders ahead, and bounded toward the south end of the battlefield. Three gigantic leaps, and the creature stumbled, left shoulder and wing taking the brunt of the impact.

Rowyn sprang clear before the injured chimaera could roll over and crush him, freeing only one of the short blades from its temporary sheath. The Strider tumbled, sprang to his feet, and rushed the wounded chimaera. Noting the blank gaze and flailing paws, Rowyn hopped inside the creature's reach and slid over its shoulder, the trailing blade slicing open the beast's neck as his left hand grasped the other sword. Standing to apply the force required to free the stuck blade, Rowyn hopped over the clumsy whip-lash of the chimaera's tail to the ground beyond. Without a backward glance, he leaned into a sprint back toward the rest of the battle.

Kevon and Carlo reached the other Striders as two more elder chimaera had almost succeeded in circling to angles that would give them the upper hand. Kevon split off to the right, slashing at the tail of the larger chimaera.

A gleaming dagger spun to the ground, deflected by the flap of a leathery wing. A second dagger found its mark, sinking into the chimaera's skull just behind the ear.

"Alanna!" Kevon cried, watching in terror as she cartwheeled over the backswing of the creature's tail to land right next to it. A blur of flashing edges and soft curves, and she was at his side, chest heaving, blades dripping crimson.

The chimaera stumbled, hamstrung. Carlo and one of the Striders pressed the advantage, dispatching the beast before it could regain its footing.

"You called, dear one?" Alanna pointed one of her daggers past Kevon to another advancing chimaera. "Can it wait?"

Kevon's mind lurched as he watched Rowyn leap at the other chimaera the Striders were engaging, his recovered greatsword glinting as he swung. Another slash as he landed, followed by a spinning back kick with a mailed boot, and the beast toppled.

"Right," Kevon whispered, turning the direction the assassin pointed. "Of course it can."

"Don't whine. At least the swelling has gone down."

"I'm not whining," Kevon whined. "And how do you..." He trailed off, glancing at Alanna's healed eye. He scratched at the bandages around his ribs, and touched the poultice bound at his side.

"Are you sure there's a portal there?" Alanna asked, nose wrinkling. "I can't see one, and we're close."

"I can feel it now, even though the Wind distortion here is worse," Kevon nodded. "It's not hidden or warded like the first one we destroyed."

"Magi don't come here," Rowyn laughed. "Why would they bother?"

"That one was orcs, imps, and leapers," Carlo fiddled with his shield, adjusting the straps a bit. "Why only chimaera here?"

"So no one would suspect?" Relaniel offered. "Chimaera are native to the Highplain. Creating only portals to chimaera habitats in the Dark realm would be a subtle way to shift the balance in their favor."

"We've got to move before we lose the light," Kevon piped up.

"Right," Carlo agreed. "Half the Striders, all the Riders, we'll need here with the Potentials, and our noncombatants." He frowned. "On second thought, Ashera's Wing would be good to have as our lookout. Ten minutes to split up and prepare. Then we move."

Kevon nodded and made his way over to where Jacek crouched facing Rhysabeth-Dane.

"This is so exciting!" the librarian squeaked. "Jacek says this set of markings reminds him of the sigils he's seen tattooed on Myrnar royalty!"

"I..." Kevon staggered, and Alanna caught his arm. Flashes of memory from years ago, faint raised lines and swirls that he'd overlooked on the arms of the male myrnar in the negotiation for the pearl. "Yes. I should have remembered that."

Alanna said nothing, but her eyes narrowed more than usual, and her jaw tightened at the mention of the past.

"We'll need to form up for departure," Kevon placed a

hand on Jacek's shoulder. "They'll want us in the center, saving up to deal with the portal when we reach it."

"Yes, yes… I…" Jacek handed Rhysabeth-Dane the sheet of parchment he'd been studying. "It's fascinating."

"Focus!" Kevon commanded. "We have the chance to set things right here that have been out of balance for two generations, rout the darkness from this place." He took a step back and sighed. "The book may be important, but the portal is *now*. Relaniel, Rhysabeth, will you join the potential Riders in the center of camp?"

"Hope you're ready," Rowyn chuckled, leading the short columns of Striders that split to form up on either side of the Magi.

"We all are," Carlo rumbled, directing Anneliese and the two dwarves to the front where Rowyn had already taken up his position.

The column began moving as the remaining Elven Hunter and the rest of Carlo's soldiers shuffled into place at the rear.

"Not too much further," Kevon commented, craning his neck to capture all of the circling Riders in his field of vision. "The center of their formation is just…"

One of the Riders cut toward the middle, diving. Two others followed in rapid succession, three keeping position in the slow circle.

"They've spotted something," Carlo called from the front. "Looks like they have it pinned down, they're not backing off." He remarked after a few more minutes of marching.

The lower three Riders flew in a braided pattern, routes twining over and through each other, taking turns swooping lower in the center to rush the unseen target ahead.

"Ten more minutes," Carlo remarked. "Eight if we hurry."

Rowyn shook his head. "Journeying to battle, keep a pace that refreshes. The Riders are spending arrows, not blood."

Kevon let his muscles relax, slipping into the gait that had carried him around the North Valley for most of his life, before he'd been a Warsmith, or even a Mage. He focused on the stiffness and tension in each limb, intentionally unclenching knots in specific muscles as he walked. Loosened up, he focused on his magic, nearly replenished from the earlier engagement. “You doing all right?” he asked Jacek.

“I’d rather be at banquet in the castle,” the Court-Wizard admitted, “Aside from that, things are lovely.”

“I’d settle for a clean bedroll and a mug of something other than chimaera tea,” Kevon countered. “But facing a Dark portal is something so far beyond...”

“We’ll handle it,” Jacek’s expression sobered. “We have to. Life up here is harsh enough without this meddling.”

“Imagine the allies they could be, once the balance is restored.” Kevon sighed. “We mustn’t fail.”

“The nest is just ahead,” Alanna advised, touching Kevon on the shoulder. “We’re to fall back, let them secure the passageway.”

“Form up!” Rowyn called from ahead, and the Striders doubled their pace, as the elves and crossbowmen slowed to surround Alanna and the Magi. “The entrance is clear. Torches!”

“They don’t waste a moment,” Jacek commented as Carlo and Rowyn led the charge down into the depths of the nest.

“You’ll want to see this,” one of the Striders chuckled, leading a trio of his companions back out of the nest’s entrance. “The commander needs both of you, now.”

Jacek formed a globe of light as he followed Kevon into the cave entrance, pushing it ahead and to the side.

“Further down,” another Strider pointed the Magi past the branch he stood in, a nesting room with dozens of broken eggs and two chimaera corpses that were visible from the main passage.

Kevon’s stomach turned as the light dimmed and the hint of Dark magic increased enough to taint all of his senses.

“No...” Jacek decided. “I don’t think I want to know what’s down here.” The Mage slowed, face ashen in the distorted light.

“There,” Kevon pointed around the bend in the tunnel. “It’s just ahead. Think of the tale it will be when you return to

Court."

A few more halting steps, and Jacek peered to where Kevon had indicated. "Not a tale for the banquet hall, is it?"

"For the Throne room, and deserving ears only," Kevon whispered. "After this, Alacrit would be a fool not having you as counsel."

The Court-Mage took a deep breath, and stood taller as he rounded the bend, stepping over the tail of a fallen chimaera. "How did you destroy the other one?"

"We had an Orclord punch it," Kevon laughed. "If you have suggestions for this time, I'd like to hear them."

"How did the portal react?"

"It expanded. The magic that was stored in the enchantment fed into the portal, and something horrible tried to come through, tried using me to make it happen." Kevon shuddered at the memory of the violation of his mind. He could still remember the grotesque features he'd seen through the portal, feel the malevolence focused on him before the doorway had closed.

"A sustained Enchantment like that would have tremendous amounts of stored magic to keep it active," Jacek mused. "Releasing it all at once..."

"I'd prefer we didn't," Kevon sighed. "Any ideas?"

"If we don't want to break it, why don't we just bury it?" Jacek suggested. "Block the passageway so nothing can get in or out."

Of course, Kevon thought. *All the time on the ocean, the odd feel of Wind magic, the twisted darkness here. I can barely feel the Earth magic over the distractions.* "I should have thought of that," he admitted. "If we can clear the area, we should be able to..." He trailed off as he noticed only Carlo and one of Rowyn's Striders flanking the portal. "Where is...?"

"Rowyn took three Striders and went further down," Carlo scowled in the flickering light of the torch the other Strider held. "We've repelled two chimaera from the portal since he left."

"We're going to seal the whole place up," Kevon explained, "but we need to be sure there is no other exit before we do."

A lightning-fast tendril of darkness flashed out of the murky arch, revealing itself as a chimaera's tail only as the fangs whistled through the air by Carlo's arm.

The Strider lifted his torch over his head, close to the ceiling of the cave. He whipped his shortsword after the errant tentacle, slicing halfway through before it slid back into the nothingness.

"There are more through there," Carlo shrugged. "We'll hold here. Go after Rowyn, maybe you can seal both directions off after you retrieve him."

Jacek edged along the cave wall furthest from the portal, speeding up as Kevon crossed in front to lead further down the tunnel. "I'd not have thought there would be such structures down here," the Court-Mage whispered as the passage opened to a cavern many times the size of the previous chamber.

"It's been designed," Kevon grumbled, pointing to three exits spaced around the twisted room, all identical in size and shape.

A glimmer of torch-light winked from one of the tunnels ahead. Kevon hurried across the refuse-littered floor to where he could see further down the occupied passageway. "Rowyn!" he hissed.

A tangled murmur of voices jounced closer, flares of light increasing as the others approached.

"This route is cleared," Rowyn announced as he strode into view. "We'll patrol the other two next."

"Not needed," Kevon corrected. "Cover our retreat to the portal, we'll close this end off when we seal the tunnel."

"And if there are other exits from here?" Rowyn asked as they reemerged into the lower cavern.

"You can handle it later," Kevon sighed. "This cave system will no longer be fed by the portal, the chimaera population should return to normal levels."

"As you advise," Rowyn directed the Striders with a brief

gesture, and they spread out behind, following their leader and the two Magi back toward the surface.

Kevon staggered from the press of Earth magic that was beginning to push through the partitioned Wind magic that had been crowding his mind for days, then continued the upward climb.

"Any more trouble?" Kevon asked as they reached the portal chamber.

"Not much," the Strider waiting with Carlo answered before tightening a strip of torn cloth around his left shoulder, using his right hand and his teeth. "We could use one of these back at the village for training."

"The very existence of this portal shifts the balance of..." Kevon stopped. "Of course, you're joking." He stepped closer to the portal, guiding Jacek before him. "If you could stand clear of the lower tunnel..."

The last two Striders walked past, poking at their comrade's bandage and laughing as they went.

"Be ready," Kevon said to no one in particular, and grasped at the power that surrounded him. He felt Jacek's spell coalesce nearby, and did his best to mirror the other Mage's construct.

Spikes of stone from every direction screeched out of the tunnel entrance walls, merging and splaying in the center of the passageway. The overlapping protrusions thickened to diameters of a foot or more. The brittle tips shattered on the opposite ends of the tunnel, but the intact bases left a dense barrier that looked formidable.

"That should hold," Kevon shrugged as he pushed back to release the spell. "I'll start the other one."

"Retreat," Carlo chuckled. "The Magi are covering our escape."

Kevon frowned at the sarcasm as Carlo walked into the upper tunnel, keeping one eye on the portal, and another on the two Mages.

"Back up," Kevon admonished, shooing the armored Striders further up the cramped tunnel. *"Back up!"*

Carlo remained ahead of Kevon and Jacek, the last line of defense against a possible incursion.

"Beginning now," Kevon advised, dropping the safeguards he'd built to protect against the increasing Earth magic he'd started to feel. Reaching down into the massive reserve of earth and stone beneath them, Kevon latched onto a buried boulder. He cajoled it upward with his Art, spinning it around solid formations through the looser packed sediment. He ignored Jacek's offered assistance, tightening his focus on his own spell. "Here it is."

Dust and sand erupted from the earthen patch ahead of them, as the boulder rose into the tunnel. The spinning stone lurched forward, bouncing on tunnel walls twice before lodging itself in the mouth of the entrance to the portal chamber. Kevon ended his spell as Jacek funneled more debris from the broken passageway floor to pack around the obstructing boulder.

"Enough," Carlo turned and waved the Magi to a stop. "Let's get out of this tomb."

CHAPTER 40

Kevon blinked at the morning sun, eyelids crusted with the unfamiliar residue of a full night's sleep.

"There are almost too many of us," Carlo had laughed the evening before, after the whole of the raiding party had converged on the purged nest. "I'll leave it to each of the other commanders to work out their schedules, but anyone committed to the retaking of the camp tomorrow will not stand watch tonight."

"This place has been a crucible of violence for generations," Jacek commented. "The least of the Striders could be a Watch Commander in Navlia. I hope the relief we bring them is not a disservice."

Those words echoed through Kevon's mind as he rose and moved to where the support crew had breakfast ready. Stringy roasted tubers and tea were all he could stomach.

"Two hours march," Rowyn mused. "And we shall have our retribution." He finished off his second mug of tea. "If you'll excuse me," the Strider handed his empty mug to a nearby Meek, and began barking orders at his men.

"He thinks the fall of Cliffside Camp was his fault," Ashera sighed, pouring the dregs of her own cup out onto the ground. "If they had held that day instead of retreating..." She shook her head. "Their numbers were so unnatural, we know now it was the Portals. If he'd stayed to fight that day, he'd have died the next, and our hope of continued survival with him."

"Born with a blade in his hand, that one," Carlo agreed. "If swordplay is my art, it's his breath. He and his men are a sight to behold. The real beauty of it though, is that he's not had to take up arms against men." The Blademaster grimaced. "I envy him that."

Ashera nodded, her eyes straying to the western sky. "My scouts return. I'll report back soon."

"*Bya, bya, bya...*" the Stoneguard shook his head, stood, and ambled to the edge of camp.

"He's bored with yer talk," Kylgren-Wode shrugged. "Fer once, I agree with the brute."

"Training entire lives under the mountains, for this." Carlo chuckled. "I'll wager your people on the frontier have pushed the orcs back further than our troops can run supply lines."

The nearby grouping of stones, twigs, and tied grasses caught Kevon's eye.

"That wasn't here last night," he commented, moving closer to view the arrangement. "Is this a map of the camp?"

"As they left it, yes," Carlo nodded. "The rocks are the solid structures, more likely to have survived the occupation. Breaks in the surrounding wall in at least these three places." The Blademaster pointed to the groupings of twigs. "These are the places we expect them to be the thickest. Buildings with large entrances. The town hall and smithy. We'll drive them there with aerial attacks from Ashera's Riders."

"Sooner than later," Ashera chuckled, rejoining the group. "Three chimaera hunting parties left earlier, two headed west, and the other is fifteen minutes from us. Only five strong, it'll get the blood flowing, at least."

"Here," Kevon pointed at one of the breaks in the wall. "There is not much open space between this opening and one of the larger shelters. We can use surprise to gain the advantage."

Carlo squinted at the layout. "Mmm. Could work."

"The town hall is on the north end," Ashera clarified. "My Riders and I will attack and distract from the south."

"Anyone?" Rowyn whispered, grinning.

"Not if you're counting the three you got this morning," Carlo hissed.

Kylgren-Wode and the Stoneguard argued quietly for a moment.

"He didn't know ye were keeping tally," the ambassador explained. "He was trying te be polite, and share."

Kevon groaned under his breath.

"So, the three of us?" Rowyn's eyes glinted mischievously. "Losers pack the winner's burden on the return trip."

"He's starting a rock collection," Kylgren-Wode translated the threat as the Stoneguard muffled his laughter with a mailed fist.

"There's the signal," Rowyn announced, standing and stepping clear of the grass that still concealed the rest of the attack force. "They're all pinned down, eyes to the south. It's time."

The fifty yards from cover to the wall passed in a half-minute of muted rustling in the short grass, peppered with chuckles from the Stoneguard as he picked up a handful of small, jagged rocks on the way.

Seeing Kylgren-Wode's glare of disapproval, the dwarf opened his hand, and the stones pattered to the dirt. "*Meh.*" He readied his axe, and began taking deep breaths, eyes closing to slits.

"Ready?" Carlo asked, but Rowyn was already leaping through the gap in the wall, a pair of his Striders close behind. He bit down on the curse that came to his lips, and followed, the dwarves at his heels.

Alanna and Anneliese hopped through, stationing themselves to either side of the gap, weapons drawn, scanning for stray enemies.

Kevon glanced down to where the other group was squeezing through a smaller entrance. The last of the Striders was slipping out of view. "Just us, then," he told Jacek, and stepped into Cliffside Camp.

Carlo, Rowyn, and the dwarves were already sliding along the side of the town hall, the Striders staying further clear of the building, following the worn path that meandered further into town.

Beginning to step off the path to follow Carlo, Kevon wobbled as his foot almost crunched down on a sun-bleached bone. He shifted, throwing an elbow to rebalance, maneuvering his foot back onto the path. He pointed to the bone, then put a finger to his lips in a *shushing* motion, looking over his shoulder toward Jacek and the girls.

Alanna pulled her eyepatch free, slipped it into a pocket, and blinked as she adjusted to the change in vision. She nodded, and Kevon continued down the path after the Striders.

Kevon and the others were midway down the side of the building when Rowyn reached the front corner and peered around it. He motioned for the Striders, now only a little ahead of Kevon, to leave the path and follow him around the front of the town hall. Rowyn, Carlo, Kylgren-Wode, and the Stoneguard slid around the corner, out of sight.

The wind shifted.

Kevon's head whipped around at Alanna's sharp intake of breath. She was staring at the wall of the building beside them, eyes glistening and unfocused.

"*They can smell us*," she whispered, "Go." Her voice rose as she pointed to where the others had disappeared. "Now."

Kevon and Jacek sprinted in the direction she indicated, bones and weeds crunching and rustling beneath their headlong rush.

Anneliese's long-legged stride devoured the distance as she barreled past where the Striders had departed the path, drawn bow tracking around the corner.

Kevon's last glimpse of Alanna as he rounded the corner was drawn knives, closed eyes, and the smile she'd affected lately that seemed to belong to Marelle as much as her assassin alter-ego.

Fire and Control runes leapt to the forefront of Kevon's

mind, shimmering in and out of focus. Lacking power and a target, the glimmering mental constructs were almost more distraction than comfort.

Stepping away from the building into the bone-strewn grasses, Kevon looked around the Striders to where Carlo, Rowyn, and the dwarves edged toward the gaping hole in the wall that the chimaera had torn open around the building's previous doorway.

Rowyn's head tilted, as if he'd heard a strange noise. Carlo spun away from the wall, words of warning forming on his tongue.

Planks buckled and cracked as a section of wall failed to resist the charging chimaera on the other side of it. Two upright beams snapped in quick succession, and a slab of wall five feet across slammed into Rowyn's right shoulder. He wobbled two steps, brushing aside a large splinter that had managed to lodge between the riveted plates in his armor.

An instant later, the chimaera was through the breach, its weight slapping the ruptured wall down flat on Rowyn's greatsword with an ominous *thunk*.

Rowyn dropped and rolled backward. He kicked upward with both feet, planting them in the creature's abdomen as the beast's curled horns slammed the dirt a foot past his own head. The Strider stretched the kick as far as he dared, the extra force unbalancing the chimaera. He arched his back and let the force from the kick's recoil roll him back to his feet. He whirled, drawing his shortswords, as the chimaera roared and twisted upright.

The Stoneguard pushed Kylgren-Wode further toward Carlo, as he stepped into the center of the new opening. "*Donk!*" he announced, smashing the next chimaera that charged through squarely between the eyes with the flat of his battle-axe.

The larger female's rush hesitated only a moment as she bowled him over on her way toward Rowyn.

The Stoneguard tumbled backward once, and landed in

a sitting position, spattered with hot blood from the disembowelling stroke. He glanced toward Carlo and Kylgren-Wode, lifted one finger, grunted, and clambered to his feet. "*Gogo!*" he shouted, hurling himself through the breach, into the unknown darkness.

Carlo slashed at a chimaera that had emerged from the other doorway, ducked a swing from a whipping tail, and severed the appendage as he spun his iron-bound shield into the side of the building. Kylgren-Wode ducked under and past him, delivering a swift axe-stroke to the beast's exposed neck.

Kevon tried to control the second chimaera through the new doorway, but its fury, and then its pain, were too strong for the spell to overcome. He let that rune fade, and poured energy into the Fire rune. He watched helplessly as the second chimaera crashed into an unsuspecting Rowyn, and the first jumped into the midst of the pile.

The Striders leapt to their leader's aid, greatswords flicking like tongues of lightning, laying bare long slices of flesh, or severing limbs as the crash of bodies continued tumbling.

The pent-up Fire magic burned through Kevon's veins, blurring his vision, threatening to reduce him to ashes if it was not released. Three more chimaera rounded a corner of another building across the camp, and Kevon unleashed the conflagration raging within him.

The spray of flames engulfed the two chimaera nearest to Kevon. Two arrows to the neck, then a dagger to the heart as it recoiled from the pain, and the third chimaera fell alongside its burning brethren.

Sounds of battle echoed from the direction the other group had entered. Kevon could feel the Fire magic building within Jacek, and he extended his own power to share even as he dashed toward the entrance the Stoneguard had taken, a globe of light forming and floating ahead of him as he ran.

The outward jolt of magic barely preceded the concussive force of the spell, and the wash of heat as Jacek incinerated a chimaera leaping from a nearby rooftop. Kevon pulled back his offered magic, and spun into the town hall, Fire rune once again at the ready.

The Stoneguard limped toward Kevon, palm outstretched, stepping around one of the four large corpses illuminated in the Mage-light.

Kevon threw his own hands up, and backed away at the warning.

"*Ahhm.*" The dwarf sighed, shaking his head, the severed tail spiked to his neck flopping as he did.

"What..." Kevon peered at the Stoneguard as the dwarf closed and reopened his hand, once, then twice more, with eyes wide, urgent. "Stop? Close? Open?" Kevon's tensed shoulders dropped as the realization hit him. He outstretched his own right hand, running his left index finger across each outstretched digit. "Five?" His sullen look was lost on the dwarf.

"*Hah!*" The Stoneguard pulled the tail-fangs free from his neck, and slapped his hand over the wounds, dropping his greataxe to the ground to lean on for support. "*Huh.*"

"Alanna!" Kevon shouted, backing out of the building. "Quickly!"

The assassin flicked another dagger, laughed, and sprinted to Kevon's side.

"He's hurt, badly. Is there anything you can do?"

"I'll stay with him, and see," she shrugged. "You have more work to do out there."

Kevon nodded, and drew his sword, the last bits of his magic sighing away into the blade's hilt. He saw Carlo and Kylgren-Wode surrounded by three chimaera, and charged back out into the battle.

CHAPTER 41

Splintering planks and creaking timbers summoned Kevon from his sleep. He blinked at the barest glimmer of dawn, and rubbed his eyes. He cast aside the rough blanket that had been placed over him, stood, and staggered toward the sound of work.

Two hours later, well shy of noon, the remains of the town hall were wholly dismantled. The stacks of nearly whole boards and beams dwindled as workers hauled the reclaimed lumber to repair the breaches in the outer walls.

Kevon handed the stack of planks he'd been carrying to one of Carlo's men as the Blademaster signaled to him from halfway across the camp.

"Is she going to be all right?" Kevon asked, brushing the dust and splinters from his tunic as he approached. "I haven't had time this morning to..."

"She wouldn't be Claw if she were weak," Carlo rumbled. "Three lost in a battle this size is unheard of. One of them was even ours. If it hadn't been..."

"Her brother," Kevon nodded. "Giving his life as he helped retake the camp he blamed himself for losing."

"Yeah."

"Has she left his side?"

"She's organized air patrols," Carlo said, shaking his head. "And details of Striders to gather brush for a pyre. Their dead, and my lieutenant will be given a proper Griffinsworn's funeral at noon."

"They needed three more leaders when we reclaimed the camp," Kevon sighed. "They'll need an extra Fist."

"More than that," Anneliese interjected, stepping alongside Carlo, "Rowyn was Fist of the Stonespire Camp. The leaders of the central clan are considered to be the default heads of their factions. Rowyn had no clear successor. One of the other Fists may move to take his place, if none from Stonespire can bring a strong enough claim to the title."

"What would that mean?" Kevon asked.

"I'd rather not think about it," Ashera commented, approaching the group from a knot of workers. "The ceremony is about to commence."

The pitch treated pallets the fallen were arranged on burned hot enough to reduce even bone to ash in less than a quarter hour. No words were spoken, but when the last flame flickered out, Ashera thanked all that were present, turned, and walked away.

"The resettlement group will be here in two days," Anneliese announced to the few that remained, minutes of silence later.

"We leave for the caverns tomorrow," Carlo grunted in amusement. "We'll miss all the politics."

"The secret," Ashera called back to the others, "is keeping your feet closer to the edge than you're comfortable with. It lets you lean back in easier."

My feet up against the cliff face is more than I'm comfortable with, Kevon thought, glancing at the frothing sea far below him. *She wants me to step closer toward falling?* He edged his feet out another few inches, and felt the shift in balance. A few more halting steps, and the ledge widened enough for two people to rest without fear of falling.

"Hold my hand?" Rhysabeth-Dane offered. "This is not so much different than the deep caverns in the Hold. A bit windier..." She shrugged.

"We should all..." Kevon clutched at the fear-knot in his

chest. "Do this ourselves. We still need to prove..."

Flynn and another of the Aspirants scampered past Kevon and the librarian, laughing and shoving as they went. Yusa stretched flat against the side of the cliff, and Kevon could feel a Movement rune pinning the sailor there until the youngsters passed.

"That we're worthy of their help." Kevon finished.

Rhysabeth-Dane nodded, and trotted off after the squealing children.

Cursing his broad shoulders, Kevon sidled out onto the ledge again, and continued down toward the caverns.

The cavern mouth loomed ahead, the path narrowing and widening in stepping-stone fashion as it neared the entrance.

"Easy," Ashera cautioned from inside. "The Unbound are congregating this afternoon.

Kevon leapt from the last ledge into the solid footing of the cavern. Two steps in, and he recoiled as a wild-looking young griffin hopped his direction from further in the cave.

"This way," Ashera pulled Kevon into a smaller tunnel that skirted the cavern, opening to it in several places as it curved around the outside. "The Gallery," she announced as they reached the back end of the second cavern the tunnel led through.

The large flat area lay open enough that they could see the whole cavern from the chiseled stone bench against the back wall. Pairs of griffin occupied most of the visible niches in the contoured walls, fussing over squawking young. A large male griffin descended from above the cavern mouth, flapping his wings laboriously as he carried a fish of enormous size, still flopping in distress. He landed near the refuse pile at the entrance, and spread his wings over the kill, proclaiming his ownership before tearing at the fish's soft grey underbelly, and picking at the organs that spilled out. As he stepped aside to preen, the nesting pairs split to claim their shares of the remains, and bringing hunks of the scaly flesh back to their nests.

"We're late..." Ashera shook her head. "We should have

been here a week earlier. There may not be time enough for the griffin to imprint on our Aspirants."

"The Seat is further to the south," Jacek pointed in the direction Kevon felt the greatest concentration of the altered Wind magic. "Does this tunnel lead much further?"

"Into two more caverns. Long abandoned, previous nesting sites, filled with bone piles and filth," Ashera explained. "We tidy this cavern up after the nesting season to keep them coming here."

"Let us hope the Seat is not more than two caverns away, then," Kevon sighed. "I can't decide which is worse… the groaning of the earth, or the whisper of the caged Wind magic."

Rhysabeth-Dane settled onto the stone bench, elbowed enough room from the fidgety Aspirants that she could spread out her research, and began reading by torchlight.

"Let's do what we're here to do." Kevon looked back to make sure Alanna and Yusa were following, and started further down the tunnel.

CHAPTER 42

Two crunching steps carried Kevon through the strewn bones that surrounded the half-buried Seat of Wind into the blustery portal that opened beside it. Two spongy steps away from the portal on the other side, and he was jostled by Alanna and Yusa stumbling into him from behind. He toppled face first into the thick mist that swirled around their feet. He pressed down on the squishy medium beneath his hands as he began to stand, wondering what it was made of.

"Hey, is this a cloud?" he heard Yusa ask, and felt Alanna's arms wrap around his legs as the surface below him dissolved into a bright nothingness. The wind tore his scream from his lips. He twisted around to see the terror on his companions' faces before returning his attention downward to the rapidly approaching surface below them. He threw his arms in front of his face, closed his eyes, and braced for impact.

The cushioned surface gave enough to prevent injury, and Kevon rolled half a dozen yards before coming to a stop. Gazing across the white-streaked blue expanse that surrounded them, Kevon spotted a large eagle perched on the edge of a cloud, craning its head to look at them. Another eagle burst through the cloud from below and behind the first, and landed next to it, squawking.

So soft... he thought, resting on the pliable material beneath him. As he relaxed, it grew softer, and he started sinking further through it. "Wait!" he shouted, leaping up from the suddenly firm ground. "The clouds are what you need them to be! Concentrate!" He spread his intent to the cloud surface the others lay groaning upon, solidifying it further until they could focus on it themselves. "It isn't magic, it's just how this works here."

The billowing surface writhed and coalesced into firm, pale cobblestones.

"Ouch," Alanna complained. "What is going..."

"I'll focus on keeping us aloft," Reko's voice rasped from nearby. "You figure out where we need to go next."

"You should be able to see it easier than any of us," Kevon squeezed Alanna's hand as he helped her up.

Alanna removed her eyepatch, and put it in her pocket. She blinked experimentally, and covered her healed eye with her hand. "No," she announced. "Not here."

"Right. Naturally." Kevon looked at Yusa. "Any ideas?"

"Curves. Lots of them. It's a proper maelstrom in here."

"That's..." Kevon looked to his right, and saw the whorls fading outward in the distance. Above and below, the impressive formations stretched to the edge of his awareness. "Too much to search. Anything important might be at the center." He turned to his left, and tried to deduce where the center of the pattern could be.

"The clouds thin out below us, thicken above," Yusa observed.

"A lot of movement up that way," Kevon agreed. "I can't tell if it's..." He choked on the words as another cloud slid past, engulfing them for a few tense breaths. "I don't know if it's where we need to go, but we can't stay here forever."

"Quickly, then," Reko's voice urged, his sudden image pointing at the trailing edge of the cloud they'd just emerged from. A wide ledge and ladder-slats formed on the retreating cloud. The cobblestone pattern under their feet raced along with them as they sprinted closer to the fleeing mist.

"Go!" Kevon felt the clouds softening under his feet as the Mage shifted his concentration to their new objective, and pushed Alanna along behind Yusa, focusing on their footing as he followed his friends' mad dash. A Movement-fueled leap, a violent gust of wind focused by Reko, and Kevon joined the others as the cloud they had been on dwindled from view behind them. He followed them up to the top of their new platform, and sat to catch his breath.

"It doesn't feel like we're moving..." Alanna frowned, not bothering to mask her discomfort. "I may be sick."

Most of the clouds now appeared to be spinning slowly around the center to the right, and down. The apparent motion seemed to verify their target destination as the most likely center of the formation.

"There!" Alanna pointed to a stretch of cloud above and to their left. "Not moving as fast as this, but it stretches in toward the center."

The cloud passed under them on its way by, but was wide enough for the three to tumble down onto with yards to spare on either side. Its trajectory took them lower before they could hop onto one of the more 'stationary' clouds on an inner rung.

"Watch your feet," Reko cautioned as he stopped focusing on the 'ground' below them. A minute later, his commanding voice led them through a series of leaps and rolls, landing them three clouds nearer the cluster, but still too far below it to be able to see anything for certain.

Birds and griffin tore through the sky at more frequent intervals, nearing the party, but never stopping for more than a quick screech before disappearing into the surrounding cloud cover.

"Close your eyes, this is the fastest way." Kevon could feel Reko's concentration overtaking his as the three of them huddled close on the small, fast moving cloud platform the Mage had directed them to. "Not you, Yusa, I need your eyes."

"I miss my boat," the captain groaned.

"We'll be out of here soon," Alanna reassured him. "Of course, we'll still be underground, along a cliff face really far above your ship."

Kevon buried his face in Alanna's hair, and waited for further instruction from Reko.

CHAPTER 43

"It's time," Mirsa squeezed Bertus's hand, straining a breath to move past the pain.

"It should be… weeks…" the Seeker leapt to his feet. Are you sure…"

"It's. Time."

"Relaniel! I'll get…" Bertus shook his head in frustration. "No, Aelion… Relaniel's… Um. Going now…" His fingers slid free of hers, and he sprinted out the door. "It's time!" he shouted at the top of his lungs as he stumbled along the suspended walkway that led toward the Elder's home. His heavy steps rippled along the sky-bridge, building in amplitude until two elves cried out, wrapping themselves around the vine railings for security.

"Sorry!" he shouted, slowing as he barged past them. "It's time!"

Aelion sat basking in the midafternoon sun just outside his dwelling, and stood as Bertus staggered into view. "It's time?"

"Here?" Bertus asked, inching the bed further toward the center of the window-light.

"Yes, right there. Sun… helps?" The Elder's firm hand on Bertus's shoulder was almost too reassuring. "All will be well."

After what seemed like hours later, the baby's cries split the tortured silence, and Bertus barged back into the dwelling. Aelion cradled the quieting newborn close as the last rays of light from the window slid off Mirsa's still form.

"Is she…" Bertus lurched to a stop, face frozen in horror.

"Resting, child. Merely resting." Aelion rocked the swaddled infant slowly. "Would you like to hold Maisy?"

The Warrior circled around to where Aelion stood, and gingerly accepted the baby, instinctively cradling her neck, supporting her tiny head, swinging her in close. His feet shuffled and he leaned side to side, rocking to calm her, as well as his own nerves.

Maisy yawned, and blinked twice. She focused for an instant, the intensity of her gaze reminding him immediately of Waine. *Let me tell you a story about that,* he could hear the fallen Warrior say.

"She has your eyes," the Elder commented as he slipped out the door.

"No, I…" Bertus began, but the elf was already gone. He walked as he rocked, getting near enough to Mirsa to see the rise and fall of her chest before making his way to the bench against the far wall. He sat and leaned back into the corner, intent on memorizing every movement, every wrinkle of her tiny nose as she yawned and fussed.

"Put her down!" Mirsa scolded, as she dumped the brace of pheasants she'd been handed on the hearth. "She's only just gotten back to sleep, and you're filthy from the hunt!" For emphasis, the Mage flung a pointing finger at the open door of the cottage. The muddy boot-prints Bertus had left on the hardwood floor peeled themselves up and sailed with considerable force out into the glade.

The Warrior touched the tip of his nose to the baby's, breathing in the newness of her, all but oblivious to her mother's fury.

"Bonk bonk!" One of the Stoneguard rapped his knuckles on the doorframe, and poked his head around to peer inside.

"*Papa!*"

"Why must they always learn the wrong words first?" Bertus sighed, moving back to the cradle, and depositing the infant back in her place. "I'll tell him we can practice later."

Mirsa smiled at the yawning Maisy, and shook her head. "She'll nap a while longer. Go play with the boys."

"I'll be back soon," he answered, planting a quick kiss on Mirsa's cheek. Bertus unstrung his Elven longbow, and traded it for the ancient sword that rested in the corner.

Bertus followed the two dwarves out into the clearing, and the unicorns, familiar now with the routine, faded into the surrounding trees.

"*Ha!*" One of the Stoneguard whirled and thrust the spear-tip of his axe at Bertus.

Bertus rolled to the left, retaking his feet as he drew his blade and cast aside the scabbard. His evasive movement put the other dwarf behind his aggressor, giving him a brief respite as the pair swiveled and sidestepped to stand shoulder to shoulder against him. He gripped the sword with both hands, and took two lurching half-steps toward his opponents, looking for a sign of weakness or panic. Seeing none, he charged ahead.

The Stoneguard on the left acted first, shifting his axe back in preparation to swing. Bertus zigged to the left, leaned into the run, and took two more quick steps. He hopped over the kick the right Stoneguard aimed at his shin, and kicked at the shaft of that dwarf's axe. At the same time, he parried the spinning axe of the other, who had turned the shifting motion into a backhand stroke. Changing grips, he smashed the left dwarf alongside the head with the hilt of his sword, spinning a backfist at the other as he twisted on landing.

The second Stoneguard ducked the attack, and whirled about to strike at Bertus's weapon with his own. The Warrior twisted his wrist, swinging the weapon out of range, and tucked into a roll that gave him a bit of distance from the dwarves. By the time he'd stood and turned, the Stoneguard had split and were trying to circle him.

All right, he thought, turning toward the one he knew to be a marginally better fighter, while shifting a portion of his awareness to listen for the other dwarf behind him.

Obvious fakes, Bertus thought of the two quick thrusting jabs of the dwarf's axe point, and the nearly silent crunch of grasses behind him confirmed the suspicion. He dodged forward and to the right, sidestepping the third, the only *actual* thrust of the weapon. He seized the weapon's shaft, and pulled it further along its existing path, pivoting on his left foot, and kicking at the dwarf's shoulder with his right.

The combination of the unbalancing *yank* and the leveraged kick tore the weapon free of the Stoneguard's grip. Bertus slashed with the sword as he completed his leftward revolution, trying to spin the liberated weapon in his left hand to bear as he did so.

The dwarf crouched and bobbed to avoid the blade's simple arc, then leaned and stood, leading with his right shoulder. The attack struck Bertus just above the small of the back, and launched him into the air, clutched weapons flailing as he tilted headlong past the dwarf.

No! Bertus gritted his teeth, and finished spinning the appropriated axe into a steadier grip. He turned his shoulder and his weapons so that he would roll when he hit, and not impale or cut himself. He sprang to his feet, face contorted in a snarl that helped him summon the strength to brandish the heavy Dwarven axe in his off-hand. He flicked the weapon upward, his hand sliding to the correct grip, and he shifted forward and to the right, squaring off toward where both the dwarves were gathered again.

The trailing Stoneguard's knuckles whitened as his grip increased on his axe. "*Ororo...*" he whispered, beginning to step around his compatriot, weapon raised in a manner that hinted at something more than friendly practice.

"*No!*" the other dwarf extended his right arm, slowing his advance. "*Behr-toos Ororo?*" He shook his head. "*Behr-toos papa. Behr-toos... o-kay.*"

The Stoneguard lowered his weapon, but the fury in his eyes did not abate. "*Ororo.*"

Bertus cried out as his grip failed, and the axe tumbled to the earth, nearly striking him in the foot. He hopped back, sword still at the ready.

"*Pffft. Ororo.*" The weaponless Stoneguard shoved his comrade aside and strode up to recover his axe. As he stood, he tilted his head toward the cottage. "*Papa. Go.*"

Lesson's over for today, Bertus thought, recovering the scabbard and sheathing the sword. *I'd never seen what fear looked like on a Stoneguard.*

"Never heard the word before," Mirsa set the plate down in front of Bertus, and swept across the room to scoop up Maisy. "If they'd left us with a translator, we would know."

Bertus watched the slow twisting movements Mirsa used to rock her child back to contentedness, and noted the hint of sadness on her face. "I miss Rhysabeth-Dane, too. She wanted to be here for all of this."

"They'll be back soon enough," Mirsa whispered, placing her sleeping child back in the cradle. After standing over her a bit longer, she crossed the room back to the table, and sat beside Bertus. "And there will be more hard decisions to make."

CHAPTER 44

"Oof!" Kevon hit the platform harder than he thought possible, but recovered and scrambled out of the way before Alanna and Yusa tumbled down after him.

"I believe we have arrived," Reko's voice whispered from somewhere between them. "I cannot affect the surface below us. It is… somewhat of a relief."

"Get some rest," Kevon answered. "We may need you again soon."

"Can you believe some of the things that have flown past us in just the last few minutes?" Alanna lay on her back, staring up into the whirling expanse.

"A few, almost *into* us," Yusa clarified. "Curiosity, it seemed, more than malice."

"Birds of all kinds, griffin, half a dozen things I cannot begin to name…" Kevon agreed. "And beyond this central platform, before we were carried above it…"

"A dragon." Alanna sat up. "I'd hoped my eyes were deceiving me."

"Hope instead that they are as benevolent as every other creature we've encountered," Kevon offered, helping the assassin to her feet. "We're nearly there."

Kevon led the way into the mist that obscured the view of the center of the vast central platform.

Hours into the journey, the mist thinned, and a twisted shape became visible in the distance.

A crystalline structure, resembling a gigantic frozen dust-devil grew out of the firm cloud surface. Deep sapphire at the base, fading to translucence, and eventual transparence at dizzying heights, the spire was the only solid looking thing they had seen in this realm.

"The base flares out to the left," Kevon observed, after the others stopped beside him. "There may be an entrance there.

"We've gathered an audience," Alanna pointed skyward to the scattered avian forms circling above.

"Watch them, but let's keep our pace up." Kevon decided. "This realm is far more dangerous than M'lani's. Best to finish our business and move on."

"There is an arch!" Yusa called over the wind that had grown steadily as they approached the crystal spiral. "We should run for it!"

Something not right about this, the thought coming unbidden to Kevon's mind as he sprinted behind Yusa and Alanna into the increasing gale. A dozen yards from their destination, his fears coalesced into reality as the wind snatched Alanna up, her scream all but lost in the fury of the vortex.

"NO!" Kevon poured all of his surprise and anger into a Movement rune, and lashed out with his mind, but the symbol dulled twice as he tightened the magic around the flailing assassin.

Then she was gone.

Kevon stumbled the last few steps into the crystal archway, nearly swept off his own feet in the final yards. The tempest subsided to a whisper inside the entrance, and Yusa seized his arm when he tried to rush back outside.

"There she is!" Kevon tried the spell again as Alanna whirled by, just outside and above the entranceway. The runes darkened as before. "Steel!" he exclaimed. "She's touching metal!"

"Stand aside," Yusa slid along the side of the arch to where the breeze began picking up, looked up and into the wind. He twisted his head as Alanna sped by again, then reached out for Kevon. "Be ready!"

Kevon joined hands with Yusa, and hugged tight to the

wall as his friend edged further out into the roaring winds. He felt Reko's spell begin, and mirrored it with symbols of his own, joining their power together under the other Mage's control. The sudden power drain wrenched at his senses, as the impact wrenched at his arm.

Yusa caught Alanna with his right arm, nearly breaking free of Kevon's grip in the process.

Kevon grabbed on with both hands, and leaned back, hauling both Yusa and Alanna into the calm interior of the crystal whirlwind.

"I'm glad I woke up for that," Reko's voice rasped above the whisper from outside. "Shall we continue?"

"I thought you were..." Kevon pushed past Yusa to encircle Alanna with trembling arms.

"You told me to get rid of my weapons," she whispered, "And I knew it would be all right."

"Time was short," Reko chuckled. "I felt using your voice would help."

"It worked," Kevon grasped Yusa by the shoulder as he released Alanna. "That's what matters."

"I saved a few," Alanna's voice lifted as she drew a shortsword and a dagger, eyes toward the back of the crystal structure as Kevon backed away.

Large azure dragons, shimmering in and out of view as they blended in with the surrounding crystal, shifted and stood near the clear dais that was the focus of the chamber.

"Well, it's no safer out there," Yusa shrugged, stepping further into the room.

The others followed, watching the dragons settle into upright, imposing stances, not straying from where they had been resting.

Not even halfway across the chamber, the dragons standing guard roared, throwing their heads back and howling upward. The deep bellows merged, and changed to a twisted parody of the screeching vortex outside.

"Something is happening," Yusa and Reko spoke in

unison, stopping and motioning the others to a halt.

The dragons quieted, settling back into their state of staid composure. The howl of the wind subsided slowly, ebbing and spiking into nearly discernable whispers.

"Up there."

Kevon craned his neck to see what Yusa spoke of; a fluttering speck of brown far above, where the twisted crystal became transparent. *Or ends?* He wondered to himself. The cavorting shape whirled and contracted. It seemed to pause for a few moments, before it became evident that it was falling at a tremendous speed.

Scintillating wings of the brightest blue unfurled as the falling figure streaked toward the dais. The attending dragons bowed their heads while the new arrival made half a dozen laps around the room, skimming the outer wall, slowing with each turn.

Yusa dropped to one knee, inclining his head as the strange figure before them alighted between the dragons. "Milady," he murmured.

Kevon and Alanna bowed, and Kevon stepped ahead, taking in the wonder that stood before them.

"Lady M'phes," he began and the goddess before him craned her neck to get a better look at him. Her folded wings hung like royal banners behind her, fluttering as she moved. Her talons clacked softly on the walkway beneath her, savage looking claws flowing upward into well-muscled, feather-clad legs that were beyond question feminine.

How is it that I am known to you, yet you are strange to me? The creator's beak opened as the thought-runes flowed into Kevon's mind.

"M'lani bade us find you, ask for your help." Kevon explained.

M'lani... It seems an eternity since... M'phes uncrossed her raven-feathered arms, smoothed the orange ruffles on her stomach so that the bright oval of color that extended nearly to her neck was perfectly uniform. *Come closer, servants of Light, and speak to me of my dear sister.*

"Servants," Alanna muttered, straightening and striding forward, nearly passing Kevon.

"Easy," the Warrior cautioned, taking her hand, evening their pace. "We're guests here."

As they drew closer, the size of the goddess of Wind became more evident. Half again the size they'd seen M'lani manifest, her talons were large enough to encircle a full-grown man.

Men, M'phes thought at them, leaning down as they approached. *Enchantment endures?*

"Yes, your majesty," Yusa volunteered, mesmerized by the blue, gold, and green ovals surrounding her eyes, reminiscent of a peacock's feathers.

M'lani knows, yet has not told any of us?

"She is trapped in her personal realm," Kevon explained. "Fearful of L'mort, as she assumed you all were."

The Plane of Magic has grown darker, I am loath to venture there myself, M'phes nodded, standing to her full height. *Our brother has always been... Difficult to be around.*

"M'lani thinks that L'mort's influence on the Plane of Enchantment has increased his power elsewhere," Kevon continued. "She wanted us to bring this news, and this weapon, in hopes of..."

M'phes's wings extended fully to each side as Kevon touched the hilt of the sword. She recoiled as the magic flowed out of him into the blade, the shock of her sudden movement booming through the chamber. The dragons at her sides stepped forward in unison, fangs bared.

"No!" Kevon raised his hands in front of him, shaking his spread fingers to show he held nothing. "This is what M'lani wanted me to show you!"

Kevon waited a moment before reaching for the weapon again, slower this time. He drew it halfway from the scabbard, then gripped the blade, and pulled it free, offering the hilt to M'phes.

A step off the dais, and a lean forward put the sword, and

the rest of the group, within arm's reach of the goddess. As she reached forward, her nearly human hand grew crimson-tipped talons. Ripples of blue ran up along her arm as raven feathers stood, stretched, and flattened into scales that matched the dragons to either side of her. She pinched the hilt between two claws, and drew back in pain, snatching the blade from Kevon's hand, sending it spinning to the floor.

The blade whooshed through the previously solid surface as though it was not there.

"It cancelled the magic." Reko chuckled. "We have another plan, correct?"

I'll get it.

The platform behind M'phes swirled into mist. The goddess backflipped, flapping her outstretched wings at the correct instant to send her hurtling downward, after the falling sword. The thunder of her exit shook the room once again.

Wish she'd said something to the dragons before she left, Kevon thought as the two beasts advanced, voicing their displeasure.

Kevon felt the Illusion rune form as the crude replica of M'phes rose from the vortex she'd descended into. "Do you really think they'll..." Kevon trailed off as the advancing dragons turned to inspect the slowly improving image.

"Doesn't look like it will delay them for long," Yusa commented, as one of the dragons turned to look their direction. "We may want to..."

The illusion and corresponding rune winked out in Kevon's mind as M'phes, sword clenched in her outstretched claw, burst through the mist and the false image at unbelievable speed, banking around the upper reaches of the main chamber to slow herself before landing in front of them.

My sister's touch lingers on this abomination, M'phes's thoughts reverberated through their minds as she advanced with the blade held before her, arms shifting back to raven-feathered covering as the mental volume of her speech lowered. *I do see that her power has faltered, more than even mine. If she claims this will help restore the balance... Please, continue.* The creator's claws flowed back to finger-forms as she shrank to merely double Kevon's height, and handed the blade back to him.

My name is inscribed alongside hers, now. Use them to combat the darkness.

Kevon looked at the sword, and could see no change in the blade, feel no difference with his dulled magical senses. "I don't..."

M'phes clasped both hands around where Kevon held the sword, and tilted her head to the side, an audible squawk escaping before her thought-runes resumed their thrum.

Truly, you do not. Until then, other measures must be taken.

Releasing Kevon, M'phes turned to the dragons that stood behind the dais. The breeze in the room stilled for a moment, and both roared, advancing toward the suddenly enlarging goddess with thundering footfalls that shook the chamber.

Kevon sheathed his sword, not keen on appearing a threat, or having the weapon fall through the floor again.

Transformed clawed fingers received the catlike nuzzles from first one dragon, then the other, as M'phes hissed in an oddly soothing manner.

The dragons stepped back and lowered their heads. M'phes stretched and fluttered her wings, and the magic in the area shifted.

Kevon felt spiraling proportions of Wind magic restrained further than the restricted magic surrounding either Seat they'd visited crackle and flare into the service of the deity before them. The release of power made him giddy just being so near, and he struggled to keep his eyes open as the spell built.

Twin cyclones enveloped the dragons, the focused vortices building in power until they warped the very fabric of the realm, twisting inward on themselves, folding down to a fraction of their original sizes.

The flow of magic slowed, and the winds fractured and dissipated from around the two light blue spheres that remained where the dragons had been.

Love them as I have, and they shall serve you well.

Updrafts lifted and carried the spheres to her outstretched claws, and she cradled them close for a few moments before turning and offering them to Kevon and the others.

Kevon winced, accepting the first sphere M'phes offered. "I still… don't…"

A sound not unlike the tinkling of wind chimes filled the air, and Kevon realized the goddess was laughing. He smiled and shrugged, clutching the warm life before him as tightly as he dared.

"I'll pack this out of here for you," Yusa glanced at Kevon as he took the other egg from M'phes. "But they're not going on my boat."

CHAPTER 45

"Whoa!" Kevon shouted, tumbling over the smooth stone floor, cradling his delicate cargo close to his chest. He rolled to his feet, and stepped aside as Yusa exploded through the portal, turning to slide on his back, holding the light blue sphere he carried aloft.

Alanna hopped through the blustery tear in the world, shifting her balance, finding her footing, and sliding less than a handsbreadth once she touched down. "Amateurs," she muttered, watching her companions struggle to their feet.

"You weren't carrying..." Kevon protested.

"Precisely." Alanna peered at Jacek. "We're all here. You can stop that now."

Jacek groaned and released the magic. The portal closed with a *whoosh* and a whistle.

"How long were we gone this time?" Kevon asked. "And where is everyone else?"

"There has been some added excitement the last few days. The new Riders are training." Jacek straightened and started out of the room. "Oh, and you were gone three weeks this time."

"A lot less crowded than when we left," Alanna observed as they entered the observation shelf above the hatching area.

"All of the nesting pairs have left, the young have taken wing." Jacek explained. "There is much to celebrate, including your return. Seven new Riders were Chosen. Only one aspirant remains for next year."

"I thought there were only seven Aspirants," Kevon frowned.

"Yes," Jacek laughed. "That is an interesting story."

Frantic shadows smeared across the cave entrance, but were gone before Kevon could turn his head. "Training?" he wondered aloud.

"They've been out for a while," Jacek offered. "They should be returning soon... Are those.... What I think they are?"

"We can discuss that later." Kevon placed the package, already wrapped in his outer cloak, on the stone bench near another bundle. "Can we find something to wrap the other one with?"

The exhausted Warrior sprawled down next to his cloak on the bench.

"It's nice to be able to relax without focusing on the medium beneath you," Reko whispered in Illusion-sound. "I may rest awhile."

"Magi can have good ideas, after all," Alanna purred, sliding down beside Kevon, twining her arm around his, lacing her fingers into his hand. "Rest elsewhere."

Kevon's laugh died in his throat, as the flight of novice Riders returned from their training. Ashera and Stormclaw led, the Claw of the Riders guiding her steed in a wide circle around the back of the cavern, wingtips brushing the wall before alighting below Kevon and the others.

"Aha!" Flynn shrieked in triumph as he and his griffin touched down, taking the direct route toward the back, the first of the group to land. "Ah... ahhh!" He tumbled over his mount's head, spinning as he shook free from one of the stirrups a second earlier than the other.

"Flynn!" Ashera fumed. "I don't care if you bust your head open, but you need to protect your griffin!"

"Sorry, sir!" Flynn hopped up, and extended a hand to calm his now skittish charge. Seconds later, his arms were around her neck, face buried in her feathers as she squawked happily.

The other Riders were filtering back toward Ashera, exuberant chatter mixing with the griffin-noise the chamber had felt empty without.

"Lean more into your turns," Ashera advised one of her students. "Take a few more seconds to land," she admonished Flynn. "And you, stop showing off."

"I fly how I feel," Rhysabeth-Dane giggled. "*We* fly how *we* feel," she corrected herself, adjusting the shoulder strap on her riveted plate armor. "Oh!" she squealed, noticing the others watching wide-eyed from the bench. She rushed toward the back, slowing as she reached the edge of the shelf. "Guess what happened?"

"Lost interest in the book, then?" Alanna teased, finishing loading her plate with two slices of bread. "Can't say that I blame you."

"No, quite the opposite," Rhysabeth chuckled, setting her lunch down on the makeshift table in the carved dining chamber. "I've gotten nearly all of this set of symbols translated. In just two days."

"How is that possible?" Kevon asked, sitting down between them. "You've spent so much time researching with no progress, then everything makes sense?"

"The second set of runic symbols are more artistic, emotionally charged, than the others," Rhysabeth-Dane explained, gazing past the others. I couldn't even catch a hint at their meanings until I flew with Brightwing for a while. The Unbound fly in patterns that reminded me of things I'd seen in the book. Knowing the emotion, finding the context..."

"A language based on the flight patterns of griffin?" Yusa's face scrunched a bit, then he let out a sigh. "Not the strangest thing I've experienced today."

"Riders are connected to their griffin," the librarian continued, between large bites of food. "I'm not sure if I feel it more, or less, because I'm a dwarf. The connection is there."

"How did you get chosen, at all?" Kevon gaped, giving in to his curiosity.

"I sat and studied, on the bench above the cavern," Rhysabeth-Dane explained. "The Aspirants were situated much closer… present, but trying not to interfere with the griffin. I would help take food and water down to them, every so often. It caught Brightwing's attention."

"You're fitting in nicely with the locals, I'll give you that," Alanna teased.

"Not as much as some," Rhysabeth-Dane admitted. "Broma-Dhug, the Stoneguard? He's the new Fist at Cliffside Camp."

"How did the rest of that go?" Kevon turned to listen closer.

"Ashera's second in command is now Seacliff's Claw. The previous Hand of the Meek has been restored to his position. Stonespire's Fist…"

"We knew that was going to be the most difficult," Kevon assured her.

"Rowyn's rival from Fallenlake Camp. Ashera has not said much on the matter, but she is not pleased."

"Where is Kylgren-Wode?" Alanna asked. "He's usually not far from…"

"Teaching the Seacliff Striders to speak our tongue," she grumbled. "Broma-Dhug was not learning Common quickly enough."

"The training is nearly complete," Ashera announced, entering the dining chamber, followed by the rest of the new Riders. "Two days, and we will move back to the camps. Your return was timely."

"After the meal, we would speak with you alone," Kevon met her questioning gaze without wavering.

"Double time!" Ashera barked, goading the young Riders

through their meal, and back toward the rest chamber. "Now," she turned and faced the five that remained. "What is so important?"

"Follow us." Kevon stood and led the way back to the observation platform, where the two wrapped spheres lay on the stone bench next to Rhysabeth-Dane's research.

"You know, as well as anyone, of the darkness that spreads across the realm," Kevon paused, turning to address the Griffinsworn. "We're combating it by destroying the portals that we've found, eradicating creatures of darkness when we encounter them."

"A war we've been fighting for generations," Ashera frowned. "Not for a belief, but for survival."

"Your people are strong, skilled, and principled," Kevon nodded. "They have shielded even their enemies from the blight of the chimaera, which makes you all the more fit for this task."

"You burden us with yet another task?" Ashera's hand shifted toward the knife at her belt.

"A glorious task, a dreadful responsibility," Kevon nodded. "A terrifying reward."

"Your riddles try my patience," Ashera warned.

"My apologies," Kevon offered. "This is something I trust no one else with. The elves are worthy, but lack your experience."

"Huh," Ashera's eyes narrowed. "The only thing the elves are possibly less experienced at is riding griffin."

Kevon unrolled one of the spheres, and held it out to Ashera. "Or dragons?"

"You gave her *what*?" Carlo turned, and lurched as a rock slid from underfoot, sailing off the narrow path and tumbling down to the sea far below.

"Easy," Kevon cautioned, reaching out to steady his mentor. "No one else has the experience needed to manage this. They already have the power to conquer the lowlands, now that the darkness in their midst has been cleansed. They've never acted on it before. The elves trust them, and so do I." He looked up and to the west at the clusters of Unbound circling in uncharacteristic formations for a moment, before continuing up the path.

"You bring dragons back into the world, and *give them...*"

"They were his to give," Alanna interrupted, moving up behind Kevon. "I'm glad we're rid of them. Keep walking."

"Rider patrols report no chimaera groups between here and Seacliff Camp," Jacek reported as the others made their way off the winding path, up through the narrow notch at the cliff edge. "We should be there well before the light fails."

"The new Riders are taking shifts in the skies above us," Anneliese glanced at a whirling speck high above. "Your dwarf seems to be enjoying herself."

"The Griffinsworn will not disappoint you," the Huntmistress added, jostling into Carlo as they began their walk. "They have never failed me."

"I don't disagree with his decision," Carlo rumbled. "But I don't answer to him."

"If your prince does not see the wisdom in this..." Anneliese trailed off, and shrugged.

I'm just glad that Ashera was here to hand this burden off to, Kevon thought, leaning against the stone slab that flanked the path back down to the nesting grounds. *We have enemies enough without adding dragons into the mix. I'd lose Alanna for certain.*

"Are you going to stay here, or coming with us?" Alanna stopped and turned to tease Kevon. "We don't have all..."

Griffin-screeches and sudden wingbeats were broken up by the *thudding* of a dozen or more Unbound landing between Kevon and the others. The unbroken griffin milled around in a semicircle, surrounding Kevon. More Unbound landed every few seconds, and the circle tightened as they crowded in closer toward him.

"What the..." Kevon slipped back into the crevice that led to the path below, limiting the creatures' access to him as they continued to close in. He stretched to catch a glimpse of the others, and saw Anneliese standing between the now two-score griffin and the rest of the group, motioning for them to remain calm.

'Enough griffin to scour us from the face of the Highplain', Kevon recalled Ashera's words. *More than enough here to account for all of us,* he sighed at the grim thought.

A dozen feet from where Kevon stood, the moving wall of Unbound griffin stopped, and a single battle-scarred male continued forward. He stalked to within a sword length of Kevon, and sat.

Kevon jumped at the sudden squawk in the waning clamor, as the sitting griffin screeched his displeasure. A wave of murmured hisses and chirps roiled through the milling audience, but faded to the dull rustling of feathers.

They're waiting for something, Kevon thought, pushing his words into an Illusion rune so that the others could hear. *If they wanted to hurt us, we'd be dead already.* He took a deep breath, and stepped forward to where the griffin waited.

As Kevon approached, the Unbound before him lowered its beak, shuffling its front claws forward, leaning until its head was waist high when the Warrior stopped at arm's length. Kevon reached slowly, and scratched the griffin's feathers above its beak, between the eyes. It hissed, a low steady exhalation, and stretched its neck forward. Kevon smiled and scratched harder, unable to think of another response.

The griffin's beak clicked around the grip of the sword at Kevon's side, and lifted it, starting to pull the blade from its sheath.

Kevon's hand slipped instinctively to the hilt, and he finished drawing the weapon as the griffin released it. He took a step back, dropping into a defensive stance, blade held across his body, as the griffin before him spread its wings and began hissing loudly. The others surrounding them copied their elder, completely obscuring the rest of Kevon's group from his sight. After a few seconds of the annoying, yet frightening noise, Kevon whipped the sword straight up, and let out a battlecry.

Every griffin within eyesight threw its head back, screeching to the heavens. Kevon could not help but think of the dragons that had called M'phes to her temple on the Plane of Wind. He half expected a portal to open, and see the creator hurtle through it to answer this summons.

Moments passed, and the front ranks of the surrounding Unbound began launching skyward. In the span of a few breaths, every griffin was gone, a dizzying vortex of tan and white spiraling up and away, their implied threat vanished.

Kevon lowered his gaze to the remaining griffin before him. He slowly sheathed his sword.

The elder griffin stood a few seconds longer, squawked, and launched himself after his fellows.

Kevon made his way over to where the others had stopped, glancing up at the slow spiral of Unbound that still whorled overhead.

"What in the world was that about?" Jacek asked as Kevon rejoined the group.

"I have a feeling it's nothing from this world," Kevon answered, resting his hand on the sword hilt at his side. "Let's move. I doubt the Unbound will turn on us. If they do, there's little we could do about it."

"Well before the light fails?" Kevon asked Jacek, peering at the crimson skyline. "Seacliff Camp is still an hour away."

"You can't walk as fast when you spend half your time looking up," the Court-Mage grumbled.

"We had no delays to combat chimaera," Yusa offered. "Kevon's pets made short work of them."

"They're not..." Kevon sighed, stopping to look up at the dozens of griffin that still circled above them. "I don't know what they are, really."

"They're a gift," Alanna laughed. "And a curse. Just like what I..."

Kevon followed Alanna's gaze as she quieted and stared toward the southwest. A bright pinpoint of red winked out of existence, and she shook her head.

"I see so much more now, but I can't always tell..."

"That was real," Kevon interrupted. "I saw it. It looked like..."

Something tickled at the edge of Kevon's awareness an instant before the light reappeared, no more than half a mile distant. The rune for Fire splashed into Kevon's mind, solidifying and sharpening for a moment before dissolving, along with the distant light.

"Pholos..." Kevon felt the magic and the heat from the portal at the same time, hot on the back of his neck. A tug on his jacket, and he fell backwards into the inferno.

CHAPTER 46

Ash and steam clouded Kevon's vision, the surrounding heat surpassing that of his frontier forge in a matter of moments.

"Quickly!" Pholos rasped. "They're coming! They're both coming!"

Kevon climbed to his feet, and wiped at his eyes. He sprinted after Pholos, along the rocky shore of a flaming lake, across a crumbling stone bridge that spanned a flow of molten stone that flowed into the lake. He could feel an oddly familiar sensation, something he'd felt only twice before in his life. It was as different from the other two as they had been from each other, but he could tell what it was immediately. He stopped, and turned toward where he felt it. "But it's..."

"No time!" Pholos cried over the booming eruption of a nearby volcano. "We've all been betrayed! Hurry!"

Mindful of the differences of time between his world and the other Planes, Kevon rushed to where Pholos stood, deep in concentration. He opened his mind to his friend, and the magic flowed into the runes that opened the portal.

"Go!" Pholos shouted, shoving Kevon before him, leaping in after.

Kevon stumbled through the water to the shore of the stream, glad of the cool soaking after the heat of the previous few minutes. He moved to where Pholos had fallen on the shore, curled in on himself, sobs of suppressed pain convulsing through his body.

A sharp intake of air, and the Mage steadied himself, rolling to a seated position. "The cold burns worse than the fire," A few breaths later, Pholos stood. "They're not here yet. That's good. There is still time."

"Time for what?" Kevon asked. "You tear me away from our friends, bring me here? Where are we even..." Kevon glimpsed the two ships anchored off the shore to the northwest. "The beach. Camp is that way."

"Wait," Kevon stopped in mid-step, holding Pholos back at arm's length. "Who is coming? We've been betrayed?"

"Holten." Pholos's breathing was almost calmed down, but his eyes belied his composure. "I haven't found him, but I've felt him. *Over there*. I've felt the signal, between the worlds. Felt the thing that's been hunting us both."

"If that's what I felt, I don't think..." Kevon shook his head. "What signal?"

"Fires, in a pattern," Pholos explained. "I've felt them off and on, gone to investigate. They were burnt out, abandoned, in random places. I thought. Then I found a campsite near one of them. Then another. It looked like your campsites. I couldn't catch up on my own, even when I could tell which way you were going."

"All right," Kevon sighed. "Someone was signaling Holten?"

"From just out of sight of the camp." Pholos pushed past Kevon to move up the hill before them, crouching as he neared the top.

"Martin," Kevon whispered before his friend even came into view over the crest of the hill.

"I've been able to stay ahead of Holten, having more experience with the Plane of Fire. Crossing the ocean through it really slowed him down." The reflections of Martin's signal-fires shone in his eyes. "But he's going to be here soon. And the other one. It's never followed me through to here, but..."

"It can't," Kevon reassured him. "Let's deal with Martin right away though. He stood, looking toward the fires.

"He's gone!" Pholos cursed under his breath. "There! Nearly back to camp!"

"You could feel the signal-fires from the other side?" Kevon asked, stepping down the hill so that he could stand without being seen. "That's where Holten should emerge, then?" he asked at Pholos's nod.

"We'll circle down by the shore, work our way toward camp," Kevon decided. "Maybe we can draw Martin back out, discover what else he knows about Holten before he arrives."

Without waiting for an answer, Kevon began the descent to the shoreline, peeking over the hill toward the camp every few steps.

"Kevon!" Pholos hissed, throwing himself at the hillside, inching up to peek back toward the signal fires. His normally raspy voice cracked more than usual. "It's too late!"

Feeling the Fire magic build, Kevon fell to the ground. He crawled up near Pholos, peering over the top of the rise to where the portal had opened.

Holten appeared, a twisted and haggard version of his former self, but recognizable even at this distance. He reduced the size and glare of the portal with a gesture, but kept it open, and began gathering power from it.

Kevon watched in awe as the power built, ghostly flames playing over Holten's flesh and clothes as the magic grew in strength. He watched for an opportunity to move against his former Master, to turn the spell against the now hellish figure only a stone's throw from his hiding spot.

A Movement rune stirred in Kevon's mind, and the Fire rune flared to unbearable brilliance. Kevon smashed his forehead into the damp sand, unable to handle the intensity of the nearby spell. The magic waned, and Kevon saw Pholos doubled over in pain, clawing at his face.

"What was..." The whisper had barely escaped Kevon's lips when he saw it. The streaking glob of molten sand struck the Imperial ship, Carlo's ship, broadside near the mainmast. Flashes of light peppered the side of the stricken ship seconds before Kevon could hear the explosions of the barrels of cannon powder from the hold.

The magic began building again, as cries of alarm began sounding from the camp.

Rolling away from the accumulating power, Kevon stumbled to his feet, and staggered into the sea. He could see tiny figures leaping from the sinking wreckage of the Imperial ship, and longboats moving from Yusa's ship to recover the swimmers.

Insulated somewhat by his contact with the sea, Kevon turned as he felt another release of Fire magic. Pholos crouched near the crest of the hill, just out of view of where Holten had been. Smoke and steam hissed from where the misfired projectile had landed, near the shoreline where Kevon stood.

Magic built from two other sources near the camp. Magi were on the move, circling away from the shore, taking cover behind the hills and boulders further inland. Elven Hunters stalked close, loosing arrows to no apparent effect, rolling away from lesser splashes of lobbed fire.

A familiar feeling spell began to take form. Kevon and Pholos locked eyes, each remembering the last time they had worked that particular flavor of magic. Holten was transforming himself into living fire.

Kevon looked at the blade at his side for a moment, but the sea called to him. Memories of training on other shores echoed through his mind, and runes formed. Concealment. Enhancement. Water. Movement. Kevon isolated his focus, brushing aside the mental tickle of the opposing Fire magic building around Holten, emanating from the portal.

The spell deepened. The Water rune glowed deeper than the others as the sea rose around Kevon, surging forward, circling around Pholos. The water deepened, rising to just below the crest of the hill. Kevon's efforts to conceal the spell became more taxing as it expanded, his magical reserves draining swiftly. The balance of building power and waning control tipped, and Kevon forced the wave over the hill toward Holten and the portal.

A flash of steam, and a shriek of pain sent Kevon scrambling ashore, dodging the muddy torrent that washed back down to the sea from above. He crested the hill, and charged down to where Pholos had fallen to his knees.

"Darkness..." Holten whispered, lips trembling, eyes rolling back in his head.

Kevon gagged at the sight of what remained of his former Master. Half of the Master Mage had been extinguished, washed away. What remained when the spell ended was wavy, distorted, incomplete. The menacing distortions that Holten had given himself in his fire-form were not fully corrected with the spell's sudden cancellation. A jagged line from his left shoulder to right hip was where he ended, warped bits of skin and bone kept his insides from spilling out, in some places.

"The Darkness... is... coming..." A last, ragged rattle shook Holten's body, his face curled into a final, hideous grin.

Kevon kicked at the remains, making sure there was nothing left in the devious Wizard's body. "Martin," he growled, leaping over the twisted remains, running toward camp.

The Elven Hunters stood down immediately, calling out to the rest of the camp's defenders.

"Alma!" Kevon shouted, running to the center of camp. "Alma!"

"She and Martin fled when the fighting began," one of the Magi pointed further down the coastline toward the cliffs that led up to the Highplain.

"He brought Holten here to attack us!" Kevon yelled, barreling past the stunned Mage. "He has my sister!"

The Mage and two Hunters chased after Kevon as the others started crewing rowboats to rescue survivors from Carlo's ship. Kevon cut through the rest of the camp, angling toward the rising cliffs at top speed.

"Let her go, traitor!" Kevon called into the shadows of the jagged depression he'd tracked Martin and Alma to.

"You're the one that betrayed us!" Martin cried, stepping out into the dying rays of sunlight, holding a struggling Alma at knifepoint. “After all he taught you... All he gave us...”

“It was difficult for me, when I found out what he really was...” Kevon stepped closer, circling slowly to get a better view. “Now that he’s gone...”

“He told me the truth of what you were, before he set out to hunt you down.” Martin shifted his grip, keeping the knife at Alma’s throat, fumbling in his pocket with his other hand. “I stayed my hand at his request, he always thought you might be saved. Now...”

“There is nowhere for you to go,” Kevon took another slow step toward Martin. “Release her. It’s the only way you get to live.”

Martin manipulated the wooden trinket he’d located with his left hand, tightening his grip around Alma as he did so. “You won’t get away with this so easily. “You’ll...”

Kevon felt the shift in magic as he heard the pieces of the wooden device *click* into place.

“You’ll pay for murdering the Master.”

Sensing her moment of opportunity, Alma used the seconds after Martin’s perceived victory to grab the hand holding the knife, and pry it from her neck.

“Not so easy,” Martin remarked, tightening his left arm around her neck, keeping the knife poised in the hand Alma held away and down, at arm’s length.

“You’ve lost,” Kevon shook his head. “The elves can react to any move you could try with lethal bow-fire.”

“Wait...” Martin’s grip slackened. “It doesn’t have to end like this...”

Kevon felt the Dark magic before he saw the portal begin to open.

“Ahh. It may, after all...” Martin smiled at the visible reactions of Kevon and the other bystanders, and squeezed Alma’s neck tighter in the crook of his arm. He shook his knife-hand free of hers as her breath rattled in her throat. Her other empty hand flew reflexively to Martin’s arm, tapping at it and pulling feebly as her strength waned.

"No, don't fall," he cautioned, pressing the knife-tip into her ribcage. "Just a little further…"

Two menacing figures leaped through the portal before it finished expanding. Curved sickle-arms and segmented black chitin armor flashed with muted glimmers in the evening light.

The portal's expansion stopped, and through it stepped a slim, middle aged man in a tailored black suit. "Something merits breaking my rapport with…" The newcomer peered around Martin to the forces gathering around.

"Master Holten has been…"

"Defeated by this rabble, I'm sure," the man interrupted Martin's explanation. Responding to his swift gesture, the two Obsidian Reapers slid past where Martin held Alma, chittering their menace to those standing before them. The new Mage's face twisted in disgust. "Flee, fool."

Shielded from the archers and Magi by the creatures of darkness, Martin hauled Alma backward past the newcomer, into the writhing vileness of the portal.

"One of you would be Holten's student?"

"And his executioner," Kevon added, conjuring up a fistful of flames. "I'd be pleased to serve you in that capacity."

"Perhaps," the Mage laughed. "Should we meet again…" He gave a mock bow from the cover of his dark retainers, and stepped backward into the liquid gloom. The portal squelched closed, and brightened out of existence.

Freed from the influence of their master, the terrors that remained leapt into action.

Kevon loosed a blast of fire at the whirling figure that charged him, and tumbled to the side as the flame slid off his attacker without effect.

The focused jet of fire that Pholos directed at the other horror caught an exposed shoulder joint, and the chitin flared and popped, the menacing limb spinning free of its body to glance off the thick armor of one of the Dwarven Stoneguard.

More dwarves scrambled to the forefront, past Kevon and Pholos. Elven arrows and bolts from Imperial crossbows peppered the attackers, fracturing a section of armor here, piercing a vulnerable joint elsewhere.

"Blind them!" Kevon shouted, remembering Carlo's account of his run-in with the beasts. "Their eyes are up top!" He turned to where the archers still angled for shots at their adversaries, and covered his eyes for a moment.

I hope they figure that out, Kevon thought as he turned back and began his spell. The power built, unconcealed. Kevon could feel the Light energy coursing through him, and the other Magi responded, offering their own power in kind. Kevon embraced it, his concentration faltering only slightly in the deepening evening.

Unable to hold the magic any longer, Kevon released it just behind the line of dwarves that stood axe to scythe with the nightmarish creatures birthed from the darkness itself. The wash of light poured through his closed eyelids, searing the negative of the scene before him into his spirit. He staggered, blinking away the twisted tapestry that overrode his mind.

Leaping backward, crashing into each other in the confines of the narrow space they'd been pushed back into, the creatures spun, lashing out with back legs and awkward slashes of their scythes, with the sight that remained to them.

Kevon reached deep, and detonated a weaker flash of light, hoping to disable the beasts even further. The spell was not strong enough to pierce the afterimage from the previous attempt, and the power fled from any further attempt Kevon made to bend it to his will. He dashed past Pholos toward the line of Stoneguard at the front, and drew his blade. He skidded to a stop and leaned back to dodge a backhanded swing of one of the reaper's scythe arms, then lurched forward and to the right to sidestep a kick and aim a cut at an exposed knee-joint. The blade bit deep, and a flying wedge of carapace, a spray of ichor preceded its wobbling retreat.

The Dwarven line split, hemming in the one-armed reaper on the right, sliding by on the left to pursue the limping one to the back of the depression. The dwarves called back and forth in their native tongue more than Kevon had heard before, coordinating the unnaturally solid defense of the Stoneguard front ranks with timed incursions by the Dwarven regulars. The reaper on the left had spiderweb cracks in its chitin surrounding the charred arm-socket, and two deep gashes where Dwarven axes had struck true.

As the line surrounding it tightened, the one-armed reaper seemed to wilt, it's body jangling back and forth on unsteady legs, slumping ever closer to the inevitable final rest upon the sand. The dwarves quieted, advancing as one to finish their flagging adversary.

The reaper sprang over the Dwarven line, cartwheeling outward nearly to the archers, single scythe flashing in the Mage-fire that swung to bear on it. Pholos let loose a focused inferno that funneled into the beast's chattering maw as it landed, twisting and flailing.

Kevon turned and continued after the limping one, hoping its wound would prevent a similar maneuver. Feeling the rhythm, the ebb and flow of the Dwarven attack and defense, Kevon inserted himself into the line. After a few miscues, he blended his strikes seamlessly with the rest of the Dwarven regulars, and in a few short minutes, the heavily wounded beast fell to a Stoneguard's savage counterstroke.

"Finish it!" Kevon shouted, making crosswise slashing motions with his sword to convey his point to the dwarves. He spun to run back toward the open beach, and the remainder of the battle.

The knot of fighters was untangling, a lone Stoneguard kicked at the mangled carcass, lecturing in his native tongue. As the Imperial soldiers and elves cleared the area, Kevon spotted Pholos.

Kevon knelt by the still form of his friend. *Not the first time I've lost you,* he thought, looking at the rust-colored rivulets that led away from the body. *But there's no escaping it this time. No portal into the realm of Fire to flee the destruction I've brought down upon you.*

"Where is the commander?" Carlo's second in command demanded of Kevon as he brushed closed the eyes of the slain Mage, and stood. "How can such a thing have happened?"

"Focus on the survivors," Kevon answered, pointing out to sea. "Save who we can."

EPILOGUE

"Come with me," Alanna insisted. "You haven't slept since we returned from the Highplain."

"I'll be fine," Kevon argued, shaking his head. "There are still some things I need to figure out."

"You know where I'll be." Alanna's fingers slid off of Kevon's, and she retreated into the stairwell that led to the cabins below.

Kevon climbed the stairs to the aft deck, and sat down beside Carlo. "Your men are adjusting well to the ship?"

"The surviving crew is working well with Yusa's," Carlo agreed. "The soldiers are feeling cramped, getting restless. Given the circumstances, I don't blame them." He motioned over his shoulder to the aft railing, where Rhysabeth-Dane sat reading, nestled behind the shoulder, under the wing of her sleeping griffin.

"Once they find the rhythm, they'll settle in," Kevon chuckled. "Constantly hauling in fishing nets should help with that." He shaded his eyes and looked up at the handful of Unbound circling the ship.

"What about you?" Carlo asked. "You haven't really talked much about what happened."

"I couldn't..." Kevon shook his head. "I couldn't open a passage to the Plane of Fire like Pholos could, even to travel so short a distance back up to the Highplain. I'm outmatched in the only realm I could open a portal to. *He could control reapers.* It's a wonder he didn't return with more to finish the job."

"You sure you didn't recognize him?"

"I've been through it in my mind for the last two weeks,"

Kevon sighed. "I'd never seen him before, and there is nothing he did that connects him to anyone..."

"We'll find him. We'll get her back."

"The mission..."

"Which one?" Carlo asked. "Translating the book for Alacrit? Rubbing elbows with the gods? Tracking down your former Master?" Carlo squinted. "Oh, right. You don't have to worry about that one any more. Should free up some time for this other fellow."

"We don't have a clear direction for any of them," Kevon admitted. "Hopefully the Myrnar will be able to help us more."

"It will be good to see the boy again. Even the witch."

Looking forward to returning to the Glimmering Isle is my new idea of getting back to normal, Kevon stood up, and started back down the stairs, memories of the last two weeks running through his mind again. Getting the attention of the Riders with flashes of Light magic, burying Pholos and the others as they recovered the dead from the sea. Waiting helplessly while the others trekked back down to the coast.

I'll find you, Alma. I promise. Martin and the others will not get away with this. There is no realm they can flee to that we will not follow. Kevon's resolve welled up through his growing exhaustion. He pushed through the doorway and stumbled down the stairs and hallway to his shared cabin. *Rejoining Bertus and Mirsa, gaining the Griffinsworn as allies. We're headed in the right direction, at least.*

Kevon's scabbard clunked into the cabin door as he reached for the latch. He fumbled with the handle for a moment, and it opened of its own accord. *Definitely the right direction,* he thought, and Alanna caught him as he staggered into the darkness.

ABOUT THE AUTHOR

Chris currently lives and works in western Idaho. He writes full(ish) time, and consults with other local authors and businesses on the side. When not working, he spends time with his wife and two daughters, and his group of table-top and card-gamer friends. He enjoys hunting and fishing, collecting swords and armor, and striving to improve his barbeque techniques. He regularly volunteers with the Micron Foundation, helping with the Science Bowl at both the Middle and High School levels. He donates to school and public libraries, enabling book purchases and special programs that support other artists. Chris has recently begun sponsoring local youth sports teams, and hopes to expand on that in the future. Other than that, he's kind of a jerk.

Influenced heavily in his youth by the works of Jack London, Lloyd Alexander, Stephen R. Donaldson, Isaac Asimov, and Louis L'Amour, Chris still consumes above average amounts of Science Fiction and Fantasy. His favorite author is currently (and for the foreseeable future) Jim Butcher.

For more information on *The Blademage Saga*, updates on Chris's other work, visit sleepingdrake.com.

Made in the USA
Middletown, DE
30 June 2019